GOBLIN CURSED

ERICA REEDER

FERRY TALES, LLC

Cover by Bookfly Design

Editing by Book Nook Nuts

Get new release updates and exclusive content when you sign up for my mailing list!
Oh, and you also get a FREE BOOK!

ACKNOWLEDGMENTS

Thank you to Ken Vahn for being there to support me in my writing journey, not only during the good parts but also in the beginning when no one else even knew it had started. You pushed the boundaries with not only your incredible cover art but all of the behind the scenes work most people didn't even know about. There will never be enough thanks.

May your kindness and heart bring incredible people into your life whose souls sync up with yours in a way that brings a smile to your face always, like you bring smiles to the faces of everyone who knows you. I know at least a solid half of our son's goodness comes from you. And for that I will be forever grateful to you.

QUEENS & KINGS

To all of the Queens and Kings out there, thank you for coming on this journey with me.

CHAPTER 1

Flames licked Gaige's body in a dance that twisted her in agony. My heart slammed in my chest. Sweet Danu, please no. I had to help her. My pulse tripped over itself as my feet worked double time to get to my best friend. The ornate foyer wasn't made for anything more serious than someone storming out after a dramatic love affair, so my combat boot's traction gave way. I slid on the floor, my cheek hitting hard marble with enough force that it made me wonder if it would have knocked me out before I'd been marked by a vampire.

I was only down for half a second though and went from prone to running even quicker. There wasn't time to give my new-found vampire powers any more thought because I was in front of Gaige before my numb mind could catch up. Wouldn't you know it. In my job as a Bounty Hunter slash Private Investigator, I could wrangle a skip while simultaneously rescuing a baby from a burning car- yes, it had happened. I was an expert like no other. People called *me* in when things got hard. But when it came to someone I loved being in danger, my head was a bowl of rice pudding. Dumb brain.

Or maybe it was the fact that Gaige was close to unrecognizable. Her former red hair that had attracted men like a moth to a flame had all but entirely burnt off. It was a fitting frame for the nightmare that was starting to become her face.

Her eyes locked on mine. My heart staccatoed in my chest. There was no time for words. Not wanting to let her see the horror on my face, I broke eye contact. I had to find a way to help her. My movements were jerky and desperate as I looked around the huge and surprisingly bare second floor. Where were the fire extinguishers? It was a regulation that one should be up here. Who knew how big this place was and we were running out of time.

A four-poster bed caught my eye from a nearby doorway. Dashing in, I yanked a thick coverlet off in one fluid motion. I rushed back to her. When I got in her view, her expression made me falter. She had the oddest look in her eyes. Pity. How could someone on fire pity another person? Her actions confused me even more as I came to stop in front of her.

Her previously adept fingers pushed clumsily at my shoulders. It looked like she was trying to turn me away. A feeling like a gut punch sucked the air from me.

"Don't worry. I'm going to take care of you." I assured her in a voice I hoped didn't sound panicked but I was suspicious it didn't work because I had to strain to get the words out as I went to throw the blanket over her.

The blanket stopped. Sweat poured down my back as I wrenched it again. But again it was stopped. Mind racing, I looked around to see what it was caught on. Gaige's hand clutched the blanket. Her long fingernails were splintered and charred. Skin had started to melt off the delicate bones of her hand.

Didn't she know what I was doing?

"I'm trying to help you," I pleaded with her.

She tugged the blanket again, pulling it away.

The act pulled at my heart. It took me a few seconds of staring at her to realize she was no longer screaming. She wasn't trying to commit suicide, was she?

"What in the hell are you doing?" I begged. "You have to let me help you. You just have to."

Her jaw set in her quickly deteriorating face.

"Stop." I screamed at her, feeling insane for screaming at someone who was burning alive. "I need to help you. I have to. I can't lose you!"

Instead of arguing with me, she brought up a hand. At the end was a gold coin with a silver phoenix in the center. She reached out to me, her hand a burning beacon. I was at a loss. I didn't know what to do.

"I don't want your fucking coin." I said angrily, tears streaming down my face to sizzle on her outstretched hand. I started to lift the blanket again. And this time it was the sadness in her eyes that stopped me. I wanted to wrap her in the biggest hug I've ever given anybody in my whole life. My arms became so heavy that I dropped the blanket. It fell, heavy on my boots. I couldn't believe this was happening. Why? Why did she want to leave? It was an undeniable fact: she did want to leave.

"Fine, you win." I said, starting to cry harder. My shoulders shook with quiet tears as I took the coin. Pain welled up. The hot metal burnt my hand. It may have branded me for all I know. It was just as well. At least I'd have something to remember her by. That and this shitty coin. For her, I did my best to quiet my sobs so her last few moments could be in peace.

"We had some good times didn't we?" I asked, my jaw trembling. A slow blink and the slightest curve of the tips of her lips was her only acknowledgment, before her body crumbled. It fell to the ground in a heap of bones and burning flesh.

I sank to the ground next to her. Letting the sobs overtake my body. At this point, I could hear the sirens outside. I knew I was in no danger, but at that moment I would've almost relished it.

The firefighters burst in through the doors. I heard them, more than saw them. Felt the wooden floors shake under the weight of their emergency feet and the snake of the too-late fire hose.

Hands cupped my shoulders as they tried to lift me. "Miss, we have to get out of here."

I understood the practicality of his words, the fire had spread to the blanket and was climbing up the curtains. But I didn't want to leave. I didn't want to leave the one person that had been my friend on the outside, even knowing I was a faerie. She was the one person who I had truly been able to share everything with. The one person I could trust. My best friend.

"There's nothing you can do to save her now." Said another, his hands digging into my shoulders less kindly and dragging me to my feet.

I felt tiny pieces drop from my body and I looked down to numbly realize they'd pulled me from a pile of purple sift. I didn't even bother to wonder what they thought of that. What did it matter?

He had clearly seen the blanket I tried to smother the flames out with. He knew, just like Gaige had known, that it was a useless battle. Why was everyone so quick to give up on the ones they loved?

A blanket was thrown over my shoulders, and I was steered out of those same bitter Gothic doors I had burst into just a few minutes before.

CHAPTER 2

"*O*K, we're done here." The booming voice jerked me out of the first blessedly sound sleep I'd gotten in the last couple weeks.

I rolled to the floor, dropping to a crouched position. My heart ricocheted in my chest as I surveyed my living room. Who in the hell was that? Eggplant colored throw pillows lay haphazardly on the floor in their new home. I'd tossed them on the floor days ago- wait, was it days or weeks?- and I hadn't been bothered to retrieve them since. The fuzzy Spanish comforter I'd been wrapped up in lay half-covering the coffee table. A mug of coffee lay overturned on the carpet, its contents creating a stain Jackson Pollock would have been proud of. No one was here.

How could that be? Rubbing my eyes, I tried to shake the spiderwebs of dreams from my head. If I couldn't see them, that meant the intruder had to be in either the kitchenette or the bedroom. I looked to the ceiling. Why now? Wasn't it bad enough that I was mourning my best friend's death? Did I have to deal with an intruder too? I leaned forward, my elbows on my knees to push myself up. Maybe kicking someone's ass would make me feel better.

"God, you really are a hoot when you're not being such a stick in the mud." The Voice came again.

I flattened myself against the carpet. The coarse fibers scratched my bare arms. I still couldn't place where the voice was coming from. Fuck it, I was out of here. I knew too many supernatural baddies to give them the cover of my apartment. Sift from the last couple week's misery-fest pressed into me as I military crawled towards the outside door.

"That's the spirit. Finally, we're getting out of this hole", commented the voice, clearly approving of my actions.

The disembodied voice cleared the fog from my brain quicker than acid. How the hell was that possible? Was it a brownie? A Mogwai? Or just an annoying incubus steered wrong? Whatever it was, I would be better prepared to face it head on, now that I was more awake anyway. Why couldn't I be one of those people who were instantly awake the second they woke up? Putting thoughts of my inadequacies aside, I pulled energy from the Leylines up through my spine. It flowed, uninhibited, out to my hands. Lightning licked and danced around my palms up my forearms. Putting them in a firing position, I slowly rose to my feet. Considering the lack of exercise I've had for the last two weeks sitting in bed since Gaige's death, that was no small feat in and of itself.

Without making a sound, I stood on tip-toe to peer into the kitchenette. It was empty. That only left one place. Changing directions, I went to the bedroom. I threw open the door with a crash. Styrofoam cups crowded on the side table and fast food wrappers were thrown around the room like confetti. It was the same as I'd left it. Don't judge. Not taking anything to chance, I whipped around the edge of the bathroom door. Still no one. Puzzled, I walked as quietly as I could, which considering my training was pretty quiet, placing one foot softly in front of the other as I made my way to the other side of the bed. Hiding behind a bed was a classic move. I feinted into full view, hands at the ready. More nothing. Holding one hand up, more as a protective measure this time than anything, I made quick work of poking the clothes rack, flipping up the bedskirt that Gaige had told me I should buy from a secondhand store, and saw a lot more of nothing.

"See? I knew that wasn't going to be so bad. Just had to get you up and running, and then we are ready for some fun and games." Came the voice again.

What in the Hellfire was going on here? I looked around, feeling more and more gone by the minute. I walked around the room tossing aside the coverlet and throwing pillows to the side, as the voice continued speaking.

"Don't get me wrong, I love the site of a crying fairy just as much as the next person, but there's only so much one can take before it just gets a little old, you know?" A chuckle went off in my head that was most decidedly not mine. Fear dropped like ice in my veins. "I mean even you have to be sick of it by now, aren't you?"

Goosebumps ran down my arms. I wrapped my arms around myself and rubbed them absently, taking no comfort in the warmth.

"I'm not going crazy," I said to myself out loud, not trusting I was alone in my head anymore.

"You're definitely not crazy." assured the voice in a matter-of-fact manner.

I groaned and sank onto the bed, dropping my head into my hands.

"But I just might go crazy if you don't get me some food. You're starving me here. Is there any way to treat a guest?"

There was no misunderstanding this time. The voice was in my head.

"Oh, no." I dropped to the bed, pulling the covers around me. Purple specs of sift winked in the low light as I pulled them over my head. "No, no, no."

"Now, you're freaking out. That's just great. I supposed this means no food for me, huh? You're just gonna starve a fellow? I tell you, I thought you had better manners than that, being a princess and all."

I ignored the voice in my head and I whispered, "fuck, fuck, fuck, fuck. Get a grip Cy. You're losing your shit."

The voice, oblivious to the fact that I wasn't talking to it, responded and said, "I am quite surprised by that, to be perfectly honest. Considering the situation, you think I would be the one losing my shit. But here you are, instead of getting me food, sitting there freaking out. Another breakdown. Don't you have anything better to do with your time?"

Instead of talking out loud, which was making me feel even more insane, I tried to talk over the voice in my head. I must have lost my shit. Finally, I cracked. It wasn't surprising, all things considered. I had hoped to get a couple of more years of living like a normal person before my mom's crazy came and visited me, but I guess that wasn't to be the case. I mean sure, she had never told me about voices in her head, but what else could explain her erratic behavior? Apparently, all it took was losing all of my friends, opening a portal to a magical world which was the equivalent of a metaphysical time bomb, and watching your friend die in front of you to trigger it. Who knew?

"Well, I'm sorry, honey, but I'm done just sitting here watching you melt yourself down. Can we at least get some of that delicious sweet stuff from that box if you're going to do that?"

I was getting kind of hungry. I decided. I told myself it wasn't because the voice told me to. I got out of bed on numb legs, walked to the kitchen, pulled a bowl, spoon, and a box of Life cereal. The voice was blessedly silent as the cereal poured loudly into the ceramic bowl. Funny, I've never noticed how loud the squares hitting the smooth edges had been before.

The relief was temporary though, as I sunk my spoon in and brought it to my mouth it started again at the first cold splash against my lips.

"Oh, honey." It said with a moan of pure pleasure. "That's the stuff. Give it to me."

I couldn't take the craziness of it and dropped my spoon back into the bowl. Milk splashed out onto the counter, drops spraying my hand.

"What in the hell?" As the voice angrily.

I could tell it was getting nice and ramped up, but I didn't even care. I got up and went back to the living room. The couch groaned in protest as I plopped down.

I couldn't take it. It was too much. How could I not distinguish between what I wanted versus what the Voice wanted? Was this what people meant by multiple personalities? I'd heard the term bantered about like people whispered about elves getting drunk on cream.

"They do, you know." piped up the Voice.

"Do what?" I asked, not believing I was having a conversation with myself.

"Get drunk on cream." He said with a drawl that hinted I might be dim witted.

I merely grunted in response. It was hard to say what I disliked more: that the voice in my head had answered my unspoken question or that I had a conversation with it out loud. Or him, more to the point because the Voice in my head was definitely male. Why couldn't I have a nice female split personality? I'd always wanted to be more feminine. Danu knew I didn't need more help being more masculine.

A laugh went off in my head. I gritted my teeth against the sudden, grating sound.

"Oh, bokkie. You have so much to learn." It said with his laughter echoing around in my head.

The sound was loud in my jumbled thoughts. Jumping back up, I started to pace the small space between the kitchen and the living room of my beige apartment. Beige, did it get any worse?

The Voice in my head confirmed it probably had gotten as bad as it was going to get as it responded to my mental ponderings, "I don't know," It said assessingly, "I kinda like beige. I mean, don't get me wrong, it's not the peace of a warm, dark cave, but it does have a little bit of Geluksalig to it."

I sat back on the couch, sinking into the thick cushions and grabbed one of the velvet pillows from the edge of the couch. Again beige. Why so much beige? Holding it against my chest, I pulled my knees up. It was fine. The Voice was obviously just my mind's way of giving me a little bit of compassion, company, and dealing with all of the bullshit I'd just endured. It didn't make any sense to sit here and get mad at it for just trying to take care of me. Ok, so I had to take care of myself and the Voice would go away. That made sense. That would mean the quickest way to get the Voice to go away would be to show my mind that everything was ok. That I wasn't alone. That way whatever voice in my head-

"Bab," The Voice in my head interrupted, "my name is Bab."

Like I was saying, I reminded myself, trying to keep on track so the Voice could go away.

"I said my name is Bab, or Loki, if you prefer," said the Voice its pitch rising a couple octaves. "Just in the name of the Great God, stop calling me the Voice. It makes me seem creepy. And I'm way more fabulous than creepy."

Great God? And did he just say he was fabulous? Despite my best intentions, I couldn't help respond to that.

"That certainly remains to be seen, and quite doubtful," I answered the Voice, I mean Bab. Since getting into an argument with myself seemed like the height of crazy, I gave in. "Considering Loki is already taken, let's call you Bab."

I could tell Bab was confused as he asked, "Taken? But how can that be? It is my name. It is not taken. How can it be taken, if it is mine?"

"Cool your shorts, there. People share a lot of names, and I wouldn't be surprised if you WERE a bit of a trickster of, but Norse mythology already has a Loki, and since it was popularized by Marvel in Thor, I'm sure there's copy infringement or something if we call you Loki," I said, trying not to feel like I was talking to a spoiled teenager. Exactly when did my subconscious become so childish? "Since you wanted to be called Bab, we'll just call you Bab. I think that suits you anyway, since you do seem to be a bit of a babbler."

"I am most certainly not a babbler. Everything I say has merit and is noteworthy. You try being alone for so long. It gets boring, why once..."

He launched into a story I tuned out. When I was on full Overwhelm Mode the last thing I wanted to do was psychoanalyze a story my subconscious had made up. I closed the cereal top and dumped the rest of the now-bloated squares into the garbage disposal. Flicking the switch on, I couldn't get over the fact that I had to call my split-personality another name. I couldn't think of any less ridiculous solution, though. I mean I didn't know how long we were going to be... living together. It could be for the rest of my life. I suppressed a shudder.

Still it was probably best that we might as well have a way

to distinguish ourselves. Besides, I quite preferred being able to call him something other than the Voice in my head. It made me feel a little less insane. I couldn't help but wonder if that's why my mind had come up with the solution. I shoved that thought away, no sense in thinking about that right now.

"...and when he pulled himself over the pile of rocks, he slipped and tumbled all the way down, his ass jiggling in the fire light like squirrels fighting under a blanket..."

Sweet Danu, forever with this? I slipped the bowl into the dishwasher. Could I just sleep away the next thousand years? No, I had to find a way to make him go away. I had to convince my subconscious I didn't need its help. Well, it had just come on and nothing had happened in the last couple weeks. What was the one thing I hadn't done in the last two weeks that I could do to show myself I was ok? I threw the pillow onto the couch with conviction. It bounced onto the plush carpet and skittered away, as if disturbed by this new course of action.

The best way to convince Bab would be to get out of the house. I strolled into my bedroom and snatched a ribbed tank from the floor, stretched it over my head, and rolled it down. I really should take a shower, but I couldn't bring myself to take one. To be honest, I didn't really feel like going anywhere. However, I had to do something. Bab couldn't stay around. I was far too sane to have a split-personality. With a determined stride to the other side of the bed, I snatched my rumpled jeans off the floor and jammed my legs into them, one at a time.

"Don't tell me we're finally getting out of this misery pit," Bab quipped.

I tightened my jaw as I thrust my shirt into the top of my jeans to tuck it in. Going somewhere, yes. But where? I started to head towards the door but stopped. After a second thought, I slowly picked up the coin Gaige had given me from my night stand and slipped it into my pocket, trying to convince myself that it wasn't a silly thing to do.

"Anywhere is better than this hell," said Bab as I shoved my hands into the leather jacket I had grabbed from the chair on the way out the door. Where did one go when you felt depressed and more than a little insane? It only took me a couple of seconds to come up with the answer as I shoved the key in and locked the door behind me with a bang. I was going to Bounty-ful Hunter and Private Investigator Services, aka my job.

CHAPTER 3

*D*espite my best intentions, I found myself in a taxi pulling up to Gaige's place. To my relief, Bab had stayed blessedly silent while I rattled off the address to the cabbie. Was it a morbid fascination that had brought me back here? Granted, almost nothing else had been on my mind since her death. But did I have to come back to the scene of my nightmare?

Men in black overalls with gold phoenixes whose majestic wings spanned the entire width of their backs buzzed in and out of Gaige's charred front door, into a matching van, and then back again like bees to their hive hoarding all of Gaige's worldly possessions.

"What in hell?" I asked no one in particular as I threw a foot out of the still moving car and jumped out.

I barely registered the "hey!" of the driver as I dashed up to the closest set of people. The two closest ones to me were carrying out her beloved Victoria baroque sofa. I jumped into it. I bounced as the extra, sudden weight sent it crashing to the cement.

A man with dark features looked from me to his cohort

and back. After he regained his ability to speak, he thrust a hand to the sidewalk from where I'd just catapulted. "Hey lady, get off the couch."

"What's your name?" I demanded, not moving from my outraged perch.

He crossed his arms over his chest as if to say, *Oh, here we go.* "Stewart."

"Well, *Stewart*," I said, coating the single word in as much ice as I could muster, "I demand to know the meaning of this. If you're stealing my friend's belongings, I swear to all that is holy, you will have me to answer to."

"I'm quaking, lady. Really, I'm quaking." said Stewart, this time with genuine laughter.

Frustration fired my veins, I did not like to be laughed at. I dropped my head and counted to ten, knowing it wasn't making a difference as purple specs of sift started to dot my flesh. Before I knew what I was doing, warm Kundalini energy seeped into me. I hadn't even realized I had been pulling a ley line.

"Excuse me, what is the meaning of this?" Asked a man who walked up with more calm than I'd ever possessed in my entire life.

He wore a black suit and shirt combination that was identical to the coveralls worn by the other men except he had a tiny phoenix on his lapel and a gold tie that glinted in the afternoon sun like it was made of the sun. He had an unmistakably Italian nose, a swarthy complexion, and an easy manner. His presence bathed me in a balm that instantly soothed me. What was I doing? I let go of the magic in a whoosh, like water being let out of the tub. It was so quick Stewart looked at me with a cocked head. Had he felt that? Impossible.

"That's exactly what *I* was wondering," I said, attempting

for the same level of anger I felt earlier but failing. Instead, I felt childish. It wasn't a feeling I liked.

"Well, cara, that is easy enough to explain," he said reaching his hand out to me.

Unaccustomed to and uncomfortable with the gesture, I took his hand, and he helped me to my feet. He led me a couple of feet away.

"My name is Navarro. And you are?" He asked politely.

I could tell he wasn't interested in my name, but I gave it to him anyway.

"Cy, I understand you are grieving for your friend but you should not. She believes, as we do, that she is not dead. She is merely brought to life again, in another space and time," Navarro said, his hands panning out to the sides as if he could reach out and wrap his arms around space and time.

I resisted the urge not to roll my eyes. Not that mumbo jumbo. Here I was with my heart broken, and I had to listen to this nonsense on top of it. People sucked at consoling you when someone you loved died. What could they really say? Nothing would make it better. Sometimes, it felt like nothing would ever be better again. My heart aching, I reached into my pocket and pulled out Gaige's coin.

My eyes went to the piece, the only link I had to Gaige still. The shiny silver and gold of a phoenix reflected the sun back at me. Wait. Was that the same phoenix on this guy's pin? I held it up. Sure, enough. Even though a phoenix was a common enough design, the tipped wings that looked like knives formed a distinct shape that couldn't be ignored. Maybe, Gaige had been trying to tell me to contact them. That they would know what to do with her stuff. To give her closure. That had to be it.

Rubbing the warmth of the coin between my hands one final time, I turned my hand over and presented it to him.

"I'm sorry for my rudeness. It's been a crazy couple of weeks. I think Gaige had been telling me to get in touch with you."

When he saw the coin in my outstretched hand, the color drained from his face.

"Where did you get that?" He asked, his hand coming up to clutch at his throat.

His reaction made me step back. Reflexively, I pulled the coin back and clutched it at my heart.

"She...she gave it to me." I said, my mind flashing back to the horror of the day she gave it to me.

He stepped forward, his hand blinding fast as he reached for me.

"Hey!" I shouted as my mind registered, he'd actually grabbed the coin. I held my hand out. "That's mine. Give it back!"

He held the coin between his two pads of fingers, turning it back and forth in the light. His head shook over and over as he put the gold between two of his fingers and tried to bend it. When it didn't bend, his fingers started to tremble. His reaction put a cherry pit of foreboding in my gut.

Then he closed his hand around the thin disc and squeezed his eyes shut. After a few seconds, he dropped the coin into my open palm as if it had burned him. I looked back and forth between the glittering coin and the perspiration dotting his brow, trying to process what had just happened. He didn't offer any explanation but he was working hard to bring his face back to a neutral expression. Instead, sorrow lingered.

"You...don't want it?" I asked, feeling stupid for asking the question, but hoping for some sort of explanation of the disturbed look that had darkened his face.

He looked positively...panicked. His lips pressed together.

"If Gaige indeed gave that to you. I won't be taking it from you. If I were you, I would keep it on me. Always." He thought for a few seconds and then seemed to come to a decision as he pulled his cell out of his pocket and hit a button on it. "If you would excuse me, I have to have some...words with someone."

"I need immediate transportation," he said into the phone as he turned on his heel, and walked to the curb.

No sooner had he stepped to the curb that a pitch black Lamobrgini with tinted windows pulled up in front of him. In 5 seconds flat, he was in the car and had rounded the corner, out of sight.

I shook my head and turned back to the coin that still sat seemingly innocent in my outstretched hand. I looked at it with new eyes this time. What did Navarro's reaction mean? What did this coin mean? With those questions ricocheting in my head, I gave Gaige's home one last look and then turned towards home.

CHAPTER 4

A fry appeared in front of me on my pockmarked desk. The movement pulled me out of the daze I was in. 'Welcome to My Nightmare" boomed quietly from the Bose speaker I left in my office to keep myself focused on what I was doing. Welcome to My Nightmare was right. I counted to 10 before looking up from the file I was holding. Admittedly, I had stopped reading the words on the page at least 25 minutes ago, but that was beside the point. After 2 weeks of total isolation, the last thing I wanted was interaction. Wasn't it enough that I was out of the house?

With what I hoped was a convincing smile, I looked past the bag of peanut M&M's, the freshly-straightened yellow folders, and the burning candle. The person who was responsible for all three of the items on my desk stood there with concern pulling at her eyes and a sensible shoe that tapped below my desk in a steady morse code that spelled WORRIED. Sandy pushed a stray hair behind her ears. Because her hair was cut short in a style that had been fashionable some 12 years ago, the thick strand popped right back out. The stuff on my desk wasn't even half of what she had offered, it was just what I had forced myself to accept out of kindness. Kindness that was wearing thin.

"I know it's your favorite," she said with a smile that barely cracked her lips let alone reached her eyes.

For the love of the gods, I wish she would just go away. I couldn't stand all of the pity that I felt leaking out of her. I felt positively caged by it, and it made me as sick as a patient in bed with the flu.

"Aren't you just an asshole?" Bab said in my head.

My fingers found their way to my pocket and I rubbed the coin Gaige gave me. Surprisingly, it brought me a measure of peace.

"Thanks, Sandy. That's really nice of you." I said and smiled to prove I meant it, but I could feel it flicker. When her lips flatlined, I added earnestly, "I mean it."

I don't know why people bother to say 'I mean it.' It's not like that's going to be the final thing that convinces whoever you're talking to that you really do mean it. Either they buy what you're saying when you first say it, or they don't. Not much you can do about the rest. Lucky for me, I didn't really care that much.

"I knew it, you are an asshole." Bab said with a smirk I could feel. "Maybe, I'm going to like you after all."

"Well, isn't that a fucking relief." I said out loud. Sandy gave me eyes the size of saucers.

Heat climbed up my neck. Great. If that didn't make me look insane as hell, I didn't know what did.

"I mean, I've been going through these case files and I just can't seem to find anything that I'm interested in, so it's really nice to have something to kind of wake me up. They've been putting me to sleep," I said with a too-high laugh.

To add validity to my statement, I grabbed the cold fry and jammed it into my mouth. I chomped furiously on the salty stick, vaguely surprised that it was still tasty. I shoved another one into my mouth. Sweet Danu, how I had missed fast food. I made a mental note to stop and grab some more hot fries later as I tossed a third in my mouth.

Sandy didn't look convinced. No surprise there. Nothing I had said or done in the last two hours that I'd been here had made her expression change from that perma-worry crease she had in her forehead. I wonder if this was what it felt like to go crazy. You wrestled with the demons in your head while people just looked at you with endless pity on their faces. If I hadn't already visited hell, I would think this was it.

Thankfully, at that moment, the only other thing on my desk besides the Pity Display in front of me, shook. The phone.

"Sorry, Sandy. I have to get this. Do you mind?" I said inclining my head to the door with a small smile that attempted to be apologetic but I'm sure it came off as the unabashed relief it was.

I picked up the phone and answered in my best business voice, "Bounty-ful Hunter and Private Investigator Services, how can we help?"

"You're welcome," said the unmistakable voice of my boss, Sully.

I'd just seen him on my way back from the bathroom, so I knew for a fact he was in the next office. I dropped my head. My shoulders shook with what were the first beginnings of laughter I'd had in two weeks. It felt good. I gave a little sigh of relief.

"For what?" I asked, like I didn't know what he was talking about.

"Getting rid of Sandy. I just saw her walk past my office on the way out of yours," he said.

I could almost hear his smirk. Tipping back my chair, I watched the afternoon sun play on the water-stained drop ceiling.

"Yeah, she was starting to become a little bit of a pain in the ass." I admitted, which really wasn't much of an admission considering he's seen her come in and out of my office at least a dozen times over the past two hours. He knew I wasn't that interested in 'conversation' on a regular day, let alone when I had taken a leave of absence from the shop for a month and a half. Funny, how people didn't question the length of time when someone close to you died. Which was just as well, all of the days seemed to bleed together. If it hadn't been for Bab's sudden POOF! into my life I could easily see how I could have sat on the couch for a month and a half. There was delivery, after all.

"I figured." He must have realized he sounded like he cared because his voice gruffed up and he said, "now get back to work."

And he hung up the phone. Sully liked to poke fun at me. He knew damn well if I was going to do something it would be on my time, not his.

"Not a chance in hell," I shouted through the wall.

Placing the absurdly old phone back in its cradle, I went back to the stack of yellow files. As I slid the top one off the pile, I had to admit I was starting to feel a little bit better. Maybe there was something to this getting out of the house thing.

"See, what did I say? You needed to get out of that place. Not to mention I had to get out of there. I'm not living cooped up anymore," piped up Bab.

I groaned. Well, I had been starting to feel better anyway. I ignored Bab after he started to go on about all of the reasons why my house was like the inner circle of hell. If Bab went away from my working, I might be tempted to pay Sully psychiatric fees.

"You aren't listening, are you?" Bab asked petulantly.

"Nope," I replied, my jaw clenching as I smiled and opened the case file.

Bab grumbled as I skimmed over the case file for a drug dealer who had skipped on his bail.

"Are you telling me all he did was give people things that made them feel good?" Bab asked, his voice rising enough octaves that I winced. I ignored him as I threw down the cool folder. "You people would probably have a harry over what I've seen. Once, I saw someone get dismembered for stealing a chicken. We're talking intestines out on the ground, strewn up over the door as a warning, and everything. Now, that was a sight to be seen. You bet your sweet ass no chickens went missing after that."

Yikes. Talk about overkill, not to mention an overactive imagination. Wasn't getting out supposed to be helping? A dull ache throbbed at my temples and I grabbed a file. The edges of this one was worn compared to the other. Cases that were passed over tended to have intangible pieces of information that were hard to find and therefore not result in any arrests.

"James D Hunter. He bailed on his bond after a bank robbery, huh? Kak, that's boring. What's the purpose of money anyway? Why not just take what you want?" came Bab's unwelcome commentary.

I bit the inside of my cheek. Well, that was ruined.

"You know, I don't have to hear all of your opinions about everything." I said as I closed the folder with more force than was necessary causing wind to blow the little pieces of hair that had escaped my ponytail into my face. Throwing the file on top of the last, I raked my nails over my face and over my head to push the stray hairs back out of my face.

"Maybe not, but yissus, a bank robber? I'd rather be sitting on the couch contemplating gremlin balls," Babs said.

And then before I mentioned that could be arranged, he hurried on, "what else have we got?"

For the next hour we tossed one case after another to the side with Bab's helpful comments of "stupid", "boring", "no way", "not a chance", and "you want to take me out and do what?" I was starting to rethink this whole leaving the house business, when the phone rang.

I snatched it off the ringer before the first ring had finished. I swallowed back my gut reaction to snap, "What?"

Instead, I took a deep breath and said, "Bounty-ful Hunter and Private Investigator Ser-"

A nasally voice I instantly recognized cut me off, "Where the hell have you been? I'd started to think that you had been snuffed by the cartel after you'd nabbed one of their own last March."

Wesley was as good as a paycheck as far as skips were concerned. He always knew a sure thing, and since he was a little sweet on me, loved to send the easy ones my way. I didn't feel special. He was sweet on any girl with a pulse.

I smiled into the phone, relaxing for the first time in weeks. It felt good to drop into old habits. "Wesley, good to hear from you. How have you been?"

"Like shit "Wesley snarled, "my hemorrhoids been flaring, my sciatica's rearing up, and I have an ex-wife who won't die already. But that's that. Do you want a case, my rabbit foot?"

Because I drug back every skip he'd ever brought to me, he called me his rabbit foot. Every once in a while, I took a dangerous case to remind him it wasn't just like- I was damn good at my job. Hence, the cartel case.

I stood up and walked around the desk, putting my hip against the back of it, my interest flaring at the thought of being back to work again. Maybe, I really had needed to get off the couch"

"Hit me. "I said in response.

"I've got a real dumpster fire of a jack-hole here. Burglaries, armed robberies, murder, you name it. Did them in disguises too, because apparently, we can't just have nice and normal crazies anymore. Anyway, you know the drill, the cunt skip town. You want him?"

"Disguises, huh?" parroted Bab. "I love disguises. I remember when an old coot who lived in the railtown used to dress in old ladies' clothes and flash people who went by. Of course, I paid him, but it was the best 50-"

"We'll take it." I said, interrupting Babs' thoughts.

I didn't want to get any more of a clear picture than was already in my head. Wait, did I say we? Damn it. Wesley was going to think I was off my rocker.

"Perfect, I will see your happy ass here in about five then," he said, thankfully ignoring my slip.

"Yeah, I'll get there when I get there. I said with a smile into the phone as I threw it down into the receiver. Maybe, there was hope for me after all.

"Don't count on it," quipped Bab.

CHAPTER 5

*O*h, yeah. Things were definitely starting to look up. I unwrapped a sausage egg and cheese McGriddle from a greasy yellow wrapper and placed it to the side before unwrapping a second.

"Great God, you're not really going to eat that are you?" asked Bab, his voice lifting in horror.

"Oh, you have no idea," I said as the same greasy acid assailed my senses, burning my nose hairs as I popped the slick goodness of the McGriddle top into my mouth. Sweetness gushed between my teeth as I rolled it's deliciousness into a ball with my tongue and swallowed it. I could almost feel the tension and sadness melting away with each moist bite. Gods alive, that was good.

Bab's shock splintered through me. "What in the name of all that is holy is that?" he asked, his voice laden with reverence.

"That, my friend, is a McDonald's McGriddle breakfast sandwich. There's nothing like it." I said, taking the now open faced sandwich and squashed it on top of the other.

Squeezing the two together, with a blissful sigh, I wedged it between my lips and took another delicious bite.

"Geluksalig," marveled Bab.

I had know idea what Geluksalig meant but I didn't have to know he was experiencing utter bliss. I felt it to my core.

"Mmmmhmmmm," I agreed between mouthfuls.

I didn't care that I was talking to myself out in public. People in New York City had seen crazier things then somebody talking to themselves. Case in point, there was a homeless guy wedged against the wooden planks covering the wall to my left who periodically left his post to pace around the table next to him where ketchup and salt packets were placed in random geometric patterns. From overhearing his frenzied murmuring he was trying to solve the Hodge Conjecture. He noticed me staring and I raised my double McGriddle in salute. More power to him. He was quick to avert his gaze. I loved the clientele at McDonald's, or in any fast food chain for that matter. It was a snapshot into the real world.

Fast food was an invention of the gods, no question. I looked around the 70's style McDonald's, and gave a contented sigh. To the naked eye, there was nothing special about the white Formica counters laid perpendicular in an odd resemblance to a pirate plank. This was my go to restaurant whenever I had a serious case of the downs. It was white washed, gleaming modernism at its best. Probably the most intriguing thing about the whole restaurant was the DJ stand set up above Greece-printed glass doors. The mediocre music was still a welcome relief and a reminder of the beauty of dance, of letting yourself go. There was nothing that took me back quicker to my roots faster than dancing. I closed my eyes to let the muted base slip over me. This is what I've been needing for about two months now. Just an unabashed, unadulterated, lustful bliss inside my mouth and nothing more complicated than keeping the grease inside the rapper and not on my clothes.

Bab had other thoughts. "For all the heavenly bliss of the food, the place leaves a lot to be desired. Kak, there aren't even any stacks of bones anywhere. How can you be at home without a stack of bones?"

His comment made me pause. Well, that was more than a little disturbing. I guess since I'd created him from a place of horror and sadness the commentary made sense. It still bothered me though. Shoving the rest of the sandwich into my mouth, I touched a napkin to the sides of my lips, trash in a ball, and threw it on the tray.

"That was fun," said Bab as I headed out the door with a nod to an extremely bored Italian who manned the DJ booth. His posture screamed that he wished he had made better life choices. My attention made him stand a little straighter and he gave me a wink and a rock on hand sign.

It left a smile on my lips as the cool late November air hit me. I loved making a difference in people's lives, even if fleeting.

"Don't get me wrong, it wasn't exhilarating, or exciting, but I do like the new taste of this world. Different. Intoxicating."

I ignored my split personality's musings as I changed my thoughts to what lay in front of me. A tentative smile curved my lips. I didn't understand how it was possible after I'd had to practically drag myself out of my apartment, but I felt...ready.

Hi ho, hi ho, to the bail bondsman we go. I took a left onto Liberty. The giant, red cube in front of the HSBC building drew my eye, like it always did. It stood out, too bright, too cheerful of the black and gray landscape that painted the city. But maybe that's what the artist wanted, to make us think, to make us feel...something anyway. I wasn't much of an art lover.I couldn't tell you the intellectual intricacies, nor did I care to.

"That weird center, silver circle, makes me want to slide down it. Can we? I mean what else have we got to do?" Bab asked what I'm sure he thought was a convincing tone.

"You're in my head, just like I am," I said, turning pointedly away from the sculpture. "We have a job, remember? "

"That still doesn't sound as fun as sliding through a silver hall, coming out the other end, and pretending like we are invaders going to terrorize all those people in their stupid crisp white shirts and black slacks," grumbled Bab.

I agreed with him but said nothing as I passed the Seven Stars Talent Agency. I ignored the building as I walked past, just another place where people were promised their dreams would come true but in reality, it was just another money-grubber that wanted to use you.

I felt Bab pull back at my thoughts. "That sounds terrible."

"Oh, it is." I agreed, my anger rising. "There is a reason they are right next to the bank. Those places are just about taking your money."

Thankfully, Bab was silent. I resisted the urge to wonder if split personalities could have thoughts of their own, and if he possibly could be thinking about all those people in their lives and how they could change them for the better. The more I start to think about him as a separate person, the crazier I would become, Of that I was sure.

I stepped off the curb that represented the small alley that was Liberty Place. The strangest prickle skittered up my spine. That wasn't normal. I brought my foot back.

"Where you off to in such a hurry-do?" asked a growly, catlike voice from the darkened alley.

No, way. It couldn't be. In a flash, I engaged the base of my spine and drank the magic from the Ley lines in.

"Hey, what do you think you're doing?" Bab asked, his voice climbing in anger.

Turning to the alley that seemed dark even in broad daylight, I spotted them immediately: two little goblins standing between the dirty-beige brick walls. In downtown New York City. The surprisingly tall goblin outfitted in battle gear, stood a mere foot away, her feet braced for battle. The other one, the speaker, had his foot raised one in front of the other, like he was preparing to launch himself at me. Where the first was tall for a goblin this one was short. Almost pint-sized. If it weren't for his extremely long ears that folded over like a puppy dog's, I would have thought he was a youngling. Goblins ears and feet grew as they aged.

How in the hell were they here? I'd never seen a goblin topside before. The last time I'd heard they'd been above ground had been the turn of the century. I thought they'd given up on us topsies, as they liked to call us. Their angry presence made it pretty clear that wasn't accurate, though.

Regardless of their reasons, two goblins weren't going to single-handedly take me down. Then again...I stopped and looked at the big one again. Even if she could take me down, she wouldn't in broad daylight. Goblins preferred most species not to know they existed. If it weren't for their lucrative diamond mines, most probably wouldn't. So importantly, why were they here?

Weighing the risk of her attacking me versus me blowing up this lovely city block if I kept the Kundalini Energy held, I decided to let it go. Instead of letting it go completely, I released most of it and kept a steady trickle of it for glamour. It poured out of my heart chakra like a dripping faucet. It almost felt wet too. They lifted their arms, the shadowy form of a homeless man stitching itself around and over them. They stepped back, shocked at the illusion. The smaller one batted at it. The projection swayed but held. It was nothing like Mother's illusions that could make you feel and acted as if whatever she conjured was real. Glamour was more like a disguise, you bought it because you assumed something was as is. To any unsuspecting person passing, it would look like there were two drunk, homeless people I was just talking with. It was clear the goblins didn't like it one bit.

I'd counted on their reactions. After they tried to take me and Anthony when we were in the caves, I wasn't feeling too generous towards them.

With a condescending smile I said, "I was just going to slay some little goblins. But it looks like you're right here. Lucky me."

"No, you weren't," said Bab with a snort.

His words wiped the smile from my face. Of course he would try to ruin this for me. He'd ruined 99.9% of the other stuff I'd tried to do since he'd "showed up."

"Hey, they don't know that. Keep out of this, would you?" I said to Bab, crossing my arms.

The female's pink, thin lips twitched.

The little ones football shaped head cocked to the side and speculation. "Why, you're bat shit crazy, aren't you, Pretty Pretty Princess?" He asked, an appreciative gleam in his eyes.

"You have no idea," I muttered under my breath, then I realized he'd called me Pretty Pretty Princess. That was actually quite funny. I couldn't let on that I thought that, though. You didn't get any badass points for joking with your enemy.

"Oh, very nice. Pretty Pretty Princess. Where did you hear such a modern reference? Last I had heard goblins hadn't come out from underground for nearly a century. Not after you gave the secret of machines to humans. How did that work out for you anyway?" I asked with a smirk.

This time, the bigger one was not laughing. That had

clearly hit a pain point. I wasn't surprised to see such a strong reaction. Humans taking the knowledge of goblin's machinery and not giving any credit to them was one of the big reasons goblins had decided to move underground and stay there. They had no patience for people who weren't willing to give credit where credit was due. I knew that.

This time the bigger one had lots to say, "First, you disrespect our queen. Then you disrespect what we hold sacred. Now, you have the audacity to throw our shame in our faces? These things are not so easily overlooked."

Bab piped up with what sounded suspiciously like a teary voice. "Look at her, sticking up for all goblin-kind. Such a beautiful thing. That's what we need more of: pride and a willingness to stand up for the things that really matter."

My blood pressure spiked. "Tor Mór, would you just stop? Can't you see I'm in the middle of an argument?"

The goblin with the puppy-dog ears answered me, even though I wasn't talking to him. With a puffed chest, he pulled himself tall and said, "it's the way of the goblins, you aren't in an argument, princess. You're in a battle. We are coming for you. And we will get what's ours. As we speak, we have hundreds of goblins amassing below the sewers of New York City-"

He stomped with a hiss, cut off by a jab of the elbow, attached to the long stick-like arm of the other goblin. "Oh for the love of Ba, would you just stop?"

"What do you mean, 'we're in a battle?' As far as I know faeries and goblins, while we've never lived peacefully, haven't been enemies either. Unless, you're butt hurt about my escaping. Though, I don't know why you would be. I hadn't broken any laws."

My jaw ticked. The whole thing irritated the piss out of me. If they said something ridiculous, like I was trespassing, I was going to lose my shit.

"Aren't you forgetting something?" Bab asked in my head with an incredulous laugh.

Before I had a chance to respond to him, the biggest one cocked her head at me and said, "You know what you've done. What it means."

A quiet, assessing look passed over her face as she stared at me through the thick braids that fell over her face. She was trying to figure me out. Good luck there, chick. I couldn't even figure myself out.

Pebbles scattered to ping against my shoe as the little one, who to my irritation I was starting to think was rather adorable looking, smacked his spear against the pothole ridden cement. "I'll tell you what it means. It means we're coming for you. It means the next time you come to these paved ways, we're going to swarm you like gnats in the jungle."

"Mabye!" the other goblin swung an incredulous look at the little goblin, her braids falling down the left side of her face swinging over her shoulder.

The little goblin blinked big, what I'd surprisingly realized were so-ugly-they-were-cute, eyes at her. "What?" he asked, surprise written across his features. "She doesn't know that we brought the entire clan with us and are ready to take her out if she doesn't...hey- what are you doing? Let go of me! We've got her right where we want her!"

The last part he'd shouted at her as she drug him by his big, floppy ear down the alley.

When they reached the end of the alley, I let go of the steady stream of glamour. The additional energy needed to pull the magic was a little more than I'd bargained for and I could feel the drain eating at the edges of my consciousness like I'd been up too long.

I couldn't help the smile that twitched my lips as they popped out the other side of the alley onto the next street, falling over each other. Maybe slapped at the air as the female picked up, righted him, and then poked him with her own glowing magenta spear. He blinked up at her and glared at her as he started away. Not watching where he was going, his canoe-sized feet caught the curb. He caught himself before he went down and bumbled out of sight around the corner.

I swallowed a laugh. If you could overlook the halitosis the whole species seemed to suffer from, their slightly disgusting mannerisms, and the fact that their bodies didn't seem to know if they wanted to be pointy and sharp or round and protruding, they were almost...cute.

Bab snorted in my head, "Don't ever let them hear you say that. They'll gnaw you to death with their 'adorable' razor-sharp teeth."

I remembered the way Mabye's teeth had gleamed with ferocity and I laughed out loud this time.

"Mabye's right. You *are* bat shit crazy." Bab said with a delighted laugh.

Said the voice in my head, I thought ironically with a laugh of my own. Bab joined in and we laughed together. I mean I laughed, with myself, as I continued on to Wesley's. How did that go again? We're all a little mad here. Just call me Alice.

CHAPTER 6

"You look like hell," Wesley said by way of greeting as he looked at me with squinty eyes from over his spectacles.

It was an apt description. I felt like hell. What little happiness I'd squeezed from my date with my McGriddle had left about two city blocks ago. I was back to square one: abject misery. Not surprising when you think of how my life had snowballed to hell in the space of a month. I'd found and simultaneously lost a love I couldn't ever imagine finding again, I'd gone and fucked then lost a good friend, and watched my best friend die right before my eyes. She was right there and I hadn't been able to do a thing to save her. Not one fucking thing. To top it off, I had the joy of living with that sobering thought 24 hours a day, 7 days a week. Yeah, it did feel like a waking hell.

Instinctively, I reached into my pocket and found Gaige's coin. I rubbed my finger over the raised bird on the coin. After a couple swipes, I felt a piece of tension break off and slide away. Maybe that's why she'd given it to me? Maybe she knew it would bring me a measure of peace.

"Good to see you too, Wesley. I'm great. Thanks for asking. You too, I see," I said with a raised eyebrow, as I propped a fist on his desk and leaned against it.

I was being completely facetious. In the space of 3 months, he'd somehow managed to find a belly, which now had a big hand print sitting on it proud like a coat of arms. I assumed the print was a stain from the half-eaten pizza that sat on the paper plate in front of him that was protecting a mess of papers from prying eyes. I was willing to bet a Marco's pizza that those cases were half-filed. Wesley tended to be a bit "squirrel." He couldn't stay focused to save his life unless it had tits, ass, or a bank account.

"Charming," Bab said with a snort.

Blinking, I pulled my hand off the table. I snuck a look at Wesley. His posture hadn't changed. Thank Danu, I hadn't done anything embarrassing like respond to Bab.

"Wise ass," Wesley said in response to my sarcasm. He leaned forward and looked at me over his spectacles. Hard. "Honestly, I don't know what it is, but even though you look like hell, you seem as strong as the greyhound I had when the ex took her." Pulling back he gave me a disapproving look. "Are you taking pills or something?"

Any other day, I would have laughed at the subtle poke about lack of my working out. But I knew why I looked healthy. It had nothing to do with pills and everything to do with a certain drop dead gorgeous vampire's mark.

"Nah, I don't do that shit," I said, taking a seat on the plastic lawn chair that served as his client's seat.

He'd once claimed that hobos had broken in to rob the place and had busted up all of his pretty furniture. He 'didn't see the point in replacing it just to have it busted up again.' I didn't believe a word of it. Wesley was a bullshitter through and through. I half thought he bullshitted so much because he was bored. He got a kick out of a good story and you never know if what he said was real. He liked to think he had the upper hand on everyone. Nine times out of ten I could spot his bullshit though. For example, I was betting that particular furniture story didn't have a shred of truth to it. I think it had more to do with his ex-wife taking all of his money.

I let him think I believed the stories, though. It was good for business and didn't cause any harm. He'd found the file quickly enough, but he was busy shooing away a fly the size of a house rat that had landed on his pizza. The fly wasn't moving, though. Maybe he was stuck in the congealed grease.

"Umm...you're employed by this clown?" Bab asked, as Wesley's makeshift fan blew pieces of hair out of my face as his waving became more intense.

My only response was the chair legs staccatoed scrape across the peeling linoleum as I stood up. There was no way I was falling into that trap. Clown or not, this man essentially paid my rent. I was tired of sitting around watching Wesley recreate Clash of the Titans, though. I plucked the file from Wesley's lax grasp. He didn't even flinch, just smacked the fly on the pizza. Ewww.

Flipping the folder open, I was immediately greeted by the 3x5 picture of a man, paper clipped to the inside flap of the file. His haunted eyes turned down at the ends, like they were starting to slide off of his face, coaxed by the hollows of his cheeks. His lips were thin and wide, dwarfed by his nose, which was blunt, like he'd taken on the world head-first and was worse for wear because of it. I pulled out my phone and snapped a picture of it for quick-reference.

Wesley wasn't phased by me. He picked off the fly and tossed it at the trash can. Not bothering to see if it made it, he scooped up the hard pizza, tore a chunk off it like jerky, and popped it into his mouth.

"John Jeffries," he explained between horse-like chomps. "Quite the freak show. Apparently, lost his mind when his daddy died of cancer. He was 17 at the time. It didn't take him long to drop outta school and commit a whole slew of crimes. Eh, he started small: crimes against property, burglary, and whatnot. Then he dipped his toe in robbery, motor theft, and a little bit of aggravated assault sprinkled in for good measure. He finally settled down and dazzled in the arena of fraud and extortion." Having thrown his pizza back down, he made little jazz hands. "Of course, no nut job would be complete without a murder on his rap sheet. That's how he was caught, actually. Our man isn't a natural killer. Unless, it turns out if you threaten his family that is. A local detective had apparently gotten on his tail because he realized Jeffries had been committing all of these crimes in disguise and that's how he'd never gotten caught. He'd confronted Jeffries and threatened to confiscate everything he'd ever stolen, which essentially was everything his family had. Well, a bullet in the head solved that problem easily enough. But Jeffries didn't consider the detective's partner though. Welp, two and two equalled four, and before you knew it, Jeffries was behind bars."

I'd been flipping through the pages in the file while he'd been talking. From the information I'd gleaned, it turned out Wesley wasn't actually full of shit on this one. In fact, he was quite spot on, for a change. I let out a low whistle.

"Poor guy. Tough break. He was just trying to take care of his family and got on the wrong side of the law." I'd felt the same deep sense of love for my own family once. When I'd had one. My stomach twisted. I pushed the thought away to the same place you put pedophiles and mass-murderers. The place you didn't visit until truly horrific things brought the stench of the memories back into the air again.

"Yeah, that serial criminal and murderer sure had it rough." Bab said, his voice dripping with sarcasm.

"Have a little compassion," I thought to him, trying to remind myself we were all just human.

Bab laughed, "We sure aren't human."

Humanity, human. Excuse the fuck out of my slip. A girl was allowed to get away with a little bad grammar in her thoughts at least, wasn't she? Did I have to be perfect *all* of the time?

I must have had a crazy look on my face because when I looked back at Wesley again his head was pulled back.

"You sure you aren't on them pills?" Wesley asked, sliding the POA documents through the maze of paperwork to me.

My lips thinned. "No." I flipped the papers over, busying myself by signing in all of the required places. "What happened to his family after his lockup?"

There was a hesitation like maybe Wesley didn't want to let the pill question go so easily. After a few more seconds of paper sliding over paper, he finally sighed.

"The detective's buddy was true to his word: he took everything that could be linked to any case or robbery. The family is close to paupers at this point. In a way it's a damn shame. Taking care of his family was what he'd sacrificed everything for. Hell, he lost almost all touch with humanity after his pa died. Not even a girlfriend to speak of."

Having everything taken away from you was bound to push an already imbalanced person off the edge. For that matter, any man on the edge was dangerous, no matter what his mental state was going in.

Wesley scooped up the papers and cartoon-book flipped through them. Satisfied I'd done everything to the letter, he stuffed them back into the yellow folder he'd taken the other documents from.

"You have 90 days to bring back my investment." Wesley

said over his shoulder, dismissing me as the rusty cabinet behind him screeched open.

"Yeah, yeah." I said, letting years of confidence pull the words easily from my lips. "I'm going to go see if I can just knock on his door and see if he wants to go for a nice ride."

The problem was I was betting this time with a man on the edge and a multiple personality along for the ride wasn't going to be such an easy task.

With no modesty to speak of, Bab laughed and said, "Oh, pish. I make you more fabulous, admit it."

CHAPTER 7

Spiderwebs clung to my fingers as I pulled them back from the door jamb. Dusting them against my jeans didn't do much to get rid of the sticky stands. Absently, I rubbed the pads together as I surveyed the deteriorated house of John Jeffries. Places in the wood siding were caved in and other places in the worn planks were missing altogether. Even if you hadn't told me a murdering con artist lived here, I probably could have figured that out for myself. It was crazy how people didn't wake up to recognize when something was so wrong around them.

"Should I get you a nice cup of coffee?" said Bab in a droll voice.

His tone made it pretty obvious I didn't want to hear what he was going to say next, but sheer perversity made me ask, "Why are you asking me that?"

"Well, I figured if we were going to have a nice philosophical debate on modern society, you might want to get comfortable," he quipped in a droll voice. "Or we could get our ass moving and go in to see said psycho in action?"

I didn't like his eagerness for danger, but he did have a

point: I was dawdling too long. I'd already checked out the locks. They weren't old style like Gaige's, no these were nice and high-tech so a little bit of shockeroo wasn't going to get me into these ones. A heavy sigh escaped me. Sometimes, the old ways really were better.

"Damn right they were. Now, all of these people walk around here with these high-fluting prancing about thinking they're better than everyone else. You'd think they thought they were me, or something."

I waited a total of the space of two seconds for a laugh of a chuckle before I realized he wasn't kidding. Right. He was clearly the epitome of humanity. I fought the urge to roll my eyes. And...sometimes the new ways were better. Like psychiatry. If this PITA didn't go away soon, I was going to have to find one of them and sit down for a long talk. How exactly was I supposed to have a conversation with a human psychiatrist? Hi, nice to meet you. I'm Princess Cybil calling to make an appointment. No, not a princess of a country, a mound. You know, a faerie mound. Yes, that's right. I'm a faerie princess. I snorted as I grabbed the duffle bag at my feet and stepped off the sloped cement doorstep into the dead grass. Yeah, that would be a great way to get a fast-track ticket to the looney bin. The contents of my Raiding Bag shifted as I slung the straps around my arms and pulled it onto my shoulders like a backpack.

There had to be a way into this place. There always was. I pushed on a couple windows. Unsurprisingly, they didn't budge, not many people left their floor level windows unlocked. That was ok though, I'd spotted the attached garage on the other side of the house.

The house wasn't overly big, so I was at the garage door before you could say 'are you sure I couldn't just use my wings to fly in one of the second story windows?' I pushed the thought away as quickly as it had come. That was out of the question. I knelt down. The uneven pavement dug through my jeans as I felt around for a good grip on the garage door.

"Wait, you have wings? Yissus, where are they? And yeah, flying up there does seem a lot easier than all of this 'watch this, I'm an expert' beeswax." Bab complained as I scraped my fingers along the line of where the door squatted, unforgiving like a bridge troll on the rough cement.

The question made me pause. Didn't my split personality know everything about me? I mean granted since I'd just gotten one this morning, I was by no means an expert on them, but you'd think that was the case since my subconscious had created him. Maybe that was part of my mind's defense mechanism: only sharing the parts that didn't traumatize me. That made sense.

"Yes, I have wings," I said, as my fingers caught on a soft spot in the lining.

My knuckles stung as I wedged a couple fingers in and lifted high. The door groaned in protest but inched up. Normally, I would have squeezed my other hand into the small space to help lift it the rest of the way, but I didn't even feel a strain. Vampire powers. Sven flitted into my mind. And just like that, I felt his presence, as if he were right next to me. Regret pulled at my heart, I could have used a friend right now. My stomach clenched. How I wished things could have gone differently between us. That he could have shown me the respect I needed him to. With the mental shove I was getting so used to, I pushed him out of my thoughts. Just like that, he was gone. My throat constricted. So why did my heart still hurt?

Taking my mind off Sven, I hurriedly explained to Bab, as if he'd asked, "But I cast a spell on myself and now they live in the Never."

The Never was the place where magic lived. True magic. None of this Chris Angel bullshit.

"The Never? Great God, what have you done?" Bab breathed. I could hear the awe in his voice. It was the tone usually reserved for friends discussing a bad idea like pranking a sorority house.

I'd lifted the door high enough to where it was awkward to hold the door and lift higher, so I adjusted my stance to pull the door rather than push it. That was better. Superhuman powers or not, I could still throw out my back.

"The really fun thing about that is that if I access them it will open a door to the Never, and who knows what kind of fun stuff that will bring through. So I pretty much have to consider myself wingless. Again." I said the last as I ducked under the small space between the two concrete pads. The door fell to the floor with a boom that rivaled the falling of a giant. It echoed in the single stall garage.

Even though I hadn't gotten the full story on what Iris warned would happen if I opened up a doorway to the Never, I got the gist that opening the door to the magical world would be bad with a capital Bitch.

Bab seemed to not have noticed our scenery had changed. I could almost hear his brain working as I stood up. "Yeah, you screwed up pretty good, didn't you?"

I let out a breath, more out of habit at what should have been hard work than anything, and said, "It would seem so, yeah. Thanks for that. Haven't you shown up to make me feel better? You're doing a shitty job."

I added the last part as I looked around the darkened interior. There was an old Chevy a foot from my calf. If John Jeffries' car was here, that most likely meant that he was driving a stolen vehicle. That was good to know.

"Unless, he's here," said Bab excitement creeping into his voice.

The likelihood of that being the case was tiny, but Bab was right. Squinting, I set my jaw. Well, there was no way better than to get inside and find out.

Barely visible through the reedy light shining in from the small eastern window was the door to the house. Bingo. I should really check out the car, though. People tended to get sloppy with evidence in the place they were most comfortable in. One of those places being their car. I dropped into the driver's seat and fished in my Raiding Bag. I snapped on a pair of plastic gloves and pulled out my notebook before helping myself to the glove box. Tissues. Registration. An Emergency Kit. I flipped through the kit to make sure there wasn't anything hidden there. It took all of two seconds to see it was just a kit. Nope, nothing. I tossed it back. Propping my stomach on the car's footboard, I ran the flashlight from my phone under the seats. Red clay was clumped just under the seat where apparently the vacuum had missed. I jotted it down on my notepad and slipped it into my back pocket. It was probably nothing useful, but sometimes even the most innocuous details could play an important role later.

When the light hit the dashboard Bab gasped. What had he seen that I hadn't? I brought the light back. The light shone off the plastic edges of a big-eyed, wide-hipped Hawaiian girl.

"Bliksem, have you seen anything so perfect in all your life?" said Bab, almost sounding like he was on the verge of an orgasm in my head.

"Oh, bokkie, unless we see Mr. Jeffries in there, I'm in no danger of climaxing any time soon," he said with a laugh.

I blinked a slow blink and half-whispered, "Ok, for one Mr. Jeffries is ugly as sin."

He snorted. "With those deep, haunted eyes? Are you

kidding? A guy could really lose himself in those brown wading pools."

I tried not to laugh in disbelief. So my multiple personality was gay. I shrugged. Whatever worked for him was fine by me.

Moving to the console, I pushed around loose change, pens, and papers. I pulled out a handful of papers. Receipts. I might as well take those. Any trail that led me to where he'd been could give a clue to where he is right now.

"I've always wanted to go to the land surrounded by water. Many tales have been spoken of the laughing women in their grass skirts. True freedom. To go where and when you please. It's the one thing I've wanted in this world that I could never have. Seeing her makes me feel like that could be possible for the first time in my life and it puts such joy and hope in my soul. I want to forever be reminded of that. That anything is possible. I want it." His far-off thoughts were brought back with the hard edge to his last sentence.

I wouldn't have tagged Bab for such fanciful thoughts. Then again, since he was a part of me and I loved the ocean, so I guess it made sense. Didn't we all want to just get away to the responsibility-free life islands stood for?

Pulling a plastic bag from the side pocket of my Raid Bag, I fluffed it out and stuffed the receipts in as I said," I know this is the first time you're 'here' for an investigation, so let me let you in on a little secret: we can't take anything that we don't intend on returning, otherwise, it's just what it sounds like: stealing." When Bab didn't respond, I added for clarity, "Which is against the law."

I stuffed the now quarter-full bag of white and yellow slips back into the front pocket and replaced the armrest to the console as quietly as possible. That about covered it. The rest of his car was pretty meticulous. It made sense for a guy who had countless disguises to keep things ultra-pristine. Less to hold his feet to the fire with.

I moved to reach for the door frame to hoist myself back out of the car door when suddenly it became really hard to move. What in the name of Danu was going on?

"I want it." Bab repeated, this time sounding as serious as a displacer beast.

My palms suddenly felt clammy. You weren't supposed to be scared of the other voice in your head, were you? My body flamed. I pushed the feeling down. If he was going to stay around, he had to learn who was in charge here.

"Well, you can want until the next midsummer night and dream about it just as long. I don't steal from skips, it's bad for business.

I tried to move again and this time found I couldn't shift even an inch. A sinking feeling dropped the pit of my stomach.

"Bab?" I inquired carefully.

His only response was to say, "I get what I want."

"It's not happening, so you can just get over that right now." I said my edge sharpened at the confrontation.

A switch seemed to tick inside of him and he said, "Yes, it is."

Then, to my horror, I saw my hand moving towards the dancing figurine.

"You better stop that. This second." I said, my breath coming fast like I was on the verge of hyperventilating.

I forced will into my arm, fighting for control. The progress slowed. Not good enough. Maybe, if I could intervene in another way. Shifting my focus, I centered on my concentration on my other arm. Since all of Bab's attention was on the one arm, it was significantly easier to take control of my left arm, sort of like picking up a 5 lb dumbbell instead of a 500 lb dumbbell.

My arm moved slow and then suddenly it moved in a blink like I was breaking through masking tape. I swung my hand over to my other forearm and put all of my energy into stopping my right hand's progress. It worked. My arms strained and bunched with the metaphysical tug-of-war.

"I have control of myself." I said through gritted teeth. "You cannot take control of me. I am my own person."

Even after I said the words, I could feel my muscles becoming fatigued.

"Don't fight me," said Bab in what sounded like the most reasonable tone he'd used to-date. "He's not coming back for it anyway. If he is found, he's going to be jailed for life. This little beauty will be tossed in the dump."

"It's wrong." I argued, sweat starting to bead on my forehead.

The hula girl's wide hips danced in the thin light with the rocking of the car that had started over the fight for my arm.

Sweat clustered and dripped down to my lips. We stayed like that for too many seconds, the salty wetness coating my lips when Bab finally asked, "Why is it your place to say what's right?"

With that quiet question resounding in my head, my body let go. I couldn't hold on anymore. My hand lost purchase and slipped off the cool cotton of my winter jacket. Bab's exhilaration zinged through my body as my fingers closed around the grinning figurine.

Did this mean I no longer had control of my body? I couldn't accept that. Having lost the immediate battle, I let my body go so I could store up strength for the battle that was coming. I had to have control of my body, and it seemed there was only one way to get it.

Bab, oblivious to my inner turmoil, was in awe as he brought my fingers up to caress the flimsy fibers of her grass skirt.

"Can you imagine it blowing in the breeze?" he said, the pointed plastic ends hard against my finger pads.

My fingers trailed up the smooth plastic of her tanned little body, over the hard sides of her coconut top, and up to her shiny hair that shone in the dim light. The toy was too old for the hair to be silky anymore and the tiny strands felt coarse and moved in a clump when he lifted them to pet her with my thumbnail.

Her smooth, painted smile had begun to flake. The chipped paint was the only rough part. Bab fan over it again and again as he said, "Do you think they have male dancers?"

I could feel his excitement at the possibility swell my chest and quicken my breath. I knew what he was asking: the soft and sensuous dance of the female dancer instead of the dynamic dance of the male dancers.

Still not in control of my body and this time not trying to get control of it for fear of breaking him from this spell of wonder that had overtaken him, I answered in my head, "Of course, they do. We live in a world where the strong can be anything they want to be. I can absolutely see a strong Hawaiian man out there in his grass skirts, swaying them for all the world to see."

This time there was no mistaking the grin I knew was lighting him up.

"I can see it." He said.

I could too. And for the first time in weeks, I smiled a real smile.

With what couldn't be anything other than a happy sigh, my arms went limp and darkness came over me as my head fell forward. I sat like that for a moment, the comfort of the dark and the quietness of the garage lapping at my senses. Finally, I lifted my head and stretched. I felt surprisingly good, if a little tired. Coming to a decision, I stuffed the little figurine into my Raid Bag. Warmth that I knew wasn't mine spread through me, as I zipped the zipper closed and slid out of the car's worn upholstery.

I was at the door to the house, when Bab cleared his throat..

"Thank you," he said quietly.

For once there were no snarky jokes or quips, just sincerity. At first I didn't respond. I was still mad at him for taking control of my body like that. I wanted to be my own person, have control over myself. But for some reason, the thought didn't put as much heat into me as it had.

I pulled on the handle, testing the lock. "Just don't ever do that again."

The lock was spring loaded, just what I'd hoped for. I could zap it, but we were going for stealth here. I pulled a library card from my Raid Bag.

"You can't imagine how frustrating it is to not have control of your life and constantly be the puppet of someone else," he said, his tone somber.

At his own quiet words, the image of Mother immediately came to mind. Yes, I knew that feeling well enough. I'd been her puppet my whole life. What I'd been trying to do was convince myself that his feelings and my feelings were entirely different. This was my body after all. However, since we were one in the same, it didn't make a lot of sense to shut him out. In fact, it had felt good to give in to him to give up having to be the one who made everything happen. If it made him feel good and in turn made me feel good, what was the harm?

I tested the thought out loud, "Look, we can't live in the same body and constantly be at war."

"Agreed."

The word held an eager note that made me cautious with my next words. "But you can't just go doing whatever you like." I said with a little warning in my voice. "I need my body. You can't just use it whenever the whim strikes you."

From the deflation inside me, I could tell he didn't like the idea. I couldn't budge on this though. A move like that in a life-or-death situation could get us killed.

He seemed to ponder the thought. After a moment, he hedged, "What if we talk about it first?"

I laid my ear against the door and listened for a second to make sure there was nothing on the other side. Satisfied there wasn't. I snorted at Bab's ridiculous request as I fit the library card into the small space between the door and the door frame and worked it up and down. The thought that control of my body was up for debate was insane to say the least and tightened my chest with irritation.

After a second though, I let the tightness out. I think it was about time I stopped trying to convince myself I was "sane" or "normal." What did that even mean anyway? Nobody was sane or normal. The ideas were completely subjective.

So while his question wasn't exactly an ideal response, I had to try to work with this demon inside me. Live with him. It was the only way I was going to have any semblance of peace.

With that thought, I considered his request. I'd never heard him attempt to moderate himself before. And he genuinely liked being in control. I could feel it. It was almost a relief for him. I could only imagine how much it would hurt to be repressed like that. It had to be like a cage only being able to view the world through a lens, not ever participating in it. That I was doing that to someone, even if it was a figment of my imagination, sat uncomfortable in my gut, so I found myself agreeing.

"Ok, as long as it isn't life or death, I'm up for it," The

gods seemed to be in favor of this decision because the card pushed the latch in and the door pulled open.

Success. Adrenaline rushed into my veins. With a truce and the library card both in our pocket, we walked into the house. We were greeted by a tidy, if dated, cream kitchen. At the ready, I pulled a trickle of energy up from my spine from the ley lines.

"Police!" I shouted into the shadows.

A big nothing greeted me back. To make sure the house was full of a big nothing, I crept my way through the adjoining carpeted dining room, circled past the veneered curio cabinet into the matching carpeted hallway, and came out onto the wood-paneled entryway whose thick railings were straight out of the 70's. I didn't go into the living room right away because that would have just brought me right back into the kitchen. Much to Bab's boredom, I repeated the performance upstairs. Whereas downstairs had the sterile feel of a 70-80's showroom, the upstairs had a decidedly more lived in feel: decade's worth of dirt and fragments of all kinds butted against the floorboards and a blue shag carpet perched on the toilet tank like a bad toupee. Despite the change of scenery, however, it brought us to the same nothing result, room after room.

Confident there was no one in the house, I let the building magic go. It had started to swell inside me and releasing it left me feeling wilted like after you let the air out of an over-inflated balloon. I wasn't quite finished with the upstairs yet, but I'd been through enough of these to recognize the musty smell of disuse when I saw it.

Significantly more relaxed, I found myself wondering about my newfound identity. He was so similar to me in some ways and so unlike me in others. One of the ways he was different had me baffled.

"So how does a split-personality have a sexual

orientation?" I asked as I rifled through some items in Jeffries' closet. There was too long a pause, so I elaborated.

"You assume too much," said Bab with a snort.

Danu bless it, I'd messed that up good. I stepped on a shelf to boost myself to where I could see on the top shelf. There were some suitcases. I shook them, but they weighed next to nothing and nothing rattled in them, so I left them. I suppose I had to run with my embarrassing comment to Bab, since I'd already let on my assumption. "Well, you are gay aren't you?"

"Bokkie, of course, I am. How can I not be when those men are so strong and virile." He purred the last stretching out the words like they were taffy and I couldn't help but laugh at his outrageousness.

"I couldn't have said it better myself." I agreed with a smile as I moved to the dresser. After a pause. I worked my way through the underwear and socks. That's where people always kept anything they wanted to keep hidden. I asked, "What does Bokkie mean? You've said it a couple of times."

"It's a pet name like sweetheart or honey," he said, his tone warm.

I flushed. I'd always been a sucker for pet names, leave it to my subconscious to give me a good one.

The lightness of our new bond shifted to one of fascinated disgust as I pushed open the last warped door to what would have been a second bedroom in any other house. I sucked my breath in sharply.

"Welcome to my Nightmare," agreed Bab.

He wasn't wrong about that. Mannequin heads were nailed to the far wall with no rhyme or reason. Some had faded, perfectly painted lips of beautician mannequins while others had the blank, empty stares of department store mannequins. Short, long, blonde, brown, black, all plain and unassuming. The most muted version of the hair rainbow the wigs were perched askew atop each scalp in. They looked like they were going to take flight at the slightest provocation. All of them had the look of time and wear about them.

Collecting myself, I pulled out my notepad from my back pocket, smoothing edges of the papers flat. They sprung back up as I pulled the pen out of the spine to take notes. In an effort to pull my eyes from the aviary that was the bird-wig wall, I went farther into the room. That's when I noticed the racks of clothes with shoes piled underneath to my left. I ran my plastic gloved hands in and around dresses, suits, and stained jeans. Besides the fact that it was obvious Jeffries disguised himself as a woman and a man, the search produced little more than a hollow clinking on the old pipes that made up the clothes racks. I put the toe of my sneaker into the shoes and gave them a little jiggle to make sure nothing was hidden in there.

When nothing popped out, I turned around to survey the rest of the room with fresh eyes. Adjacent to me was a plywood plank attached to two two-by-fours to a crude black vanity. Flesh colored bits of every color was thrown about the surface like an old battlefield. I picked one up and wiggled it, the loose plastic jiggled like jello. It took me a second to recognize them for what they were: prosthetics to change Jeffries' appearance. The black vanity sat atop two black cabinets that looked more at home in an office than a dressing space. The wall across from it had hats of every size, shape, and style dotting the rough-hewn wood wall. Hard hats, baseball caps, floppy hats, and blusher veils to just name a few. Those weren't as interesting though as the wall adjacent to it. Shells of torso, busts, and fat suits dangled from rusted nails.

Rubbing the back of my neck, I had to wonder at the

dedication. It had to have taken years to amass such a staggering collection.

"Or just a healthy dose of psycho," quipped Bab who, judging from how quiet he was, had been just as absorbed by the spectacle as I had been.

"You said it." I agreed as I made my way past the vacant stares of the mannequin heads to the vanity.

Here sat all manner of body parts. They were fake, but that didn't make the collection of teeth, noses, foreheads, and cheeks any less disturbing. There were also a collection of other fleshy bits that I didn't recognize. I scratched some notes into my notepad. I could kind of figure out where these were supposed to go on the body, for example, a mouthpiece looking thing clearly went in his mouth, but I didn't get the why. And the why was important to know how to catch Jeffries. I needed to know what his body alterations might look like in order to know what he might cobble together to disguise himself from capture. From the way everything was strewn about, there was no real way to determine if he'd come back for any of the pieces.

Opening the first drawer of the cabinet sent dozens of tubes rolling inside and crashed against the front of the drawer. Lipsticks. A quick perusal of the rest of the drawers produced more makeup. It made sense he'd need an extensive collection of makeup, some theatrical and some daily wear to recreate his dozen or so personas. The file had shown exactly what I was seeing: he was a chameleon confined no gender, race, or ethnicity was out of his reach. My shoulders slumped forward. How exactly was I supposed to find this guy? I couldn't exactly go around harassing every New York citizen that matched the same approximate height as Jeffries because honestly that was the one thing he couldn't change easily. You could spot a lift a million miles away. I'd lose my license in a New York minute if I tried it.

So, how was I supposed to catch this guy if I didn't know who to look for?

I blew out a frustrated sigh as I wandered over to the larger body modification turned art project on the next wall. Every nail held a body modification to change John Jeffries into an entirely different person. I stuffed my hand into my pocket and pulled out Gaige's coin, worrying the raised surface between my gloved fingers. What could I hope to find here? In a place where literally everything could be a clue, where did I begin?

My muscles tightened and then loosened as I let out a sigh. Here was as good of a place as any. I'd get everything and flip through the pictures later to see if anything popped out at me. I pulled my phone from my pocket and started snapping pictures of the clothes, shoes, wig aviary, old battlefield, art project, and was focusing my phone's camera over the wall o' hats when Bab piped up. Maybe, I could stop by the PD and see if the police had seen anything that could help.

"You put too much faith in law enforcement. They are bumbling idiots," said Bab in what was clearly dwindling patience.

I didn't blame him. The whole bounty hunting process sounded interesting, but in fact, it was wading through a lot of seemingly innocuous details in hopes that one gleaming gem would present itself.

"I mean not *all* law enforcement are," I countered as I tapped on the phone's screen to refocus the lens on a dull brown hat. It wasn't focusing because the muted colors all bled together. Good enough. I snapped the picture.

As soon as I did, the wink of a tag jumped out at me. Unlike most of the other worn costumes, the tag looked bright. New. It was my wishing stone. I did a little dance in place. I shifted the lens to the tag and snapped the picture.

"We've got something, folks!" crowed Bab.

My lips twitched as fingered the tag. I was starting to like him. Plain white lettering read Crazy Costumes. Ack. Jazzy's. I had successfully steered clear of that trainwreck since I'd started bounty hunting, but I couldn't ignore it any longer it seemed. I was out of options. He was going to flip like a street preacher at a whore house when I walked into that place. There was a reason I'd avoided him like the plague. It had to be worth it, though. Didn't it? I prayed it was. From everything I'd seen, I wasn't convinced; Jeffries' collection gave new meaning to the term extensive. I chewed my lips. What choice did I have? Either I conquered my fears and reclaimed my life, or I lived with this second-opinion for the rest of my life.

"I think that's the nicest thing you've called me to date." Bab said in a cocky voice.

The tag swung on its noose as I let it go. With my gem of a photo in my pocket to start this treasure hunt that every skip was. They were my pot of gold at the end of the rainbow. My step was lighter as I spun on my feet and headed towards the door.

"Oooo- treasure hunt. I like the sound of that. Can we get eye patches?" Asked Bab, really feeling himself.

I laughed at the insanity of it. "If I'm going to be crazy, can we at least stay with a singular instead of a plural?"

As we descended the stairs, I practically heard him roll his eyes. "Fine. Can *you* wear an eye patch for me?"

"That's still technically a plural," I pointed out as I threw the latch on the door and was met by the cold night air.

"Gods, you're such a pain." he said as I closed the door behind me.

I couldn't argue with that. It wasn't the first time, nor the last, that I'd be called that.

CHAPTER 8

There was no bell to greet you as you walked into the Crazy Costumes, which made sense. I'd never been in a less welcoming place. Caution tape-yellow linoleum followed the same blinding color onto the walls. The cold metal shelves flanked either side of the shop like sentries that screamed Stay Away. Like good subjects, the product had listened too. Each long shelf held a handful of things, at best. A plastic witch broom there, a President mask here. It was the only part of the place that might convince you this was an actual store. Too bad I knew better.

The door behind me closed, sucking what little life had managed to sneak in back out of the shop. The few hanging rags that did their best to convince you this really was a costume shop, swayed like ghosts.

At the end of the shop, a matte, black wall loomed over a display case that served as a counter. On the surface the black wall was a place to hang a selection of wigs and ghoulish masks, but I knew the black served as a very clear line between you and where danger lived.

A head had lazily rose from below the store counter.

Upon seeing me, the shop's infamous owner sneered, his lips pulling back to reveal pointed teeth. A mouth full of razorlike teeth was a dead giveaway for changelings. If they were going to be in the human world, most of them went out of their way to conceal their teeth. Changelings had created a whole existence centered around blending seamlessly into the world around them. Not this one though. Jazzy had no time to "pander to inferior beings."

I took his acknowledgement as an invitation and made my way to him. It wasn't.

"I'd heard the egregious rumor that your kind walked again. I prayed it wasn't true, but the gods have never been good to me." Jazzy said and as if something reeked, he flicked his hand in front of his nose. When I was a foot away from the counter, he hissed and said, "That's close enough, Slayer."

My jaw ticked at the insult. Breathing deeply, I let it go on the exhale. Getting into it over past disputes wasn't going to help right now.

Up close his species became even more evident. Crepey skin covered sharp cheekbones that made the perfect resting place for a rat's nest of hair. The only effort he'd made to blend in was that the unruly hair sat in a classic 80's do on top of his head.

"Why aren't you dead?" he asked the quietness of his body belaying the rage I knew simmered below his exterior.

I knew he wasn't talking about me. He was talking about all faeries.

"You are supposed to be dead," he said the force of his words ruffling the papers on the counter this time.

"I don't like his jerkface." growled Bab in my head.

I nodded my silent agreement, but since I was here for a purpose, I pasted on a smile that didn't reach my eyes and said, "Jazzy, good to see you."

If Jazzy thought my nodding was odd, he didn't

acknowledge it, instead he said, "Don't act like you and I are familiar." Jazzy said, eating his words with those big lips. His fists pumped on the counter. "Will you faeries never stop with your lies?"

Even though it was grating, his hostility didn't faze me. Stepping through that door had been an acceptance that this conversation was going to happen. That didn't stop my gut from twisting.

"We didn't lie."

The denial was out of my mouth before I could stop it. Heat tipped my ears and my eyes dropped to my hands.

Don't let anyone see your uncertainty. Mother's words floated back to me. I stuffed my hands into my pockets, so I couldn't look at them anymore. My fingers came in contact with Gaige's coin. I worried the cool metal between my fingers.

I knew he deserved an explanation. When we had come up with our escape from the vampires and fled to our mounds, we couldn't exactly make our deception public knowledge. It would have been like you telling your little sister a secret. Yeah, that was the best way for everyone to know what you were planning. It was just like that. Telling the changelings we were faking our own extinction, would have killed the plan before it even had a chance to get off the ground. Then we would have been extinct for real. The problem was we had changed the course of their race. But what could we have done? It was theirs or ours.

His eyes turned reflective. Shit. Changelings were so powerful when they pulled energy from the ley lines, it shone in their eyes. They used their magic to change their appearance and could force a change in others. Permanent change. There had been whispers of more horrific things they could do, but it was only that: whispers. While in some cases, it paid to listen to rumors, I preferred to deal with the monsters I could see. I had to distract him before he did anything stupid.

Talking quickly, I asked, "Don't you want to know why we disappeared without a word to your people?"

"I could give a shit less." Jazzy said, the reflection in his eyes shining bright like a cat in the dark.

My stomach soured. Well, crap. Of course, he didn't. I wish I'd paid more attention to Changeling Studies in school. The one thing I remembered was changelings held onto grudges like week old sap. I had to be very careful here lest I start a Faerie Changeling war.

"You're just amazing at this diplomacy stuff." Bab quipped in my head.

There's a reason I don't participate in that Princess stuff. I reminded him. I'd always hated the insinuation that because I was a Princess, I was naturally good at Princess-type duties. That was a big fat No. I'd had to work at every Princess skill I possessed. Even then I wasn't sure I was convincing anyone else. Maybe the crown could help me here though.

"How about the fact that I am Princess Cy Vanguard from the House of Aine and Manannán mac Lir? Do you 'give a shit' about that?" I asked pulling myself up to my full 5'5" of regal superiority.

At that declaration, the reflection dimmed slightly from his eyes. "No shit, daughter of the fertility goddess and a sea god?"

I swallowed the fact that my mother had lost her fertility goddess powers when my father and sister had been killed and instead nodded sagely.

The light left his eyes fully this time, leaving blessedly plain seafoam green eyes in its wake. I let out the sigh of relief slowly from my nostrils as to not draw attention to it. If you could appear all powerful and scared shitless at the same time, I didn't know how, and I didn't think this was a good time to be learning new skills.

"Ok, *Princess*," he said the word with a mocking bow. "Explain why you left thousands of my people's children without homes to die alone?"

"You did what?" Asked Bab, shock evident in his tone. "That's cold."

In my head, I told Bab, "That's not exactly how it had gone."

However, I realized that was exactly how it had happened. Cold trickled down my spine. We'd had a pact with the changelings, and upon our fleeing to the mounds, we'd left them in the forest. Alone. That was a fact we hadn't even been embarrassed enough to leave out of the history books. I got why we did it. I understood. But at the heart of it, I never could. We'd left all of those babies there, to die. My throat was thick, and I had to try a couple times to speak around it.

"Being that I am only 84 years young, I can honestly say I was not there when...your babies were left." I said a tightness in my throat squeezing off my words. Somehow, I managed on. "All I know is that we fled somewhere safe to save our species from the hunt of vampires. Up until now, it has seemed to keep us safe. But it seems as if things are catching up to us."

"In this, you speak the truth. Whispers overrun the streets once again. The vamps know blood flows through your veins still. All you have done is delayed the hunt. They hunt again. For you."

His words threw ice on my veins. When everyone who had known for sure had died in the fire at Jerrick's, I'd thought we'd contained the spread. It seemed that wasn't the case. Uncertainty and fear hung like a guillotine over my head.

"Eighty-four years. That *is* young." Jazzy had retreated inward at my words and mumbled this to himself. After some time, he finally looked back to me. "So you're about 24 human years. How long have you walked among the humans?"

"Five years." I answered dully, not bothering to mention the brief stint where I'd been a prisoner at Knockaine. I'm sure he wasn't interested in Court intrigue.

He pulled at the loose skin around his chin.

"And what brings you into my place of business, young Slayer?" This time his voice held no malice as he casually threw around the insult.

That was odd. Why the sudden shift in conversation? A small headache blossomed at my temples. I rubbed them absently. Fuck it. I probably shouldn't give a gift horse a dental exam.

Pulling John Jeffries' picture up on my phone, I asked, "Does this man look familiar?"

I saw a spark of recognition light his eyes.

"I don't know. Why are you looking for him?" He asked, holding his hands behind his back and leaning casually against all the worn stool.

He knew who he was. I explained to him the case and what I'd seen at Jeffries' house.

"But why do you want him so bad?" He asked as if it meant nothing to him.

I knew better. He was extremely interested. But why? Danu bless it, but I hated games. I gritted my teeth. This changeling was nothing but games. One minute he was ready to rip my head off, now he was interested in my case yet pretending he didn't have any information. He clearly wanted something. But what? The conversation had shifted when I'd told him about me. Maybe if I gave him some personal details along with what he already knew, he'd talk. I so did not want to do this. I wasn't exactly known for being Mrs. Tell-All. I crossed my arms.

"I have, uh," been bitten by a vampire, been kidnapped by my own kind, and watched my best friend killed right in front of me, "...been through a lot recently and as a result," my subconscious has developed a split-personality to try to protect myself and am desperately looking for a way for something- anything- to be normal again, "...going through some things. Bringing this guy to justice is the best way I know of to make things ok again."

Turns out, I couldn't bring myself to tell him. Shocker. It wasn't a lie, though. Somewhere along the line, nabbing John Jeffries had become my ticket to salvation. He was the one way I knew to make Bab go away. The one way I knew to show my subconscious everything was ok. Because Bounty Hunting was the one thing I didn't question myself about. It was the one thing I was good at. It felt like being me. And I was celebrated for that. I'd never had that before. If I could get the feeling again, maybe my subconscious would see that I was ok. I put my hand back into my pocket for Gaige's coin.

Coming to a decision, Jazzy straightened up and let on what I'd known all along. "Actually, yeah. I have seen him. He comes here all of the time. He's a master of disguises, as good almost as myself. You're going to have a harder time finding him than a changeling in a human's crib, no doubt about that."

No human could be as good as a changeling. Him and I both knew that. It was a huge compliment, though. From Jeffries' movie-quality store room, I didn't doubt for a second I had a chance in hell of finding him without Jazzy's help. It was why I was here.

Jazzy continued on confidently. "If you know the police are watching his house, he most likely hasn't gone back for any of his disguises after making a run for it."

From what we'd just come from, I had to agree with him.

Suddenly, Mr. Talkative, he kept going, "I could tell you the last few purchases he made and tell you what to look for. That way you can have a chance in hell of finding him. And to use your words, things could be ok again."

"Finally, a shred of decency." Bab said happily.

I knew it couldn't be that easy. I wish he would get to the point.

"On what condition?" I asked, prodding him.

Jazzy straightened back to a standing position, his faded Great Expectations style suit barely shifting on his gaunt frame and said, "On the condition that you honor the commitment your people made to mine to place our babies with human families."

I threw my arms in the air. How dare he get my hopes up and then turn them on me?

"'Place' them. What nice words. Don't you mean take human children from their families and place your children in their place so they can live a lie for the rest of their lives?" I said, biting on the words.

"Not for the rest of their lives," scoffed Jazzy. "Just until Manifestation, then they can rejoin their real families."

My fist rattled the glass case as I slammed it down in anger. "And what about their human families? They're never reunited with their children again. Do they mean less than yours?"

He threw his head back and laughed at that, his sharp teeth glinting off the fluorescent lights. "Of course."

What a selfish thought. Other people in this world mattered too. It wasn't just one species. No matter who that was. We all needed to exist for the world to turn like it did.

"I want to snap off his head. Let me snap off his head," begged Bab.

Oh, how I wished we could. I had to try to keep my wits

about myself, though. I needed something from him; I couldn't just leave. No matter how my teeth ground or how much he might deserve for his head to be popped off like a dandelion.

Trying to find an answer and separate myself from my anger, I asked, "Why not do it yourselves? Why do you even need faeries?"

"A new changeling mother can't know the whereabouts of her children. She would do anything to get them back, even kill another changeling," Jazzy said this last bit with a touch of admiration.

Confusion shook my head. "So why would you take them away from her in the first place?"

"Gods, you clearly know nothing." Jazzy said looking to the side, his expression pained. "A changeling mother kills her children because her Kundalini Core, her ability to pull magic from the Never is passed to the baby. When a Kundalini Core is taken the only way for it to come back into the body is to kill the thief."

It made sense, but I still couldn't get past the idea that they killed their own children. Even though I hadn't had a picture-book worthy mother, I wasn't ignorant. I knew most mothers loved their children more than anything in the world. It seemed like magic was a small price to pay for your children.

"But why would they kill over magic? Wouldn't a mother's love override the need for magic?" I had to ask.

Jazzy's hand balled into a fist. "Our magic is what makes us what we are. Who we are. Through Kundalini energy, we *are* our magic. That is why the mother is overtaken by a bloodlust until the core comes back into their bodies. Most don't realize what they are doing, until it has already been done."

"Then why would the child come back at all? Wouldn't

the mother just try to kill them again?" I asked, feeling like I wasn't getting it. My toes curled in my combat boots.

"No, because a new, mature Kundalini energy grows inside them and has taken root in the mother by then and has manifested itself so the bloodlust is gone." Jazzy explained looking like he'd rather be explaining this to a dozen litters of angry kittens.

I think I was starting to get it. "So how does the baby changeling- I'm sorry, I mean the grown changeling, at this point know to come back if they were stolen as babies?"

"Because the Manifestations are related and call to each other. The Manifestations lead them to each other." He explained like it was obvious.

I didn't know what a Manifestation was, but I think I was starting to see the problem.

I took a deep breath and explained back to him what I thought was happening. "So if the changeling babies have been with their mothers then that means generations of mothers have been killing their babies. And some day that will mean extinction of the changeling race."

"Gods, you're quick," said Jazzy with a roll of his eyes.

"Ok, but why does it have to be a faerie that Places them in a new family? Why can't another race do it?" I said, pointing at him, refusing to take full blame for their inaction.

"Because faeries and changelings are the only beings that pull magic from the Never, so they are the only ones that can hold the babies. Since they just stole their mother's core, they are so charged with energy that if any other being were to hold them, they would be reduced to a pile of ashes," said Jazzy, his eyes and his voice level and intense.

"Well, shit." said Bab.

That was putting it lightly. By faeries saving themselves from extinction, they'd unwittingly put changelings in danger of extinction instead. If I were in his shoes, I would be pissed too. My seeing his point did little to no good, though. It's not like I could do anything about it.

"I'm not in charge, Jazzy. I can't make something like that happen." I said feeling like I was pointing out the obvious.

It was a strange life I led. For all of the times I felt badass and like I had no equal, I had just as many times where I felt powerless. The image of Gaige's melting flesh seared itself in my brain. I tried to shrug it away.

"There was nothing you could do.," said Bab, trying to be comforting.

Was that true though? Could I have done nothing? Or did I just not try hard enough? Act quickly enough?

Jazzy brought me back to the present with a shrug. "You should be in power within the next 100 years, right?"

Everything in me wanted to argue, but the crown imprinted on my wrist burned, reminding me of the Will of Danu. Sometimes, we didn't choose our destiny, it chose us. I gave a slight nod.

He inclined his head. "We can hold out until you are in power for you to honor your agreement."

Everything in me wanted to say no. All changelings no doubt hated faeries at this point for what we had done to them by leaving. And personally, I didn't like what changelings did to the human children.

An idea came to me. "Would changelings be willing to raise the human children while their own children are gone and when the Manifestation brings the changeling back the human children can be returned to their own families?"

Always thinking of an angle, aren't you?" Jazzy shook his head a rueful smile on his face. "I can't speak for changeling kind, but if there is no other option, I think it is a safe bet that they would be willing to participate in the exchange. This is our race's lifeblood we are talking about."

"This is a really dumb idea, you know that right?" Bab put in. "You have no idea how many ways this could go wrong."

It could backfire spectacularly, but I couldn't just do nothing while their species went extinct at our hands.

"Then as long as you honor your part of the agreement, we will honor ours. When I am Queen, we will participate in the Exchange for you." I said, hoping I didn't regret those words later.

My words were like a switch. Jazzy shifted to the case. "Splendid. Let me show you what Jeffries purchased."

Finally, we were getting somewhere. I pulled my notepad out of my back pocket from where I'd slipped it earlier. He reached into the display case and pulled out a couple pieces.

Dropping one that was ridged like the inside of your mouth, he said, "This was the first thing in his cart. It's an artificial palette, designed to give the wearer a lisp, effectively making their speech unrecognizable."

Holy, crap. I never thought disguises could go so far. I snapped a picture of it and made a note on my notepad.

"This one is to enlarge your nose and give it a slight left crook, as if it's been broken before." he said, tossing down what I thought looked like a comically large nose.

Pointing to a brown, shag wig behind him, he said, "Along with some cosmetics, that's the wig he bought." He seemed to think and then added, "And a leg brace."

I snapped a picture of the wig and made a note on my pad before moving on.

"A leg brace? Did he hurt himself?" I asked, wondering how he might have done that and who might have witnessed it.

Jazzy waved the thought away. "No, people use it to change their stride. It's just one way they can do it. It's infinitely more comfortable than a stone in your shoe.

"That's clever." I mumbled, making the necessary corrections on the paper.

"Oh, this is a smart man you are looking for, make no mistake. It was only because of rage that he was caught at all. He's got to be provoked pretty hard to make more mistakes like that, though. He's not prone to screw ups."

I nodded my agreement. From all of the reports and everything I'd seen, he appeared to be a pretty even-keeled man.

After thanking him for his help, and after a parting response to remember my promise, I headed to the door.

Even though Jeffries was even keeled, he was on the run. People on the run did stupid things. I don't think I'd ever hoped for someone to do something stupid before. Usually, I was praying for the opposite result. Most commonly in regards to myself.

"Why don't I find that hard to believe?" Bab said with a laugh.

"Oh, shut it." I said laughing with him.

Even though I was laughing, my mind was whirring. Had I bitten off more than I could chew this time? I was making promises I didn't know how I'd begin to honor to a dying breed all for what? For the hope that I could be normal again? Even if I did catch John Jeffries, which was starting to look more and more unlikely, could I ever be normal again? Did I even have it in me? What did normal even mean anyway? With those thoughts heavy in my heart, I stepped out into the air that felt like it would never be warm again.

CHAPTER 9

The sound of my slurping down a vodka and cranberry as I tried to put it in my system as fast as physically possible was swallowed up by the thumping of bass. If only there was a way to inject the stuff. It was days like today that I understood drugs. I stared, unseeing at the empty seat across from me. Somehow, I'd found my way to Chaz's instead of home. I wasn't here, though. Not really. My mind was in another time. A time when Gaige's long nails would tap this very same table. A time where Gaige's laugh would be swallowed by the very same tall curtains that surrounded me now.

I missed her. To the core of my being. To the depths of my soul. I missed her. That wasn't going to bring her back, though. That heart-wrenching thought had me taking another sip of my cocktail. When I first got here, I didn't have any plans on getting drunk. Then, again I hadn't had any plans on coming here at all, but here I was. Maybe getting drunk wasn't such a bad option.

"Who'd have thought we could be in a place surrounded by such life and you'd still find a way to bring it down," said

Bab, his all-too familiar voice a rasp against my brain. "That's real talent right there."

"Oh, sure. Losing someone isn't such a big deal for you. You've only been a figment of my imagination for...today. It must be easy for you to move on." I said out loud, not caring who thought I was crazy.

Bab had the decency to sound embarrassed but maintained his position. "I wasn't saying it was easy. I was saying if you sit here and wallow in it, you're just going to bring yourself down....and me."

I had a feeling it was the latter that he cared most about, but instead of rising to the bait, I raised the glass to my lips.

Before I had a chance to tip the glass, I felt a presence behind me. I turned in time to see Marc stride into view. He slid into the seat across from me.

"I heard you'd been kidnapped." He said, by way of greeting. After staring at me for a few heartbeats longer, his forehead crinkled. "Apparently, it agrees with you. You look...good. Your hair looks all shiny and your skin is...flawless really."

"Gee, thanks. And you heard I was kidnapped? Did you hear about the first time I was kidnapped or the second time?" I said my voice dark with sarcasm.

It was a valid question. Since he was a werewolf, he could have heard about my escapades with the Catskill Pack. Word traveled fast in the werewolf world. And yes, that's what I considered my time at Knockaine. Wasn't that the definition of kidnapping? All of the other was strictly details as far as I was concerned. I shifted in my chair at the thought of one of those 'details'. Of the lips I'd dreamed about since childhood pressed against mine. Of the tall, tan body covering mine in sweat and blue sift. Sweet Danu, that had been a mistake. I drained the rest of my drink. A fuzzy warmth spread through my chest.

"A mistake, huh?" Bab mused. "Sounds fun."

"I have been told I look like fun before," I said with a smile remembering Sven's words to me when I'd first met him.

The memory of his laugh kept a smile on my face, but Bab was quick to dispel it.

"How does it feel to know they were wrong?" He said and snorted back laughter.

"Haha," I said drolly looking into the bottom of my empty glass.

What I wouldn't give to be at the Enchantette right now and have this thing automatically refill itself. Raising my eyes again, I noticed Marc sitting there with an expression on his face that said he was 5 seconds away from calling the paddy wagon.

"Uh...you ok?" He asked, reaching out a hand tentatively and then dropping it to the table top.

"I've had better days," I admitted around a long, low sigh.

Then a thought hit me like a Mack truck: he didn't know about Gaige. My chin dropped to my chest. My eyes squeezed shut of their own accord.

I really didn't want to have to be the one to tell him. I didn't. Gods be, I didn't. But I didn't see any other way he was going to find out. He hadn't been as close to her as I had been, but he was her friend. Ok, if we were being honest, he'd wanted to be more than her friend. That thought didn't make this any easier though, so I was going with "friend." And as her friend, he deserved to know. My gut twisted. Why did the hard things always fall on me to do? Maybe because I knew what the right thing to do was, and I just couldn't let something pass without doing what was right. The sharp pain in my stomach told me I'd hit the nail on the head.

The blue veins bulged in Marc's hands as they rubbed and twisted around each other in a dance that did nothing to help the dread knifing through me. I wasn't surprised when he blurted out, "Cy, you don't look like hell. Talk to me."

He didn't know what he was asking- didn't get it. Gods, I wish I didn't.

I went to tell him, but the words stuck, thick in my throat. Just when I thought I couldn't do it, that I couldn't take one more burden, the words did come. "She's dead, Marc."

His eyes narrowed at me and he cocked his head. "Who's-"

"Gaige. Gaige is dead." My lips tightened as the words passed them, like a door trying to keep the awful truth in.

He blinked in confusion, shaking his head to get rid of the impossible thoughts."What are you talking about? She isn't. I just saw her-"

I slammed my fist on the table and he jumped. "I'm telling you, damn it. I saw it with my own eyes. She's dead. Gone. Not coming back. Ever."

I added the last, thinking back bitterly to Navarro's stinging, misplaced sentiment. Living in a different time and place, my ass. What a crock of shit.

"But how?" He asked, his voice catching. His throat worked and his eyes blinked back what he didn't want to see: the truth that was in front of him. "I just saw her here a few weeks ago."

Sadness flattened my brow. He'd had to have seen her right before she passed. I struggled with how to tell him what happened.

"She...she...there was a fire." I managed.

Even those few words paraded her burning body in my mind. Flaming hair, golden flesh wrapped in flames.

"Let's not do that," said Bab, his words surprisingly gentle. "Well, I'm not a dick." he said with an indignant huff I was suspicious was more for effect than anything else.

This time Marc was oblivious to my inner struggles. It

was his turn to do a million mile stare. His turn to look haunted. Why did I have to tell him? Why couldn't I let him just think she'd stopped coming? Stopped caring? Because that's not how she would have wanted it. At least he didn't have the same images in his head that I did. I could spare him that anyway. Sure, he could imagine, but the truth of the nightmare was far more grotesque than anything my imagination could have come up with. I was hoping it was the same for him.

Scooting out of the booth, I went to his side of the booth. Not bothering to look up, he moved in farther. I slid in next to him and wrapped an arm around his too-broad shoulders and pulled him to me with the other. Due to the angle, the hug was as awkward as you could get, but he turned into it with the gratitude of a starving man.

We sat like that for a few minutes, both of us not knowing what to say or do with the grief that sat in each of our hearts. I was grateful for the quiet comfort of shared grief. It felt good to not have to hide it for a blessed moment. Finally, he unraveled himself from the pretzel-hug we'd managed. Tears shimmered, unshed, in his eyes. Tor Mór, talk about tearing out my heart. I dropped a hand onto the rough cotton of his bouncer's shirt. His jaw worked with all the pain in his heart, all of the things he wanted to say. His chin firmed up and I knew the moment was lost.

"Thank you for telling me, but I...I can't be here. Not in our spot. Not with you when she was always with you..." his voice trailed off as if it was suffocated. His rejection stung and I dropped my hand. He didn't give me much time to think on it because he moved to leave. The problem was I was in his way. "Excuse me."

He wanted to be alone with his misery. I tried not to let the sting of I totally understood that. It wasn't something that lent itself to a group activity. I knew I wasn't in any shape to offer any sort of help, but I offered anyway.

I fished a business card from my purse and handed it to him saying, "If you want to talk, here's my number."

"Thanks, but I'll be-"

I cut him off. "Take the damn card," I said, shaking it at him in a mock threat.

He laughed, a moist laugh, and nodded his acceptance to my demands. Only then did I move out of the booth. I'd done all I could do to be there for him. I let out a breath. As he stood up, I realized I felt a little better. Maybe coming here and finding someone to share Gaige's loss with who cared as much as I did had been the right thing to do. Maybe, I could go home now and have a little bit of peace. Maybe.

"Actually, I'm heading out. If you need me, you know where to find me," I said with a raised eyebrow, daring him to defy my order.

He gave a little mock salute and slipped the card in his back pocket. He smiled, a genuine smile and said, "Yes, ma'am."

It was quieter and more somber than it had been, but there was a flicker in his eyes at least. I'd take it, for now. With that he headed to the South side of the building. There was a single door on that side of the room that said Do Not Enter that led to the faculty room. He was no doubt taking some time to process everything. That was probably for the best.

Turning the opposite direction, I made my way down the winding stairs to the main floor. Spotlights shot colored beams in every direction, bathing me in color like the Northern Lights. The frenzy of it and the excited bodies, echoed a distant thrill inside of me. Some day, I'd come dancing again. Maybe, just maybe I'd have a whole life again. Tension left my muscles as a calm washed over me.

"Well, well," said Bab. "Could it be there is a chance in this living nightmare you call a life we might *actually* have fun?"

"Go to hell," I said with a laugh as I pushed onto the dance floor.

My good humor disappeared. Normally, I'd be happy to be here, but today the bodies sliding and bumping against me were just a little too much. Why couldn't the door be anywhere but on the other end of this dance floor? By the time I reached the edge of the dance floor the fleeting peace I'd felt was long gone. My mind and body felt crowded, like the world was pressing in on me. What the hell was wrong with me? I took the first opportunity out of there: the bathroom.

Ducking into the spacious terracotta room, my heart rate dropped almost immediately. I let out a breath I didn't know I'd been holding. It was crazy how quickly things piled one on top of the other when you were emotionally raw.

Corralling my scattered emotions back into the got-it-together woman I knew myself to be, I made my way to the line of stalls. It never ceased to amaze me how big this bathroom was. It was almost as big as my apartment bedroom. Pushing open the impressive faux marble stall door, I made quick work of my business. Just as I was done relieving myself, I heard the oddest noise. It was like a rhythmic slap-slap, slap-slap on the hard tile. I listened closer. And was that the faint sound of breathing? It sounded like it was coming through a shake straw.

I pulled up my pants. No, it sounded more like...a dog, a bulldog. What was a dog doing in Chaz's bathroom? Confused, I flushed the toilet and opened the door. There greeting me were the two goblins from the alley. And they weren't here to talk. They clutched tiny daggers in their little hands and wore grim expressions on their cartoon shaped faces. They looked adorable in their battle gear, Maybe in his little helmet and Kutulun with her hair chunked off into thick breads in a style that was designed to provide freedom of movement. She looked like a Disney warrior princess. Were you supposed to think someone who meant to do you bodily harm was cuteness personified?

"They aren't adorable. They are fierce," said Bab, sputtering over the words.

I didn't have time to retort that yes, they were because the little muffins charged me with a war cry that echoed off the walls and floors in a way that made it immediately apparent this was not a space for a battle. I flinched in an attempt to keep at least some of the sound from piercing my ear drums. That was all it took for them to be on me, though.

Their weapons weren't cute. Their diminutive daggers pierced my flesh with the efficiency of needles.

"Ouch!" I screamed, jumping onto the toilet to put some space between them and me.

It took only seconds to brace my feet on either side of the seat, but it didn't matter. They pressed on, repeatedly pulling back and jabbing their daggers into me over and over again. Needles or not, there were enough stabs to where blood started to show through the swiss cheese that was starting to become my pants. Pants that had become soaked because Maybe had fallen in the toilet in an effort to get to a more vulnerable part of me.

"Stop it!" I screamed.

"Give it back!" Maybe snarled in a voice that would have come off as threatening if it were two octaves lower.

"Give what back?" I yelled at him, trying to hold them at length with my boot.

It didn't work. Their feet slipped on the now slick surface, but they kept coming at me. I kicked at them. Kutulun ducked the blow, but it landed squarely in Maybe's face. He flew back his head smacking the stall door and throwing it open. It was all I needed to pull my Kundalini energy. A soft heat filled me as I drew the magic in. It wasn't a lot of magic, but it was enough. I took a breath and threw out my hands.

"No! Don't kill them!" shouted Bab.

My heart raced in my chest. Whether it was the force of the voice ricocheting around inside my head or a feeling of sympathy that tingled my toes I didn't know, but I changed my trajectory at the last minute and sent the bolt of lightning to the ceiling. It blew apart a cheap chandelier above. Crystals, sparks, and a huge chunk of ceiling crashed down onto the wide-eyed goblins. Their bony butts hit the ground. Sweat dripped down my brow.

"Bastard," I said to Bab. I didn't know how much I meant it, but I was hot. About his interference? Possibly. Everything seemed to be going wrong. I didn't know which way was up anymore, and for the moment, he was an easy scapegoat. I'd worry about feeling bad later.

I shot a tiny thread of lighting at Maybe's feet and then Kutulun's. Kut howled in pain and outrage. I hadn't meant to hit her, but even if it did, it wasn't enough to kill her. Sure, it hurt like a bitch. But I'd still sleep like a baby tonight. My own legs burned like they were on fire from their needle stings, so it was hard to feel bad. An interesting thing happened, though. Maybe dropped his dagger and reached to her.

Seeing the distraction for what it was, this time I aimed higher and shot her intentionally. Her body jerked and she screamed again.

"Kutulun!" He screamed, pulling at her beefy shoulders.

Despite the lightning coursing through her, her eyes blazed with determination. She used Maybe's hand to lift herself up. Damn, she wasn't going to give up was she? I shot her again. Still, she pressed on. Her legs shaking with the effort, she stood tall and proud. Again, I threw lighting into her. Was I going to break my promise to Bab and kill her despite my intentions?

Maybe's eyes were wide, the whites showing around his black irises. He got it, understood that I would kill her. Kutulun's arms, thick for a goblin's, shook as she held herself up against the faux marble stall wall. She took a step forward. I flinched and let another shot of magic fly. Her thick body lurched and she dropped to her knees.

Maybe's plaid skin flushed. Desperation clung to him as he planted both feet on the cream tile and yanked on her arm. It took the small movement to grab her attention. She whirled a scowl on him.

Never dropping her arm, he looked at her with pleading eyes and said, "We can't win this, Kutulun."

She started to pull her arm away from him, but then stopped to look back and forth between him and me.

"I don't want you to die. I couldn't bear it," he said, and I saw something that shocked me more than anything seen all night. His eyes started to well up with tears.

Ignoring the tears, he jerked harder and harder. Her upper body moved with the force, but it was clear she was the stronger of the two. Then Kutulun turned to me, daggers in her eyes, and let Maybe pull her away. I listened to the slap-slap, slap-slap of their feet fade away. The bathroom door opened and closed but still didn't move. I told myself it was so I could be ready when they came back, but I had a feeling it had more to do with the crippling anguish crushing my spirit and soul. Goblins were after me. A murderer was on the loose and I had zero prospects of finding him. And I was wholly and totally alone in this world.

CHAPTER 10

"Fuck," I said to my tiny apartment as I dabbed a soapy wash cloth onto the angry red dots patterning my legs.

The TV prattled on in the background as I studied the road map of pin pricks from those damn goblin daggers. Some cuts were clean in and out while others were jagged lines, like rivers. I know they were just little daggers, but from how much that shit had hurt, I'd assumed there was more damage. I paused dabbing at my bare legs to reach for some antiseptic gel from where it rested like a dutiful sentry on the coffee table. I wasn't a huge advocate of the stuff, but who knew what type of germs goblin daggers had on them.

"You aren't wrong there." Babs agreed solemnly. "You don't want to get the Tribbles."

Looking at the coffee table put my gauge in line with the TV.

The anchorman's aged voice caught my attention. "A new terror is plaguing New York City in the form of small creatures running amok in New York City."

A fuzzy picture, that proved someone tried to use the

zoom and failed just as badly as I do, flashed on the screen. I froze, my hand on the antiseptic bottle. Though it was hard to pick out any discernible features, I knew immediately what they were. Goblins. Shit.

"They're reported to be gray with rotund bellies. Dozens of sightings have been reported in the city limits. We'll take you to a few of them now."

"Little perverts the lot of them. They ran under my dress. And they smelled like...like...*cabbage*." said a sausage-shaped woman in a mink coat, her dogs observing her report with equal disdain.

"It's because they're cold, you dumb ass. They're used to living with lava." snapped Bab at the TV.

Before he could say anything more, the camera switched to the next person.

"Giant, hairless cats," said a scruffy man who stumbled and caught himself on the reporter. Her arm wavered under the pressure but she held firm, journalistic zeal steeling her spine. "Can't see what all of the fuss is about. Unless you count the fact that they were on their back feet. Shoot though. I can get you some of them, just name your price and I can get you-"

The camera cut him off, switching to the next witness.

"Whatever they were, they suffered from halitosis, I can tell you that, for sure." reported one pot-bellied man in a lab coat who stood outside a Fine Dental sign.

The camera cut back to the serious reporter at the studio. "Until it becomes clear what these things are. We're being advised to exercise extreme caution."

I snatched up the remote and switched off the TV. Angrily, I tossed the remote back onto the table and started dropping little dew drops of gel on the dozen achy wounds. The whole thing stunk to high heaven. From the reports, there appeared to be more than just Kut and Maybe. What were the goblins doing in the city? Did they really come all of this way for me? What had I done to generate this level of wrath?

Ok, admittedly, Anthony and I had made a little bit of a fool of them when we had been there last month, but they wouldn't come all of this way to extract retribution. Would they? It didn't make sense.

Speaking of things that didn't make a ton of sense, that brought me to Bab. Sure I'd been through a lot, but I felt like I was stronger than someone who'd create a whole other personality. Was I though? There was clearly something wrong with me. I couldn't just waltz down to a psychiatrist here. If I started talking faeries and vampires, they'd have me committed, and I'd had enough of being locked up. What about the doctor at Knockaine? My thoughts immediately went to Mother, which they did a lot when I thought about home. The last time I'd seen her she looked like she had aged a hundred human years in an instant. No, I needed to make sure I was mentally sound before going back there to do battle with her again. That left one option.

Reaching back to the rich mahogany tree that served as my coffee table, I grabbed a box of bandaids and my phone. Stuffing the bandaids between the cushions, I turned my attention to my phone.

"What is this incredible device?" asked Bab, fascinated as the screen lit up.

"It's my phone," I said as I pulled up the browser. Then I typed in something I'd never thought I'd search: MULTIPLE PERSONALITY DISORDER.

With a deep breath, I hit search. It only took a few seconds to find a reputable site. Apparently, it was called a dissociative disorder now. You had to love how there was constantly some suit in the world messing with things that were fine just as they were. I pushed back my irritation and instead focused on the medical journal. Words like "two or more people talking or living inside your head" and "unique name, personal history and characteristics, including obvious differences in voice, gender, mannerisms" formed a walnut inside my stomach.

Bab laughed, "What a great entertainment device! And here I thought phones were for transmitting voices."

"They're for way more than that." I said absently as I continued reading.

The article mentioned that children usually experienced it but "other traumatic events" could trigger it. I'd been through enough trauma in the last month and a half to last a lifetime. I found myself nodding as I saw the word "kidnapping" on the list. Isn't that indicative?

It was helpful enough to mention that "Symptoms, which can be profoundly distressing, may last only a few moments or come and go over many years." Distressing was putting it lightly. I felt like I was constantly on the verge of a nervous breakdown. I could feel panic try to crawl up my throat even as I thought it. My heartbeat accelerated at the thought that this could go on for years. How was I supposed to handle that?

Throwing my phone into the cushions, I took a few stabilizing breaths. When the feeling went away and my heart rate had returned to normal. I picked up the bandaids and focused on peeling the wrapper off each bandaid and laying them carefully to my skin, making sure to press each one down securely. After I had gotten about half of them placed, which was no small number, considering the mound of wrappers on the floral cushion next to me, I started to think more about the problem at hand. So there was hope that Bab could go away. I wonder how one made the process go quicker?

I gathered the wrappers in my hands and crumpled them

up. Maybe if I showed my brain that I didn't need the security of a second personality, Bab would go away. But how would I do that?

"If only it were so easy," Bab said. Then he brightened. "That's ok. Can you imagine all of the fun we are going to have together?"

I ignored his peppy musings and tossed the wrappers into the garbage. If I had companionship, maybe my brain would see that Bab wasn't necessary. That I had other people to rely on. I went through the list of people I knew outside of Knockaine. Sandy, the receptionist? I quickly dismissed the thought. I'd rather pluck out my eyeball with a pair of tweezers. Sully? I nixed that idea as quickly as it had come. Only two outcomes could result from hanging out with your male boss, and neither of them were things I wanted to contemplate.

Forty-five minutes and a delivered hoagie later, I had a tidy Sanity Savers list jotted down. I grabbed my phone. Feeling lighter than I had in weeks, I trotted into my room and bounced onto my bed. I snatched a pen from the bedside table and called the first person on the list. Well, to be more specific, I called The SAW.

"You've reached the SAW," drolled a familiar voice.

"Hey, Mitzi!" I said with a too-bright smile on my face.

"Who's this?" She asked, still sounding as bored as when she first answered.

"Cy," I said and when there was no immediate reply I added with a whisper, "You know the Faerie Princess."

I felt silly as hell whispering, but these walls were paper thin.

"Oh, that's right." Then after I didn't say anything after that she threw in off-handedly. "How's that vampire mark? Feeling weird yet?" She asked, still sounding as bored as if she were asking about the weather.

Odd emotions bubbled inside me at her off-handed comment. Some of them bad, some of them...surprisingly good. They were all cut off as a thought hit me. Could Bab be the result of the bite? There were just too many variables to this equation.

"You have no idea," I responded, deflated.

I was becoming increasingly deflated because I wasn't feeling any better. In fact, if it was possible, I started to feel a bit worse. I just wanted to hang up and be alone. I forced myself to continue the stilted and awkward conversation for a bit longer before I asked if Worm was there. As she patched him over, I drew a thin blue line through her name. She wasn't going to help me through this mental disaster, that was for sure.

It wasn't much later that I'd hung up from a very confused Worm. I crossed his name off the list too. I didn't want to do it, but I was out of choices. I punched in the number to Chaz's. As it rang, I felt terrible to have to be all needy with him, but I needed help and he was the only one left. I was so lost in my musings that when someone answered I jumped.

"Chaz's," barked an unfriendly voice.

"Is Marc there?" I asked, grimacing at how teenager that sounded.

"No," came the one word response.

"Is...is he working tonight?" I asked, forcing myself to continue.

"No, he's off on personal leave," he said. Then his voice thinned out. "This is that crazy ex of his is it? Listen. he doesn't want you, Barb. Get a damn clue and stop coming round here."

Before I had a chance to respond, the line went dead. Throwing the phone down, I sighed and dropped back onto the bed. The conversations didn't have me any closer to feeling any better. In fact, on some levels, I felt worse. I felt like I was trying to find a friend, unsuccessfully at that. Didn't people usually find those naturally? Was I that unlikeable that I couldn't find a friend?

"Do I have to be the one to point out that's what you're trying to do? Find a friend?" Bab asked.

I ignored Bab and my mind wandered back again to Mitzi's comment. Maybe it did have something to do with the mark I'd been given. Looking back at my list, one name was suspiciously missing from the list. Sven. Just thinking his name made my pulse quicken.

"Sven, huh?" Bab asked with a lilt to his voice.

At the thought of Sven, I could feel his presence tickle my awareness. I closed the door to him, and it went away. I was getting good at that. Despite not feeling him, my mind was certainly not done with him. It went to the image of when he was lying under me, covered in a pile of glitter. The wonder in eyes as he'd stared up at me, floating about him.

At the tantalizing image, Bab said, "Sweet, gods. Tell me more, honey."

That's all it took for my mind to play a highlight reel of what Sven and I had been through, including when he'd held me outside the burning building telling me he loved me.

Bab gasped and then said, "Oh, honey. You have to call this man."

I laughed aloud at that. Calling Sven was the worst idea. Like ever. Granted, he was all things that made me weak in the knees. But more importantly he had broken my trust. I couldn't let that slide.

"But how are you going to know if I'm a result of the bite?" Asked Bab in a voice that made it clear all he was concerned about was laying eyes on Sven.

"You're terrible at hiding your true agenda." I shot at Bab, pushing myself out of bed.

"But am I wrong?" asked Bab, knowing he wasn't. "Are there any more vampires you feel like ringing up?"

Though my words lacked conviction I said, "Thankfully, no."

I wasn't so sure they were as evil as I'd thought before. If my experiences were to be believed, it seemed like there were good vampires and bad vampires. Well, vampires and vampyrs. I hadn't known there were two different kinds before Sven. He'd introduced me to a world I'd never known existed, and I wasn't sorry I'd seen it. I felt like my eyes had been opened. It felt good to not live in fear of the unknown.

I made my decision. Pacing the living room, I pulled up Sven's contact. After two seconds of staring at the large S that sat where his contact picture would normally be, I punched his number. I pretended like I knew how to breathe, as I held the phone up to my ear. It only rang once before the gulf of silence of him picking up the phone stretched out. Then my heart hit the wall when he said, "Are you ok?"

"Oh my gods, how sweet is he?" Bab exclaimed.

Sven's question took me off guard, and I stopped in my tracks. "Ummm...what? Uh- hi, yes. No. Gods, I don't know."

I ran my hand through my hair. I couldn't explain why it felt so good to talk to him, but it did. I felt the most measure of peace I'd felt in weeks.

"What do you mean, you don't know?" Sven asked, then the speaker sounded muffled as he put a hand over it. "Not now."

Horror filled me. He had another girl there. Gods, I was such an idiot. My bare feet dragged on the scratchy carpet as I started pacing again.

Before I could stop my mouth or shape any coherent thoughts, I blurted. "I'm sorry. It's not a good time. I'll let-"

"No, it's fine. Really." Sven said, and I could hear background noises fading. "So what do you mean you don't know. It's a pretty cut and dried question: either you are ok or you aren't."

Then it dawned on me there had been noises in the background the whole time. It wasn't a girl. He was somewhere, and I'd been so bent upon hearing his voice that I had completely glossed over that fact and assumed the worst instead. Great, now I was crazy and insecure. What a confidence-inspiring place to be. I stopped at the floor-to-ceiling window and stared vacantly across the street to the buildings across the street.

"I guess I mean I'm fine physically, just not…" I dropped my head against the window and finished, "mentally."

Sven breathed a sigh of relief, and then after a second said, "Well, I'm really glad you're ok. I feel like I've been going slowly crazy knowing something was wrong but…not knowing."

I felt my breath leave me as I said, "How do you know something is wrong?"

"I can feel it." he said simply.

My brow furrowed and my mind worked on that piece of information. How was that possible? Then a sickening thought hit me.

"Is it because of the bite?" I asked, not really wanting to know the answer.

This time it was his turn to be silent. He took so long answering that I knew the answer before he uttered it.

Finally, he said, "It is because of the mark, yes."

My eyes closed. It looked like I wasn't going to be able to just ignore this whole bite thing after all. Why didn't life work like that? What else was being affected that I didn't know about?

Gathering up my courage, I asked the back of my eyelids the one thing I'd called about. "Does this bite…I mean the mark gives multiple personalities?"

"Multiple personalities?" he echoed, confusion rife in his voice.

That meant no. The knot in my stomach tightened. I didn't know if I'd wanted that answer or not. If the answer would have been yes, at least I would know what was happening to me.

When I didn't respond, Sven's voice became more urgent. "Cy, you need someone there with you. Do you have someone who can come over?"

I shook my head, numbly; it rocked against the cool of the window pane and said simply, "No."

"What about your friend from the club? Call her up. She'll come." He said, not dropping it.

My lower lip trembled. I bit it to stop the quivering and whispered hoarsely, "Gaige is dead."

He breath hissed, "God, I am so sorry, Cy."

I opened my eyes and a tear slipped off my cheek to track down the window pane.

I wiped it away and said quietly, "So am I."

We sat there for a few seconds, neither of us knowing what to say.

Sven spoke first, "How about…." then he cleared his throat and tried again. "Would it be ok if I came over?"

"Yes, 100%. Absolutely." Bab fervently responded.

I wasn't as quick to agree. Could he come over? Should he come over? It took me a few breaths to realize I was happier speaking to him than I'd been in a long time. If I was looking for a Sanity Saver, betrayal or not, he was my most likely option. If I separated all of my lustful thoughts (that seemed to be on a steady stream courtesy of Bab), I could feel in my bones that talking to Sven would give me a measure of peace. A peace that I desperately needed.

It was because of this that I found myself saying, "That would be nice."

"Do you need anything?" He asked.

"A pair of handcuffs and a whip," Bab supplied helpfully.

"No, I'm fine." I said, not sure if the urge to smile came over me because of Sven's kindness or Bab's ridiculousness.

I could hear the grateful note in Sven's voice as he said, "I'm leaving now."

"That sounds great." I said, and I meant it.

We hung up. I stood there clutching the phone, feeling a steady stream of energy start to drip into my veins. He was coming. He was coming here. Tor Mór, I was standing in front of the window in my underwear. I needed pants. I was about to turn from the window when a motion below snagged my attention. I blinked at it. It was a half-moon looking thing.

Then it did something truly unexpected and came off the window. After a few more seconds, the half moon turned into a full circle. Wait, was that a suction cup? A spindly gray arm rose into view, holding it. It smacked on the window again with a hollow thud.

"You've got to be kidding me." I said.

Two little eyes rose into view. The eyes were attached to a head I was really getting sick of seeing. It was Maybe. He was making small but energetic movements, inching up the window. I just stood there as they worked like industrious inch worms, not fully comprehending what I was seeing. It wasn't long before Kut popped into view behind him.

"Aren't they adorable?" Bab sighed adoringly.

As Kut's eyes rimmed the ledge, she made straight eye contact with my naked legs. Her mouth worked furiously as she gave what looked like an incredible bitch session to Maybe. I had to agree with that reaction, especially when Maybe's eyes made eye contact with me and widened to comical proportions. His squishy little tummy made squeaking noises like someone was squeegying the window as his body started twisting and writhing like he didn't know whether to go up or down. Kut's expression of long-suffering patience started the giggles in me as she opened her mouth. My body started to rock as in response Maybe's mouth flapped back, his movements quick and jagged. He looked like he was doing a tribal dance. Kut lost her patience and started to bang her head on the window in miserable slow thuds, which of course only made me laugh harder.

"It's not funny." said Bab, trying to hold in his laughter before he started to snort.

We laughed longer than we should have at the spectacle. It probably had something to do with the fact that Maybe had decided to retreat and was currently inching down the window at a rate that would bring them to the ground approximately next week.

Deciding to show them a little mercy, I knelt down, eye level with Maybe. I took my fist and connected it to the window a few times with increasing thunderous quakes until the seal on the first suction cup broke. His arm flailed, his eyes wide. He watched as I brought my hand up to the other suction cup. I cocked my head to the side as I feinted like I was going to hit the glass. He shook his head and I raised my eyebrow and motioned again.

"Oh for the love of the gods, if you are going to do it, just do it." said Babs with a laugh.

"Do you think it will kill him?" I asked Bab out loud.

He thought for a second and then answered. "No, but it will hurt like the devil."

That made me smile wider, "Good, I think they deserve that."

With a wink to Maybe, I gave a hard thump. The suction gave with the slightest provocation and he hung suspended for a second before he dropped. Kut, who'd seen the whole exchange, opted to simply let go of her suction cups rather than suffer the same fate. Her larger arms caught Maybe, and they dropped from view together.

I stared at the two remaining suction cups, laughing harder than I should have. Maybe it was the absurdity of the situation. Maybe it was that I felt lighter than I'd felt in weeks.

Whatever it was, it made me laugh all that harder when Bab tsked in my head and said, "That was cold."

I knew he wasn't mad, though. For some reason, that made me feel better.

"Oh, yeah. I'm going to hell for that one. Wait, been there done that." I quipped as I made my way into the bedroom to get dressed before Sven came over. I wouldn't do a great job convincing him I wanted to just be friends if I greeted him half naked.

"Take off your shirt." Bab commanded as soon as I opened the door for Sven and all of his 6' dreamy glory.

I resisted the urge to bang my head against the wall. Talk about the first thing I didn't want to think as soon as I laid eyes on the man who'd betrayed me and broke my heart. His dream-come-to-life status had been revoked. And I needed to keep that in mind when he was around.

"Can I have my own thoughts?" I complained out loud.

Sven's guarded look melted and I could feel his palpable need to gather me in for a hug as he asked, "Is it so bad?"

"Sure, you can," Bab responded. "You want him to take off his shirt too. This is a win for both of us, honey."

With a sigh, I motioned for Sven to come in. I refused to

regret having him over just because the voice in my head couldn't seem to behave. I refused to acknowledge Bab just might be right and pushed down the tingles shooting through me as Sven's jacket brushed over me when he passed.

I ignored my vagina and Bab as I stayed behind to duck my head outside and look both ways for those pesky goblins before I shut the door. Just one more thing to add to the list of things that were slowly driving me crazy.

When I came back in, Sven was surveying me with hooded eyes as he leaned a hip against the cabinet. Was he thinking of the time he'd put me on that very same counter and kissed me silly? My heart thudded in my throat. I sure was.

"Gods, just kiss him already, will you? You're killing me here," groaned Bab.

"Do you have to do that?" I complained. This time I was careful not to brush against him in the tight space as I moved into the living room. Space was definitely what I needed when Sven was in the equation.

"Do what?" asked Sven, opening his arms wide.

"Prop yourself against a random object like some sort of GQ model." I said, narrowing my eyes at him, as I sat onto the couch. I grabbed a fluffy pillow and sat it on my lap, punching it for good measure.

A grin lit his face at my words, but to his credit he did move away from the counter.

"GQ model, huh?" He prompted with a twinkle in his eye as he came into the living room.

"You're missing the point. What I mean is do you HAVE to pose?" My face got hot. I was pretty sure this was my problem, not his.

He looked to the empty space on the small couch next to me then searched the room and spotted the one other chair in the room. He only paused for a second before moving to the soft pink chair. I ignored the disappointment in my gut and the "Boo's" from Bab as he sank his lithe frame into it.

"I'm not doing it intentionally, I assure you." He said, the smile on his face still watted to a 1,000. His next words took the smile from his face though. "So why don't you tell me what's been going on?"

I blinked against the tears that suddenly found their way into my eyes. I put my socked feet on the couch and pulled the pillow to my chest.

"Gods, where do I begin?" I said into the pillow. "Well, let's start off with the fact that I was kidnapped by the Boogeyman."

Sven leaned forward in his chair. "I'd heard tales of The Boogeyman. He is real then?"

"Oh, yeah. He sure is." On one level I was proud my fellow fae was so notorious that everyone knew him, but on a more practical save-your-ass level, I wanted to steer everyone clear of him.

"I've heard mostly bedtime horrors, but there was one story that was attributed to him in Transylvania that has always stuck with me." He said with a cocked head.

I found myself nodding at our unintentionally shared memory. "Oh, yeah. How he killed invaders to his land in a fit of rage and put their bodies on posts to keep out others. Vlad the Impaler historically gets the credit for that, but it's not the truth. Vlad just took credit for it because it increased his power. The Boogeyman let him because he didn't want to attract headhunters. He hunts. He is not the hunted."

"So how is it that he came to be hunting you?" Sven asked, intrigued by the revelation.

I threw my arms up in frustration and let them drop back down to the sofa. "By some miracle, my mother apparently had a favor the Boogeyman owed her, so she sent him to bring me back to the mound."

He rolled his eyes in amazement and said incredulously, "I can only imagine what agreement led them to that end. Yet, here you are. What has happened after that, my little faerie?"

I was like a locomotive engine, after I got going, I couldn't seem to stop. I told him about everything. Leaving the part about Anthony out (there was no need to pour salt on wounds,) I told him everything about the deadly scavenger hunt I'd had to go on to get out of Knockaine: escaping Goblins, a deadly horde of werewolves on a full moon, traveling to another world, the death battle in Hell, all of it. The fact that one of my old childhood friends tried to kill me and I couldn't save my best friend from a tragic fire seemed like an appropriate segue to my new split personality friend, after all that was the straw that had broken the camel's back, so to speak.

I talked well past the sun sinking into the horizon, through the incredible colors of the sunset painting the cityscape in pastel rainbows, and through the hundreds of lights that popped on, one at a time, into the inky darkness.

"And now I'm in some messed up game of hide-and-seek with these so-ugly-they-are-adorable goblins who want to kill me. Dagda knows why, though." My gaze, which had flickered back and forth between the vampire to my left to the scene out my window that changed like a digital picture frame, rested on the darkness.

He was quiet for a long time. Right that second, I would have given anything for him to come over, wrap his arms around me, and tell me everything was going to be ok. To not think about anything more complex than his hands stroking my worries out of my hair.

To Sven's credit, he absorbed it all, adding thoughts,

feelings, and exclamations in the right places. He even gave me psychologically sound advice when I told him about Bab. It made me feel cared for, like someone gave a shit. I don't know what I'd expected when I'd agreed to let him over, but it wasn't this. Honestly, given the emotional place I was in, I probably would have had sex with him if he'd tried. I needed to feel loved, and at the base of it, that was one way to achieve that. In fact, I'd half expected him to make a move on me after listening to me prattle on for a bit. But he just let me sit in silence. Let me process it. Maybe I didn't know him as well as I thought I did.

"Oh, yeah. We'd let him ravage every inch of your body." Bab said on a half-sniffle.

The ridiculous comment was enough to take a little of the weight from my maudlin thoughts. I laughed and had to agree. "You're right about that."

Sven, who'd been listening intently, blinked in confusion and asked, "I like being right as much as the next man, but may I ask, what am I right about?"

I covered my mouth with a hand, horrified. "I didn't just say that out loud, did I?"

Sven raised an eyebrow and thinned his lips before cracking their compression with a pop and saying, "Yep, you sure did. So what am I right about?"

I couldn't exactly tell him that I wanted him to come over here and mold my body like newly wet clay. Looking down to pretend sadness, I racked my brain for the last thing he'd said and grabbed onto it.

"That I need friends." I said, hoping he would buy it.

This time he did move over to the couch. I could feel the couch dip under his weight. The fluffy cushions sank in. My abs were not up for the unexpected challenge, and I struggled not to slide into him.

"It's a dumb thing to struggle against." Bab noted sagely.

I rolled my eyes. I couldn't respond, though. I'd forgotten how to breathe because Sven had taken my hands in his. My eyes flew up to meet his. His gaze held what could have been construed as need for a fraction of a second before they shifted back to the care that I'd seen for countless hours.

"You have a friend, Cy. I'm your friend." he said, a passionate need to be heard stitched into his face.

Pretty words, but I knew when it came down to it, they didn't mean anything. When it came down to it, he was just going to do what he wanted. The memory of the all-consuming anger I'd felt when I realized what he'd done to mark me came back over me. Sure, it was an echo of it now, but I clung to it. He'd marked me. For life. Do you know how long that was for a faerie? It might as well have been eternity. The buddings of anger was enough to pull my hands from his. I knew he could sense the shift in me because he grabbed my hands and pulled them to his side fervently.

"Look, I've been doing a lot of thinking. What I did was wrong. If I could undo it, I swear by the Mother, I would. I justified it in my head that it was for you too, to keep you safe from other vampires because without a mark you were fair game for any vampire to take you and make you theirs. But while that was part of it, it wasn't the real reason. The real reason is I wanted you all to myself. I didn't want to give you up. Wanted you all for myself. And now, I don't have you at all."

He took a breath. The protest that it wasn't his decision to make sprang to my lips. It was mine. My mind. My body.

Then he continued, "It was wrong of me to not give you the choice, not let you make your own decisions. You are your own person and deserve to do so. I know you didn't list me and what I'd done as part of what you've been through, but trust me when I say I am fully aware of how all of that must be affecting you too. To fear a species and then have the one you opened your heart up to betray you like that. It must have hurt like nothing else."

On one hand, he was right. On the other, he could never know how much he had hurt me. My breath hitched in my chest.

"I've never loved anyone like I loved you." I found myself whispering before the logical part of my brain could keep the words in.

Sven inched closer, the heat of his knee searing mine. His hands came up like he wanted to take my chin in his hands. I could feel my lips part. The little traitors. His hands were only suspended for seconds before he dropped them, settling for gathering my hands up into his again. It's like he didn't know what else to do with them.

"I know and it tears me up everyday knowing that I'm not worthy of you. I'm not here to pretend I am. I'm not here to beg for a second chance. I'm just here to be the friend you need, the friend you deserve. You'll have to forgive me though. My feelings about you haven't changed. I still want you just as badly. So if I look like I am struggling, it's because I am. But that doesn't mean I can't handle it. I'm a grown ass 250 year old man. I can *handle* it."

Rather than grab the lifeline he was offering, that I so badly needed, I had to find a way to protest, so I focused on the one thing neither of us could argue about.

"We'd said we loved each other, but you can't fall in love over the course of a few weeks. We were infatuated. That was all." I said, knowing it was the truth.

His eyes wanted to protest, but he stopped to think for a second, let his eyes travel to the wall clock, unseeing. Finally, coming to a decision, he said, "You know what? You're right. But I loved your spirit, your personality. Those things you can't fake. Maybe it wasn't true love. But it could have grown into that. Could have become that."

His words hung between us like a tightrope walker. What he said was true. I could feel the possibility sitting here even now, shiny and mesmerizing, as he sat here pouring his heart out to me.

"But I messed it up. I am more sorry for that than I can tell you. I can't take it back. There's no magic unfuck button. But maybe we can move forward as friends. Maybe I can still have your sparkle in my life and be what you need: a friend." He said, bringing our joined hands to his heart.

My throat bobbed at the intimate contact.

"Oh, for the love of all that is holy, just kiss him already," Bab practically shouted in my head.

I found myself smiling a watery smile, and I nodded, feeling true peace for the first time in a long time.

"I forgive you." I said, and I meant it.

Tears gathered in his eyes too, and he nodded his head too fast. I wanted to gather him in for a hug, but I held back. I didn't want to give him the wrong impression. For now, the dam I'd built to protect myself, the dam of anger and bitterness broke. Relief flooded over me. It felt so good to let go of the fury and frustration I'd been holding onto. Keeping that in your heart, didn't do you any good. The love and caring felt so much nicer, so much warmer. I yawned, suddenly tired.

He laughed through his tears and said, "Someone's tired."

"That happens when you're not dead." I quipped.

Laughter rocked his body forward. This time when he came back, he had no tears, which is what I'd been hoping for. I was done with the tears. I'd had enough of them to last a lifetime. I looked at the clock.

I gasped and said, "Holy shit, 5 am!"

He looked over at the clock with a sheepish look.

"Yeah, I noticed that," he confessed. "I just didn't want to stop you because you've been through so much, and I knew you needed to talk about it."

My heart expanded at his obvious kindness, especially when you consider the fact that the sun was going to come up soon. My joke about him not getting tired because he was dead was just that: a joke. I knew that he would be extremely tired if not because of the sunlight because I'd kept him up all night. A tired vampire meant a vulnerable vampire. Considering everything he'd done for me, I couldn't do that to him.

"Hey, I've got an idea," I said, giving his hand a squeeze and letting it go.

"I like ideas," said Bab warming up to my train of thinking.

Bouncing off the couch, I opened the entryway closet door. A broom and some clothes that I'd shoved in there when I was "cleaning" fell out. I grabbed a pillow and blanket before shoving the stragglers back into the closet with a foot. He'd stood up when I'd left and was now staring quizzically at me.

"Here," I tossed the blanket and pillow at him.

He caught these with a cautious look on his face. "What's this?"

"A cloak and a dagger, enjoy." I said with a laugh and then rolled my eyes. "You're not going out this close to dawn."

"You got that right, sister. That would be a damn sin," Bab agreed enthusiastically.

A smile twitched at Sven's lips. "You know that stuff about vampires in the sun is fabricated, right? I can go out in the sun just like you."

I walked over and pushed him back down onto the couch. "Right, but you've got to be exhausted, and I won't have your death on my hands. That shit is messy."

"What are you doing?" Bab asked, stress thinning his words.

He laughed and shook his head. "You worry for nothing," he said, taking his shoes off, despite his words.

I loved that he protested but did what I asked anyway. That made me feel better. Made me feel like he actually respected my thoughts and feelings. He swung his feet up onto the couch. They stuck comically off the side. That wasn't going to work. I grabbed a second pillow from my room and tucked it under his feet. All he did was laugh and shake his head as I laid the thin blanket over him. I stood back to survey my handiwork. Better.

"An utter tragedy," Bab said, sounding distraught.

Sven might be laughing, but I could tell he was tired. Vampire or not, the guy needed sleep.

"Now, promise not to leave until you've had plenty of rest." I said, feeling pretty good about myself.

"Pinky promise," agreed Sven with a smile that was suspiciously stretched like he was hiding a yawn.

I grinned back at him, resisting the urge to scrunch my nose up at him to be cute. With a smile still on my face, I walked to the bedroom.

"You're the worst. Like ever," said Bab as I shut the door.

I CLIMBED *up onto the dragon, my fingers slipping under scales as they looked for purchase. Finally, I made it to the dragon's neck. I straddled it. The thick muscles stretched my thighs wide. The dragon shot into the sky with a rush. I laughed and held on with my kneecaps. His neck moved, straining to reach higher and higher.*

Elation soared through me. Never would I have imagined that I could feel such elation riding a dragon, such pleasure, such...such...hey, since when could you feel a dragon spine this high up on its neck? Wait, was that a spine? Didn't they have vertebrae? I only felt one rigid thing pressed between my thighs. What in the hell?

Working, I pulled myself out of the dream, but the movement didn't stop. Now that I was awake, I knew the motion for what it was. I was in the living room, on the couch, straddling Sven. My eyes about flew out of my head. How in the hell did I get out here? That answer soon became apparent when I realized Bab was talking in my head.

"You like that, don't you, cutie?" Bab said to Sven. He proceeded to move my hips in a circle, grinding on Sven. "What about that?"

Sven groaned out loud. My eyes flew open, blinded by the afternoon light. His eyes were rolled back in his head. A rush of sensations flooded over me. Desire. Uncertainty. Fear. I wanted this, but I didn't at the same time. I wasn't ready. Didn't know if I would ever be ready for it to be with Sven again. I felt too vulnerable where he was concerned. But even if I did, I didn't want it to be like this.

Just like in the car, though, I didn't have a say where this was concerned. Bab had control over my body. Desperation clawed at me. I didn't want to be doing this. I needed control over my life. Over myself. I couldn't do this anymore. I needed to find a way to have control over *me*. Sven had said he would help me, so I reached out to him.

Willing all of my energy into my mouth and vocal chords, I was able to squeeze out, "Sven."

I tried to convey all of my desperation into that one word.

"Yes, my love. Yes." He said, taking my waist into his hands.

His fingers wrapped around to my back as he moved me

up and down. My skin moved under his fingers as he pushed and pulled me to him, in tandem with the grinding of my hips. I took all of my will to remember why I didn't want this. This wasn't the way. I needed this to be on my terms. And this couldn't be farther from that.

"Stop," I said, hoping that word would be enough because it was all I could get out.

This time Sven's eyes flew open in confusion.

"What?" He asked, blinking the fog of desire away.

This time I couldn't muster a sound, but I used my eyes to show my desperation.

"Cy?" He ground out the question, his voice hoarse with the effort.

He knew what I needed, though. I knew it by the way his head dropped back and his eyes squeezed shut. Grimacing with the effort, he stopped grinding against me, which had to have been no easy feat since my body still gyrated on top of his.

"Stop? What do you mean stop? You aren't making sense, Cy." he said, swallowing hard.

I tried to convey with my eyes everything I couldn't say. The dawning horror in his own eyes gave me relief.

"Sweet Mother," he said, grabbing me and lifting me off him.

I had about three seconds to marvel at his strength before he had flipped me around, and I was where he had been, prone on the couch. He stretched over me, his hands pinning my waist to the couch. What was he doing? Had he not understood? My breath came fast as panic washed over me. My arms, still controlled by Bab, wrapped around his neck and pulled him closer. He smelled so good pressed against me that my mind reeled. My tongue flicked out to run up the chord of his neck to just under his ear. I sealed the act with a kiss on the lobe of his ear. He shuddered under my lips. Gods, he tasted good.

"This is a natural treasure, and we should fuck it," Bab argued, raising my hips to rub against Sven's.

Sven groaned what had to be the most tortured sound I'd ever heard. With a Herculean effort, he pulled away. Relief made my mouth dry.

Bab knew I'd won. He grunted irritated and said petulantly, "You really are the worst."

He gave over control of my body so quickly that my hands dropped, one smacking me in the face.

"Ouch!" I exclaimed, raising a hand to rub what no doubt would be a shiner later.

"Cy?" asked Sven, tentatively.

I could see he was caught between indecision on not knowing if it was really "me" or not.

Giving him a half smile, I said, "Fancy meeting you here."

He moved off me in quick order, "Cy, I am so sorry."

I sat up, gingerly, more embarrassed than hurt. "You have nothing to be sorry about. It's totally my fault. I'm the one who jumped you, remember?"

"Yeah, but am I mistaken in the assumption that was..." he searched for a word and finally ended with, "not you?"

"No, you're right. That was Bab," I said. I didn't want to tell him the rest, but he deserved some sort of explanation, so I admitted, "He has...a bit of a crush on you."

Sven swallowed a smile and finally, looking way too happy about it said, "Is that right?"

"You're liking this way too much." I accused.

He looked away, still a ghost of a smile on his face "What can I say? He has good taste."

Suddenly, he became serious. His piercing blue eyes roved over me, assessing.

Finally, he asked. "How many times has this happened?"

I tried to keep the question light and quipped back, "I've only ridden 13 guys since he's shown up, why do you ask?"

He gave me a droll look. It wasn't the question he was asking, and I knew it. He wanted to know how many times Bab had taken control of my body against my will.

Deflated, I couldn't keep the monotone note out of my voice as I answered, "This is the second time."

Sven nodded, his lips pressed tightly together, "So he's taken control of your body before."

I nodded and motioned to the hula girl who was currently sitting in a prime viewing locale on the kitchen counter.

"So how does it work? Do you always know what's going on? Do you...leave consciousness and then come back?" He asked.

It was clear he wanted to better understand this whole multiple personality thing. That made the two of us. Unfortunately, I didn't have much light I could shed on the subject.

"This was the only time I wasn't aware right away, and I think that's because I was sleeping. Normally, I am fully aware of what's going on and all of his thoughts."

"All of what I say," Bab corrected.

Oh, great. There was more that I didn't get the "pleasure" of hearing? That was a scary thought.

"Oh, forgive me. I was just corrected. It's all of what he says," I rolled my eyes as I said it, trying to make it seem less serious than the panic that was starting to inch its way over me.

Sven nodded, taking it all in. When he didn't go running for the hills, I felt a little better.

"That makes sense, I suppose." Sven said, standing up.

He grabbed my hand. I went to move my legs off where I laid on the couch, and I noticed I was only in my underwear.

Again. Great. Then I noticed one of my bandaids was flopping loose. The strange thing was there was nothing for it to cover. What the heck? I reached down and pulled my skin taut. Still nothing. Not a hole, a tear, nothing. I tore off another bandaid. Flawless skin greeted me. I ripped another and another off. More unblemished skin greeted me as bandaid after bandaid joined the growing pile on the floor. I shook my head. Where were all of my cuts? Sven stopped my sharp yanks with a hand. His cool hand sent waves of relief over me.

Sven bent down to scoop up the bandaids and placed them in a neat pile on the coffee table.

"What happened?" He asked as he pulled off the remainder of the bandaids.

"Goblin attack," I said absently, mesmerized as every bandaid came up, with no wound or even a scab under it. Not even a knick to say anything had been there. They were small wounds, scratches in some cases, but they'd never healed in a day before. Had they?

When I kept staring wordlessly fascinated by the procession, Sven finally whispered, "You're wondering why there aren't any there now, aren't you?"

He folded the last bandaid and placed it on the table.

I nodded and said, "Well, yeah. I just got...cut yesterday. Shouldn't they still be there? Or is that my imagination?"

He helped me up with a hand. I rose slowly to my feet. Not answering me, he directed me to the bedroom and tucked me in.

Understanding dawned over me, and I asked him the question I already knew the answer to, "It's because of the vampire bite, isn't it?"

"It is," he confirmed, pulling the covers up over me.

I blinked expecting to feel something: anger, sadness, but instead I felt nothing. Numbness.

"What else is going to happen?" I asked in a surprisingly calm voice.

He sat down on the edge of the bed and thought about my question.

"Increased speed, healing, durability...beauty," he said the last as he pushed a strand of hair behind my ear.

"Like you?" I asked, fascinated by the thought that these things could be happening to me, and I didn't even know it.

That made him smile, "Not quite. You aren't a vampire from a mark. Just...enhanced. It would take 3 marks to turn you."

He finished the last statement, quietly. I wondered what it would be like to be a vampire. Drinking blood, in a constant blood battle for power. The hair lifted on the back of my neck. No, thank you. For all of their failings, I liked being a faerie.

"I think I'll pass on being a vampire." I said, as if he asked.

He chuckled and touched my cheek.

"I know," he said, quietly.

With a smile and a shake of his head, he got up and went to the door.

"Get some sleep," He said with his hand on the switch he stopped and looked back at me. "Oh, and tell your friend...if he comes out again. He won't like me very much."

I could see the threat in his eyes, and I don't know why it made me feel so safe, especially considering he was threatening me.

"You two may just well be made for each other," Bab said, pouting. "You're both no fun."

CHAPTER 11

*E*asing the apartment door shut behind me, I locked it with a soft click. I hadn't had the heart to wake Sven after everything I'd put him through last night and this morning. Or was it afternoon? Anyway. I hadn't trusted myself enough to go back to sleep after Sven had so sweetly put me to bed. Sweetly? I shook my head. It wasn't sweet. It was kind. Friends were kind, lovers were sweet.

"And what's wrong with that?" Bab huffed.

"I barely know the guy. Remember?" I asked as I tiptoed down the stairs, feeling like I was sneaking out of my own apartment. I kept up the ridiculous charade. I know he had great hearing. Since these walls were paper thin, I didn't want to wake him up.

"You know he would rather come with you than sleep, and you want him here," Bab pointed out, in a self-satisfied tone.

My brow furrowed. "Regardless, there's more to a relationship than sex. Which means no more of that bullshit you pulled last night, you hear me?"

When he didn't immediately reply silent, I prodded, "I mean it. That's not fair to him or me."

"Oh, fine." he said with a grunt.

He didn't have to be happy about it, as long as he respected it.

I looked both ways before stepping out of the stairwell. No goblins. Good. After Chaz's, I wasn't taking any chances. My old Buick was parked in the same spot it always was in the busy street.

Bab cleared his throat. "For what it's worth, I'm...I'm sorry."

Scanning the front and back seat, I yanked open the rusted door.

"Apology accepted," I said as I slipped into the worn seats.

With the goblin rise, I'd have to start locking my doors. I pulled into the sardine traffic. The traffic I didn't mind, the Jeffries' case, I did.

To try not to fall asleep, I'd pulled out my laptop and did a little bit of work. I already had the easy information from Wesley about John Jeffries: his date of birth, car make and model, and social security number. I'd looked through databases for the usual addresses, phone numbers, and license plate numbers to find his last whereabouts. When I'd found nothing, I did a quick hack into the NYPD's system. A stolen car had been reported in the area. A couple screens later into their license plate scanners showed just what I'd suspected: the plate had been scanned a few blocks from the family home. It made sense. We were talking about a man who'd literally sacrificed everything for his family. That was my lucky break too. Family was the easiest place to find the possible Judas in any case. A Judas was someone who felt scorned by the fugitive and could possibly be swayed to help in the person's recapture. That's actually where I was on the way to now. The Jeffries' family home. I figured one of them had to be the Judas. They'd scrounged to put up for John's bail. They were bound to have some bitterness about him taking the last of the little money he'd left them. Thankfully, luck was on my side. My lips thinned as I changed lanes. At least there was one thing easy about this case because Danu knew nothing else had been.

Thirty minutes later, as I sat on the Jeffries' family paisley couch across from the 3 Jeffries' women, I was eating my words. This was going to be harder than I'd thought. I'd been here for 20 minutes and they were a tougher nut to crack than an unripe walnut. All I'd succeeded in was having each of them retreat in one manner or another. Nadine, the mother and matriarch (and I used that term loosely) looked like she was going to sink through the horrid couch and clear past the floorboards. She made a meek woman look adventurous. Becca, who looked like a replica of her mother with her platinum blonde hair and waifish frame, hadn't moved her eyes from the black stain that dotted the carpet five feet in front of her 5 minutes past when I'd gotten here. The only person I'd gotten any sort of response out of was Tillie. She and John must have taken after their father in coloring because she had a strong jawline, which was currently clenched in barely suppressed fury. Her hateful brown hair stood up on its ends after repeatedly being pulled by her hands as she ran them through the thin strands over the course of our conversation. She was currently in the middle of "giving it to me." I tried to remind myself they were also the victims here as she screeched on.

"...I don't know who you think you are coming here. Like we would even think about turning Johnnie over to the likes of you, even if we *did* know where he was. It should be a damn crime for putting away a man who was just trying to do the best by his family the only way he knew how..." she said, going on and on.

I don't know how long she'd been going on, but I'd tuned out long ago. When someone didn't see that a crime had been committed, you weren't going to change their mind over the course of a few minutes. In a world where people didn't like to change their minds on little issues, they sure as hell weren't going to budge on those things, we call values. I pressed the coin in my pocket between my thumb and forefinger. With the tip of my finger, I outlined the phoenix I knew by heart now. I stifled a yawn. Tor Mór, I wished I'd gone back to sleep when I had the chance.

"I say we burn her at the stake. Or better yet, throw her in a pit and let snakes eat out her eyeballs," Bab piped up, clearly sick of hearing it too.

I decided to go for a different tactic. Partially because it was against the law to do either of the things Bab had suggested, though I must admit the thought did make me feel a little better. You couldn't cure bad. But was she bad? Or was she caught up in the tornado of emotion?

"But let me ask you something," I said, knowing full well that I was interrupting her tirade.

Becca's head flew up. The disturbance seemed to shock her out of her trance. Tillie was not taken aback however. No, ma'am. She was pissed. Red rimmed eyes shot fury at me. I kept talking like we were having a pleasant conversation about sunny weather.

"Don't you think it was a little selfish of him to do this to the family?"

Tillie sputtered. "Do this to the family? He's done nothing but sacrifice for the family. Sacrifice everything. It was the only way he knew to take care of us."

I turned my head to the side, like I was actually thinking about the crazy logic she'd thrown down.

After a moment, I shook my head and said, "But was it really the only way? If he'd have just been honest everyone in the family could have pitched in, helped out. There are countless organizations that are there for families suffering loss. You all could have gone to any of those. Together."

Becca's brows furrowed at this, not like she was angry, more like she was thinking.

Pressing my advantage, I went on. "He wasn't just trying to 'help.' He was trying to prove how manly he was. That he was good enough to be man of the house, and when he couldn't, instead of admitting that, he single-handedly, without consulting one of you about the fate he was roping you into, made the decision to bring you into the dangerous underbelly of the criminal world. Can you imagine how badly things could have gone? I say you thank your lucky stars the worst thing that happened was John got arrested and some of your possessions confiscated."

"I know what you are trying to do." said Tillie, fairly spitting her fury. "You are trying to get in our heads. But it won't work. We don't know anything, but even if we did, we wouldn't tell you. We wouldn't rat out our brother. Not after everything he's sacrificed for us."

From her statement about not getting into their heads, it was clear she was so wrapped up in her own hatred that she wasn't paying attention to Becca because right about now, she looked like she was about to go all plastic-bag-in-the-wind.

"He sacrificed everything, did he? No, he didn't. He didn't sacrifice you. But that's exactly what is at stake next if you go along with him. You could be attending her funeral right now," I said pointing from Becca to Nadine.

"That wouldn't happen," protested Becca, but I could hear the uncertainty in her voice.

"Couldn't it? Why don't you read up on crime families, after I leave. So you can know what life you are signing up for when John contacts you again and you *don't* report him," I stood up and gave them all a hard look, trying not to look like I was focusing on Becca. "Or instead, you could make the decision to finally take control of your life and give me a call."

I stood up and threw my business card on the table. Becca stared at the plain white and black business card, tangible fear flowing from her. Tillie's reaction was far different. She matched me, move for move, as she stood up and snatched the card off of the pine coffee table.

She ripped it into tiny pieces and held it out to me saying, "We won't be needing this."

I shrugged like it made no difference to me, "It's your funeral."

I caught Becca's wide eyes. I gave her a meaningful look before turning to the door. I started to walk to the door, thinking I'd misread her when she popped up like a thermometer on a turkey and followed me. "You get yourself out of here."

I played a pretty good poker face and tried to appear offended as I said, "It's not like I'm going to steal anything on my way out."

"You better believe it because I'm seeing you out," she said, her face red through the lie.

Tillie, who'd eyed Becca since she stood up, swung her gaze to me. Her evil eye said she wouldn't be surprised if I tried to steal the whole house from underneath their asses.

Becca and I walked to the door in silence. It wasn't until she'd opened the door for me, I stepped outside, and she followed me closely behind that the tension in my arms began to ease.

"Look, I don't like you or trust you." she began by saying, her jaw working.

I crossed my arms and didn't bother to say anything. She'd obviously come out here for a reason. She shifted on her feet and looked off into the distance, looking at nothing but the inside of her mind and the thoughts that undoubtedly crashed around in there like mallets against cymbals.

Her throat worked and she said, "But I can't keep doing this. Since John was caught, our family has fallen apart. It's like when we lost Dad all over again. I can't keep doing this. At some point, we need to be able to heal and move forward."

Running with it, I asked softly, "Does that mean John has contacted you?"

She snorted and bitterly said, "If he'd contacted us, we wouldn't be talking right now. When he says jump, we say. 'how high?' It was the same as when Dad was alive. I can't do that again. I need to live my own life for a change."

I nodded, knowing exactly what she was feeling. Pulling another business card out of my purse, I held it out to her. "Well, when he contacts you, call me. I'll take care of everything."

She nodded numbly, not taking the card. "Do you have any information that I could use to possibly locate John?" I asked, pressing my advantage. "The more information I have the sooner we can put all of us out of our misery."

"I...I wouldn't know what to give you." She said softly, the wind almost snatching her words away. "John always kept to himself."

"Was there a place he liked to go? A grocery store? Anything?" I asked, searching for possible answers.

"No, we usually did his shopping for him, and he pretty much spent most of his time here when he wasn't...working." She finished the sentence, her mind processing the lie John had told them about him going off to a job every day. Like he wasn't really going off and scamming people from 9-5 instead.

I tried not to show my disappointment. My mind worked.

There had to be something. I'd finally got someone close who could talk to me. I had to be able to get some kind of lead. It was a stretch, but I asked, "What kind of phone did he have?"

"A...Pixel 3, why?" she asked, her face clearly said I was grasping at straws.

Maybe I was, but I had to try something.

"What about a Gmail address? Does he have one of those?" I asked.

Her brows furrowed and she cocked her head, "Well, yeah, but I don't see how that is going to be much help."

I wanted to laugh out loud, or shake her in frustration. Most people had no idea the kind of information Google kept on you. What most families did know though were each other's passwords.

Tapping the card against my lips, I said, "Trust me. It's going to be a huge help. There's a lot of technology nowadays. Do you happen to know any of his passwords?"

She shrugged and looked away as she said, "I could take a pretty good guess."

Praying she did, I pulled a pen out of my purse and handed it to her along with the business card.

She looked at the card, scissored between my fingers. She softly shook her head. After a second, she took it, scrawled some information on the back, and handed it back, her motions quick and jittery. I put it back in my purse and took out another business card. When I gave her the card this time, she took it right away and shoved it in her front pocket, like it could burn her. She might not like it, but she didn't have to. All she needed to do was call me. And I knew she would, if her brother contacted her. She didn't want to live a life that wasn't her own anymore. I understood that feeling. I lived it every time I stepped in the same room with Mother.

CHAPTER 12

*B*ack at my apartment, I heard the noises before I put the key in the front door. Someone was in there. Oh, hell no. My heart beat double-time as I focused, pulling the energy from the ley lines to coil into my spine.

"Are we going to kick some ass?" Asked Bab, ready to do some damage.

I was right there with him. "Oh, for sure."

I had a second to wonder if it was the Goblins again before I shoved the door open to my apartment. When I saw the movement to my left, I feinted to the right and outstretched my hands, preparing to take a shot. It wasn't until then that I noticed Sven standing there holding a skillet with his shirt off in only his jeans.

"Gods above!" I shouted, throwing my hands in the direction of the ground, so I didn't shoot him on accident.

"Yum!" Bab said, getting over the shock sooner than I did.

"What are you doing here?" I asked, angry at Bab's reaction and how my body wanted to go over and rub over the length of him.

He raised the skillet in a defensive gesture. "I thought you might be hungry." He said, pasting on what he obviously knew was an enigmatic grin.

It worked on me like a sucker too. I could feel my insides get all gooey. I worked to solidify them and kept my footing as I asked, "I mean, *why* are you still here?"

"You aren't happy to see me?" he asked, putting his hip on the counter in a sexy pose.

He knew it was sexy too. The jerk. I scowled at him, mostly to hide the heat starting to creep up my body. When he could see his antics weren't working on me, he sighed and put the skillet back on the stove. He ran a hand through his hair and looked at me. I mean, *really* looked at me. I felt like there wasn't an inch of me that he didn't see. I squirmed.

A whole host of possible answers flitted across his face. From the way his shoulders slumped a shade, I could tell he decided to go for the truth. I applauded in my head. No matter how content pretty answers made you feel in the moment, they didn't help in the long run. And I didn't want to feel content for the moment. I wanted honesty, so I knew what I was dealing with. Knew how to move forward. That would make me happiest of all: the ability to move on for once in my life. To not forever be stuck in the past.

"You need someone here." He finally said.

Ouch. That hurt. Mostly because it was true. I was in over my waders, and I knew it. Quickly though, like all hurt does when it tries to be processed, pain quickly turned to outrage. I may be lonely, but that didn't mean I needed anyone. I'd never *needed* anyone in my life. After all, I had been through, all of the things I had lost, it was one of the only things I could still cling to: that I was capable. Me. Myself. I. How dare he insinuate that I wasn't enough?

The nice thing about outrage is it drove away lust like red

dandelion seeds in a tornado. I stalked towards Sven. Without conscious thought, ley line energy flowed into me, unbidden, unrestrained. I let it come.

"Now, you listen a damn minute. I don't need anyone. I've survived- no flourished in this cold, cruel hell with no one else but myself." As static electricity built around me, I was dimly aware my hair had lifted off my head and had bled to purple. It was a classic sign things were getting out of control. But it didn't matter. Nothing mattered except the misery and anger knotting a tight rope inside me. "Fuck, go before that even. I didn't need anyone when my dad and my sister were killed. I didn't need anyone when I had to pull myself out of the bog of my mother's all-consuming sadness. I didn't need anyone when she snapped out of it only to make my life a living hell. And don't even get me started on living in New York City knowing no one. I didn't need anyone then, and I certainly don't need anyone now."

I felt wetness on my face. Good gods, I was crying. How humiliating. It wasn't until another splat hit my arm and then my head realized it wasn't me crying; it was raining. I looked up, and a thundercloud had gathered above us. Lightning flashed in the cloud, waiting for my call. Seeing the light dance calmed me a bit. I wasn't alone. I always had the rain. Being that the ceilings were so low, though, I really had to calm myself though. Just because I was upset didn't mean I wanted to electrocute Sven or myself. I took a deep breath and pulled the energy back inside me. I could feel it coil around the base of my spine, where it lies in wait, like a serpent waiting to spring.

When the clouds had dissipated a bit, and just a light fog dewed our skin, Sven dared to take a step closer.

"Look," he said. "I'm not here to argue that you weren't ok before. I'm not here to point out that your childhood was a nightmare. That may have been the truth. It may not be. But, it doesn't matter. What matters is that you need someone now. Between the voice in your head making you do things and these rogue goblins I've seen everywhere on the news, you're going to need backup. Because believe it or not, there comes a time in everyone's lives where they need someone." He stepped closer to me, close enough to where I had to tilt my head up to continue to look into his eyes. His hands came to clutch my arms tenderly. "Let me be your someone."

Heat blossomed where he touched me. I was pulled into the magnetism of his soul-searching gaze.

"You are a bit of a mess. I'm not going to lie." Agreed, Bab.

I laughed a watery laugh and said, "Look who's talking."

Sven seemed to know I wasn't talking to him and a rye smile hitched up the corner of his lips. He rubbed my arms, bringing me back to the moment. I wanted to give him what he was looking for, but I just couldn't. He'd killed my trust. It didn't just spring back to life with a couple of nice words. It *was* nice to have him here, though, so I gave him a concession.

"What have you got cooking there?" I asked, nodding to the skillet on the stove currently streaming an amount of smoke that guaranteed anything in it was going to be the same color as a Black Witch's magic.

His smile said that he knew I was agreeing to his sexy butt being around. For now. Looking back to the food, he started to explain what the concoction was but, upon seeing the swirling smoke, exclaimed, "Shit!"

He rounded the L-shaped counter curve at a speed that had me wonder if he wasn't going to be out the rest of the night if he knicked the sharp edge of the corner. As he sailed around it, it turned out that he was a whole lot more graceful than I was, big surprise there. I had to smile as he shoved my old spatula around the pan, a discouraged look on his face. I came over to peer into the pan. It had nothing to do with the fact that I missed his warmth.

"Right. Keep telling yourself that, honey." Bab said, a smile in his voice as I bent around Sven in the tight space.

The gooey black and yellow contents of the pan looked like a pot of melted bees. I burst out laughing. Sven's scowl just made me laugh that much harder.

"It's not funny," he said, lines etched between the usually smooth expanse of his forehead.

I doubled over at the petulant look on his face. "Ow! Ow!" I said, gasping between breaths.

"Do you know how long it took me to make that? I haven't made food for two centuries. Let alone on one of these." He gestured to the yellow stove with the spatula with a force that caused some of the blackened goo to fly off and stick to the dirty surface.

The science experiment he called food didn't even run or slide down the side of the stove. It stuck like a stubborn lump, defying gravity, like a zit. It really was a disaster. My smile widened so far my face hurt. It was the sweetest thing anyone had done for me in a long time.

"I can't tell you," I took the pan out of his hand and tossed it in the stainless steel sink with a clang and continued, "how much I appreciate the thought. It probably would have been delicious if I hadn't come in and interrupted."

A smile twitched his lips, and he finally said, "No, it looked almost just as bad before you got here."

That got me laughing all over again.

"It does have the same qualities of a war zone gone awry." I acknowledged as I took in the rest of the kitchen. A bag of shredded cheese lay sprawled on its side, pieces escaping onto the counter to run recon into the unknown territory of the speckled countertops. Flour trailed from the counter to the floor in a sizable heap, which we were currently leaving footprints in. Spaghetti poked its head out of the top of its box, surveying the destruction. A can of carrots and olives stubbornly huddled together unopened, eyeing an opened packet of gravy just a few suspicious inches away.

Shaking my head, I started to shove the curious spaghetti back in its box when Sven stopped me with a hand on mine. It burned me deliciously.

"I got that," he said with a chagrined expression.

"Fair enough," I said, setting the spaghetti into his hand in what was starting to feel very intimate. To break some of the intimacy, I asked as I was walking into my bedroom. "Do you mind if I do some work while you do that?"

"Not at all." He said with a big smile, "as long as you will let me order you a pizza, at least."

I smiled as I walked back into the room with my laptop in my hand. "Only if it's a deluxe."

"Is there anything else?" he asked with a wink.

"There sure as hell shouldn't be," I said, unable to keep the mile-wide grin off my face.

The twinkle in his eye matched my smile, and I couldn't ignore the warmth that was turning my insides to jelly. I flipped up the computer screen to convince myself that I really *was* working. I signed into Google with the information Becca gave me and downloaded the data Google saved on John. Most of my attention was on Sven, though. He rattled off the order for pizza and the numbers off his black credit card like he'd done it a million times. Did vampires order pizza a lot? As he started to make his way around the kitchen, though, my attention *was* on the screens flashing in front of me. I flipped through the pages and pages of Google information.

By the time the pizza had gotten here, I had a twinkle in

my eyes that had nothing to do with the delicious dish he was carrying to me.

"Wouldn't you rather have a bite of that sexiness? You can have food any old time," said Bab.

I could practically feel him salivating as we watched Sven come towards us. I ignored him, which was quite a feat considering I was excited about what I found. I found the urge to place his lips on mine was growing exponentially with every passing second.

"You wouldn't believe what I found," I said to the plate of food to distract myself as Sven handed it to me.

"Something good, I take it?" he asked with a smile.

"Golden," I said. "I've got a hit on two locations that Jeffries visited regularly.

"You can do that through Google?" said Sven in awe, peering around me to check out the data on the screen.

"Oh, yeah. You'd be surprised what Google collects." I said around a bite of pizza.

I licked a drop of grease that was running down my hand in an attempt to getaway. Sven grabbed a napkin from the napkin holder and handed it to me.

Automatically, I said, "Thank y-" before I realized where he'd grabbed that from.

The napkin holder sat, brimming proudly with napkins on display as if it was like that all of the time. Which couldn't be farther from the case. I never filled the napkin holder. Usually, I just used a paper towel. My eyes snapped to Sven and narrowed.

"Did you fill the napkin holder?" I asked suspiciously.

"Maybe." He said, his face breaking into a giant, contagious grin.

For the first time, I took a second to really look around the house. It looked...fresh. Pillows were placed just-so on the couch. The coffee table even had a daisy sprightly sitting in a single bud vase on it. I looked at him with an admonishing eye and disappeared into the bedroom again. Clothes were hung up nicely on the rack, the bed was fluffed and made. A peek into the bathroom revealed the same thing. I stalked back into the living room and opened the entryway closet. No pillows sprung out at me; in fact, everything sat primly on their hangers and folded onto the shelves. My mouth fell open. Though the rest of the apartment had fallen a little into disarray after the month I'd had, this closet hadn't been clear from day one. Not since I'd shoved the last of my belongings in there after I'd moved in. I closed the door, the smoothness of the door closing foreign to my brain.

"Why?" I asked, my throat constricting at the kindness of the act.

He shrugged with a smile. "Because I want to help you. I want to be your person."

He was taking care of me. I pressed my lips together. I couldn't remember the last time someone had wanted to take care of me. I responded the only way I could to such a kind, unselfish act. I walked over to him. I stopped right before I got to him, my eyes shining with unshed gratitude. Finally, I stepped into his arms, he folded me into them. I breathed into the beauty of the moment, feeling his arms cradle me against his heart. My heart was beating like a moth against glass as I struggled not to cry.

When I felt confident to speak, I said into his chest. "You know I'm not going to be able to find a thing, don't you?"

His cheeks expanded in a smile against the top of my head. "I know."

I laughed a watery burble. He pulled away to look at me. I know love and desire were shining in my eyes; I didn't care.

"Kiss him," egged on Bab.

For once, we were on the same page. Indecision warred

inside me, though. Did I really want to go down that path and be hurt all over again? The possibility was there. There was no doubting it.

Sven seemed to understand my indecision and disengaged himself, slowly saying, "So where are we off to?"

CHAPTER 13

I pulled into the pothole-ridden parking lot. The colossal sign with dancing boobs that proclaimed "Juiced" threw neon colors into the puddles that looked unending in the darkness. The Buick shuddered into the parking space next to the door. The sooner that I could get in and out of this strip club, the better. The solitary sound of my door opening and closing wasn't lost on me as I thought about how Sven had fought me about wanting to come with me. I finally had won the argument when I mentioned that the women who worked here were less likely to talk if I had an imposing-looking man in the background. He couldn't argue with that point, but he did throw in a couple comments about my being a stubborn princess and gave me a hug like it was going to be the last time he saw me. Not wanting him to come may have more to do with the fact that I didn't want to see half-naked women throw themselves at his sexy self or, worse yet, him show the slightest interest in them.

As I stepped into the low light of the club, the slow tempo of the base snaked its way into my veins. Speaking of half-naked women, my eyes went to the stage. If that's what you could call it. It was the height of a platform built out of two by fours, so it was more like a platform at a mall than an actual stage.

There a woman gyrated with all of the excitement of a woman paying lot rent. From the way her hips dropped to the side unceremoniously, you could tell she was a woman who'd seen shit, and nothing you were going to do was going to impress her. She looked like she'd been here a while. She was probably the best place to start. I tried to look as inconspicuous as a woman in a strip club on a Wednesday night could look as I made my way to the black velvet curtain by the edge of the stage. The handful of men lounging in the chairs around her looked just as interested in being there.

I tried not to brush up against the aged velvet curtain as I focused on watching the rest of her performance. Through the hazy and flashing strobe lights, I could make out that she was dressed (dressed seemed like an overstatement) in a brown stemmed hat with a black blusher veil that impeccably fell down red lips. Her top was totally bare of clothing, but she did wear a G-String in the shape of a grinning pumpkin. It seemed unfazed as the girl grabbed the pole and walked around it like she was surveying a used car she considered buying. I'd seen some jaw-dropping pole dancing videos online, but this was not it. After a few more minutes of glaring at the audience and used car shopping, the music ended as she leaned against the pole with a little kick of her foot and looked up with abandon at the ceiling. Apparently, she could never find a decent used car either. A couple of men walked up and threw some dollar bills on stage. This time the smile on her face was as close to genuine as I think this girl got as she winked at them. One guy even gave her a tip of an imaginary hat. There. Gallantry wasn't dead.

"Give it up for Pumpkin Spice!" growled an announcer over the intercom as she unceremoniously made her way to the front of the stage, scooping up the bills.

She walked off stage to a smattering of applause. This was my chance. I rounded the corner, and feeling ridiculous, I called out to her.

"Miss Spice, might I have a word with you?" I realized how silly I sounded, but I wanted to add some formality to it, to show her I was here on business.

She turned around, her makeup looking cakey this up close. She gave me an up-and-down look and asked, "You the cops?"

"No, ma'am." I answered, holding my hands up in the generally understood gesture of 'I come in peace."

After a second of staring at the silk tank top peeking out from my leather jacket, she nodded. "Go ahead and take a seat, and I'll be right out."

She barely waited for my nod before she turned around. I made my way to one of the tables in the back. With time on my hands, I surveyed the rest of Juiced. It had a far more relaxed atmosphere than I would have pegged a strip club for. With more of a diner mentality than a strip club, the wait staff wandered in and out of the handful of customers. Every so often, though, I would be reminded of where I was. A boob here, a woman leading a man in the back by the hand there. Oh, and glitter. The only time I'd seen more glitter was a gathering of faeries. If it wasn't for the disenchanted and slightly grimy feel of the place, I would have said it felt almost homey. Almost.

It might have been my preoccupation with my surroundings. Still, it felt like Pumpkin Spice was walking to me in fishnets, black hot pants, and a bikini top sooner than I thought she would be. She didn't seem like the kind of person who hurried for anyone. She would probably walk casually away from an explosion.

"Yeah?" she said unceremoniously when she got to the table. "What do you want?"

"Have a seat." I offered, trying to make her feel more comfortable.

The more comfortable someone was, the more they would be willing to open up to you.

She popped some gum I hadn't realized she was chewing until now and said, "No can do. If Marley sees me sitting on the job, I'm toast. And crappy job or not, I still need it."

I nodded. I suppose that made sense. However, it made me uncomfortable to have the bored stripper standing over me. Oh, well. It wasn't the first time I'd been uncomfortable here. Ignoring it, I pushed my gun to the side as I pulled Jeffries' picture out of my purse.

"Do you know this guy?" I asked, handing her the picture.

The dim light of recognition flickered in her eyes.

"Oh, yeah. He comes in here all the time. Though not lately. He in trouble?" Spice asked, handing the picture back to me.

"You could say that." I offered unhelpfully. "Did you have much interaction with Mr. Jeffries?"

"Nah, I didn't even know his name. He usually came in and just went straight to the bar. Didn't seem to be interested in being helped by anyone but Chastity." She said, pointing a finger to a small-boned blonde woman behind the bar. "Not too surprising there, though. Every man has their favorites."

Seeming to prove her point, she caught the gaze of a man a couple tables over and winked at him. He wiggled his fingers at her suggestively.

"Look, I've got to make some tips. Are we done here?" She asked, not making any bones about the fact that she wanted to move on.

I nodded my thanks and said, "Absolutely. Thanks for your help."

She didn't return my nod, instead made her way over to the hand-wiggling man. I couldn't look away as she curved a hand over his cheek and ran them suggestively down his jowls. He grinned wildly. Unbelievable. That shit actually worked?

Shaking my head, I turned back to the reason I'd come here. I made my way to the bar and sat on one of the surprisingly clean-looking stools. I sat purposely on the other side of the bar from the only other customer. Chastity was helping the other customer. Her outfit was very similar to Pumpkin Spice's, except hers was gold. Her hot pants showcased short legs that gleamed in shimmer stockings as she stood on tiptoe and leaned over to get the money the customer had sat too far to the edge of the bartop. He'd probably done it on purpose to see her cleavage. A quick look at his eyes said that I'd been right on the money. Chastity seemed used to it, though, because she grabbed the money and sank back onto her heels with a quick movement that offered him no more than a glimpse at best.

You could tell he was disappointed. I smiled, liking her immediately. When she was done, she made her way over to me. Her hair was in one of those sensible messy buns that screamed sexy but were also easy as hell to create. For those with practice anyway. I'd seen people do it, and it still eluded me. I always ended up looking more like your 70-year-old grandma than a sexy schoolmarm.

"What can I get you?" she asked with what appeared to be a genuine smile on her heart-shaped face.

"I need some information," I said, presenting her with Jeffries' picture again. "Do you know this man?"

"Oh, sure. He comes in all of the time." the petite bartender said, handing the picture back to me.

My heart quickened. "Has he been in here recently?"

She cocked her head to the side and then, after a brief pause, said, "You know...now that you mention it, I don't think I have."

I deflated. Nothing could be that easy, could it? I really wish they hadn't taken Jeffries' phone. It would make this a hell of a lot easier to track him down.

"Has he mentioned coming or going from anywhere in particular when he comes in?" I asked, falling back on my usual pattern of determining where he was going or where he might be coming from.

She pulled a dirty rag from out behind her counter and started wiping down the gleaming counters. "Nah, he usually doesn't say much. I get the feeling he comes here more to get away. He just orders a Coke and sips on it for about an hour. When he's finished, he leaves." Pausing in her wiping off the counter, she resumed scrubbing at a spot I couldn't see with a little bit more force. "To be honest, he's one of the last people who come in here that I'd expect anyone to be asking about."

That had me curious. "Why's that?"

"Because he doesn't bother anyone, and is nothing but courteous and kind when he is in here. I mean, sometimes I catch him *looking* if you know what I mean, but nothing more than that."

"So he's never done anything...odd?" I asked, searching for the correct wording, "Nothing out of the ordinary?"

She stopped to look at me. "No, noth- well, I guess unless you count that one time he asked me for a lap dance. That was a little strange. I'm the wait staff, not one of the girls. But when I told him as much, he never brought it up again."

"Did he get any lap dances from any of the other...girls?" I asked.

"No, just the one Coke and jetted. I got the feeling he was just lonely, so I tried to talk to him at times. He never really had much to say. I think he just liked the company more than anything." She said with a shrug.

"Hey, Chast." Called the other customer, holding up his glass and rocking it back and forth in the symbolic 'refill' signal.

Clearly, he was not appreciating how much of Chastity's time I was taking up.

With the patience of a bridge troll, she raised her finger. "Be right there, M-"

A hollow groan interrupted her. Chastity stopped, wide eyes shooting to the floor where the sound had come from. Short, staccato moans followed, and then another one that sounded like pulled taffy. A stillness fell over the room, and everyone seemed to freeze. People looked around confusion, blinking their wide eyes. Then suddenly, the faucet in front of me seemed to rise of its own accord. I jumped up, pulling ley line energy in a breath to curl around my spine.

"What in the hell?" Chastity stumbled back then stood, her feet braced.

No sooner had the words left her mouth than other pipes started to rise up. Then they came back down in a sucking motion, then shot back up.

"Oh, look, a symphony!" Exclaimed Bab.

Then he proceeded to hum along as the pipes rose and fell and swirled. He didn't stop as the tubes exploded and water shot out of every available faucet, newly exposed pipe, and drain. People ran around in a cacophonous mess of bursting pipes, spraying water, screams, and crashing furniture. More people had poured into the main room from in back. Limp penises bobbing their sadness, and boobs moved in a frenzy as people ran past in various states of undress. Water sprayed them from all directions, eliciting muffled screams and shouts. One fully nude man took a jet right in the face, slipped on the wet floor, and went down with a thud so loud it gave the groaning pipes a run for their money. People were more likely to kill themselves in the hysteria than they were by the mayhem around them. I had to do something. Since all of the plumbing was downstairs, the problem had to be coming from down there. Chastity backed up until the bottles lining the bar behind her clanked. To her credit, she wasn't running around, hysteria at her heels.

"Is there a basement in this place?" I yelled over the mass hysteria.

She nodded and pointed to where the people had poured in from the back.

I headed that way with one final direction. "Get everyone out!"

The less the damages, the less the cops were involved. The less the cops were concerned, the better. They weren't the biggest fans of bounty hunters, and anything they could even stretch to pin on my head, they would.

This time I pulled a full breath of energy into me. I could feel it expand my chest as I rushed through the narrow hall that served as the passageway from the dressing rooms to the stage. Some girls, Pumpkin Spice, included, still lounged in their dressing rooms.

One with a peacock plume in her aubergine hair pulled the cigarette from her mouth. "Gunfight?" She asked, flicking the ash onto the grime encrusted floor.

I shook my head no and kept moving. I couldn't be distracted by their apathy. I had to find out what was going on. As soon as I passed their dressing rooms, I saw a sign that said Boiler Room right next to a door that said Manager and had a crude penis scratched into the door. That had to be it.

"You sure about this?" Bab asked, clearly underestimating me as I opened the door to the Boiler Room.

The groaning and crashes intensified, along with a couple

grunts that sounded suspiciously familiar. It was the familiarity that halted my steps as I went to step in. I sent energy into my hands, enough to charge them, and made my way down the narrow staircase. A light flickered against the white-washed brick as I made my way down. When I rounded the corner, I stifled my own groan. You had to be kidding me.

There had to be a dozen goblins down here. Some had wrenches and were hammering against the metal tubes that were half the size of their bodies. Others swung from the smaller pipes like they were chandeliers. With the skull of a bird over his private area, one goblin stood closest to me. At least a foot of water lapped at his kneecaps. He was directly underneath another, and he idly grabbed the feet of his friend above. With lazy movements, he swung the unfortunate goblin back and forth.

I shook my head and continued to survey the group. My groan was swallowed by the pipes as I spotted Kut and Maybe among the rabble. Kut hurtling Maybe higher than all the rest, her arms thick by goblin standards. Slowly, the activity stopped one by one as they noticed me.

"Look at them, doing damage." Bab sounded...proud.

What in the hell? Suddenly, everyone started talking in their tongue, one over the other. The sound was almost more painful than the noise they'd been making on the pipes.

"Enough!" I shouted above the din, my noise echoing in an endless loop over the water and old brick. "I'm tired of seeing your adorably-ugly faces everywhere. Tell me why."

One of the goblins dropped from the pipes into the water with a splash. Water drenched the others near him. The goblin with a bone sticking through his earlobe raised his hand to cuff the other offender. The goblin who'd landed in the water paid him no mind.

"Look who's calling who ugly. You with that disgustingly

smooth skin and vomit-worthy silky hair," he said, the movement causing water to drip off his ears and pointed chin.

I tried a different tactic. "Maybe. Kut. You've been the worst. Why are you here, *again*?"

All of the eyes in the room centered on the two goblins. Their all-too-familiar faces had a reddish hue to them. Could they be embarrassed?

"Kutulun? Mabye? Is she talking about you two? Why are you on a pet name basis with this God Thief?" One of the burlier goblins let go of, the larger pipe and moved towards the two with untrusting steps.

He was bigger than Kutulun, which was saying a lot. She was one of the tallest goblins I'd ever seen. She looked more like a dwarf than a goblin.

"We were under guidance from the Queen," said Kut. Though her words were calm, she let go of Maybe, and her hand went to the dagger in her waist.

"Enough of this. Tell me what I want to know." I interrupted.

I wasn't interested in wasting my time on a goblin skirmish. I had other places to get to. It didn't have anything to do with the fact that I didn't want to see Kut get hurt.

"You just keep telling yourself that," said Bab, a smile in his voice.

"We don't have to tell you anything, God Thief." said one of the smaller ones close to me.

He was a lot closer than I remember him being before. He'd obviously been trying to sneak up on me. I'd have to keep an eye on him.

"You may want to rethink that," I said, putting some lightning into my palm and looking meaningfully at the water.

They all knew the subtle threat I was implying. I could tell from the way they tensed up.

"We'll never bow to the likes of you!" Squeaked a little goblin in the back.

Fury pink tipped her ears; I could see them all the way from the front of the room where I was.

"Wrong answer," I said quietly.

I knew it was loud enough in the room to where they all heard, though. I lowered my sparking hand to the water.

A goblin that was all limbs stumbled through the water towards me and screamed, "You stole what is ours!"

The smile of satisfaction that I had gotten them spilling their guts quickly disappeared as his words sunk in. It took me a second to realize he was probably babbling about that God thief thing again.

I resisted the urge to roll my eyes. "Look, I know your buddy mentioned it a couple of times, but I didn't steal a God."

As if you could. I mean, really. It was the craziest idea ever. Gods were all-powerful; someone didn't just take them like a hotel shampoo.

"You took him. Multiple goblins saw it. You can't deny it, God Thief." said the one closest to me, his little body shaking with fury.

This was crazy.

"I didn't take-" then it hit me. I *had* taken something. The bone from the altar. "Are you talking about the bone?"

"Of course, we are. What else would we be talking about?" Scoffed the bigger one who'd since turned his attention away from Kut and rested it on me.

"We have to return it back to its rightful resting place.." explained Kut quietly.

"Or suffer the wrath of Loki." Maybe added from where he dangled above Kut.

"They're not wrong." Bab agreed merrily.

"Well, fuck." I said under my breath.

As if to emphasize my point, Maybe lost his grip and fell. Kut stepped back, and he fell into the water with a giant splash.

CHAPTER 14

*S*tanding in front of the last house on my list, I knocked on the white screen door. I let out a deep sigh. Knocking on people's doors was at the bottom of my Good Time list. They treated you with all of the warmth of a grim reaper.

I suppose I should be thankful. It was only by the grace of the gods I was here. Goblins weren't a peace-loving bunch, so I'd been shocked they let me go when I told them I'd get the bone and get it back to them. Maybe it had something to do with my being stronger than they realized and their few numbers. Whatever the reason, I now found myself needing to take a trip to Iris's. Truth be told, I may have lied to the goblins. There was no telling if she even had any of the bone left after making the potion. My stomach flipped as I thought about the fact that I'd drank a thousand-year-old bone.

"Makes you feel great, doesn't it?" quipped Bab.

"Shut up," I muttered under my breath.

I'd just finished muttering when the white door swung wide.

"May I help you?" asked a middle-aged man with white hair at his temples.

"Hi, yes. My name is Cy. I'm with the Bounty-ful Hunter and Private Investigator Services. I'm in search of this man." I said as I handed the picture to him like I had at the last three houses.

I didn't really expect someone to positively ID Jeffries. After all, they could be in cahoots with him. That didn't matter much, though. I was trained in telling if someone was lying. What the witness *didn't* do and say was just as important as what they did say.

However, this man was only displaying positive indicators as he looked at the picture. "No, I've never seen this man before. I'm sorry."

Well, shit. I don't know why Jeffries had been here, but everyone up and down this block hadn't been able to positively identify him. I reached to take the picture back when a woman's voice floated to us.

"Are your parents here already, Rob?" it asked right before the source of the voice.

She was wiping her hands on a well-used apron, her blonde hair in a messy ponytail. That wasn't what held me transfixed. She looked like she could be a twin to Chastity. All the way from her petite frame to her heart-shaped face. When she saw me, her small eyes blinked in confusion, but she didn't lose the polite look on her face.

"Oh, excuse me. I didn't mean to interrupt," she said, pushing a strand of hair out of her face, holding out a hand to me. She introduced herself. "Faith Regan."

"Cy Vanguard," I said, taking her offered hand and giving it a couple brisk shakes before letting go. I hated handshakes. "You aren't interrupting. Maybe you can help, actually. I'm a bounty hunter, and I am looking for this man. Have you seen him?

I handed her the picture, my fingers tingling in anticipation. She knew something; she had to. She looked too much like Chastity for it to be a coincidence.

As soon as she laid eyes on the picture, she clutched her neck.

Bingo.

"Who is he?" I prompted, not even bothering to ask if she knew him.

At first, she tried to speak, and nothing came out, but after another try, her voice worked. "That's John Jeffries."

I resisted the urge to crow. Finally, a break in this case.

I pulled my notebook from my back pocket. "Mrs. Regan, what is your relationship to Mr. Jeffries?"

"Relationship? Well...if you can call it a relationship, I would suppose you could say...former...almost-boyfriend?" She said, her voice stilted in confusion. "But that was years ago, back when I was in high school. So what...9 years at this point?"

Former almost-boyfriend? That didn't make much sense. A former "almost" boyfriend didn't come to your house for hours on end. Maybe she was having a fling and didn't want her husband to know.

"The hussy." Bab huffed excitedly.

Put down the popcorn already. I wanted to say. This isn't a soap opera.

"Have you had any contact with Mr. Jeffries since then?" I asked, keeping a keen eye on her reaction.

Either she was the best actress I'd ever seen, or real confusion crossed her face. "No, I have not."

Instead of beating around the bush, I called a spade a spade. I said, "You'll have to forgive me, ma'am, but I have to ask: why would an almost-boyfriend from almost 10 years ago be at your house every week for 3 years for two hours or more?"

At my words, the color drained out of her face. "He... he's been here? No, surely, you must be mistaken."

I leveled a severe look at her and said, "I assure you I am not mistaken. I have tracking information that puts the suspect at this location."

"In our house?" prompted the husband, who obviously had a very vested interest in this now too.

However, to his credit, he wasn't freaking out.

"Well, not specifically in the house, no. However, right across the street and GPS is accurate up to 3 meters. It makes sense he would park there and come in here." I said, putting it out there.

"He has not been in this house." She looked to her husband, her hand fluttering around her throat. "He hasn't!"

I believed her. I didn't know why, but I did.

"Why don't you tell me what your relationship to John Jeffries was?" I asked more gently this time.

"When we were in 11th grade, I heard he liked me. It was just a silly rumor. Nobody as attractive as him was interested in someone like me. But then he started to come around and show interest in me. He helped me carry my books home. Helped me through problems with my family. Silly teenage problems, but they were everything to me at the time. Things were...perfect. I thought he was going to ask me to be his girlfriend. I would have in a heartbeat, too, mind you. But...when his dad died, he just...stopped coming around. It was like a light switch turned off. It wasn't shortly after his dad died that he dropped out of school, and I never saw him again."

All of her body language screamed that she was telling the truth. I didn't understand it, though.

"So...if what you are telling me is true, you expect me to believe after six years of no contact with you, he just started showing up at this house one day?" I asked, letting her see my skepticism. "And what does he do? Just sit outside for a couple of hours once a week?"

I made it sound ridiculous, but the idea had more credence than she thought. Chastity told me basically the same story.

"Yeah, I...guess I am." She said, letting go of her throat and shrugging her shoulders in confusion.

"No." spoke up her husband. "We just moved here 3 years ago. Who knows how long he was coming around before that. I'm willing to bet if you looked at that history of yours, you'd find this address from before too."

He rattled off an address, and I penned it down, lost in thought. Either this woman was a hell of an actress, or her life could possibly be in danger. I couldn't take the chance of either.

"Look, if what you say is true, we are looking at a man with a very real obsession with you. A man who has nothing more to lose. Your life very well could be in danger. With all of the things on his rap sheet, I wouldn't be surprised if he decided to finally make good on that obsession and add kidnapping to the list."

At my blunt words, her legs buckled, weak with the news. Her husband caught her and led her down to the chair next to a cluttered shoe rack. She stared into the distance with saucer eyes.

"What do we do?" he asked, putting a comforting hand on her shoulders.

"Do you have a firearm?" I asked, my lips pressed into a thin line.

"I do." He said, his nod tight.

"Keep it with you at all times, and make sure she does not leave your side until you hear of his capture. Keep an eye on the news. They love this kind of shit. Feel free to call the NYPD for updates too. Arm your alarm system at all times." I said, motioning to the alarm panel with a nod of my head. "In the meantime, only travel during the day and stay away from crowded places where she could be easily taken."

His eyes blinked fast to take in all of the information. Her shoulders seemed to shrink in on themselves as I rattled off the precautions they were to take.

"I'll have NYPD add you to their patrol route until the threat is eliminated," I added as a final thought.

This way, they could protect her should anything go awry or monitor the house for any suspicious activity. Though, I was betting on it being the former rather than the latter.

Minutes later, after we'd swapped information, I was back on the road heading towards my house with the ringing phone up to my ear.

Darkness pressed in around me. It would be good to get back home. Back to Sven. The thought filled me with more warmth than it should have.

The phone picked up, and a too-young voice said on the other end, "Tyler NYPD detective unit."

I fought the chuckle that threatened. He wishes he was a detective. He was just a beat cop until Burdock retired, which I'm sure he was praying for would happen any day now.

"Hey, Tyler. Cy, long time no talk to." I chirped.

"Cy. Yeah, nice to talk to you," he said though the way he dropped his voice low said differently.

The police didn't have a great relationship with bounty hunters, and Tyler had been mocked on more than one occasion for being my "friend." Friendly was a better way to put it. I wouldn't call us friends by any stretch of the imagination, but in a cop's mind, friendly was too close to a friend, especially when it came to a bounty hunter. We were pretty much the scum of the earth where they were concerned.

"Hey, I just came from a Faith Regan's house. Turns out John Jeffries' may have been stalking her." I said, pulling the Buick to a shuddering halt at the red four-way stop.

"No, shit." he breathed. Then added, "So you're on the Jeffries' case, huh? That is going to put piss in Burdock's coffee if you find him when he couldn't."

"You guys have too much to do to worry about this kind of B.S," I said, partly out of kindness because I wanted him to do me a favor and partly because it was true.

I read him off the address and asked. "Could you add her to your patrol to keep an eye on the situation?"

I could hear him scribbling down the information as a car's headlights pulled up behind me. I flipped the visor so it wasn't shining me in the eyes before accelerating down the road.

"Yeah, I can do that," he said. "Do you really think she's in danger?"

"Could be. It's also possible that she could be in cahoots with Jeffries, and he might show up later." I added as the car behind me came upon me.

It accelerated to pass me. My eyes flicked down to the gauge. Passing when I was going 60 in a 50 MPH zone. Asshole.

"You think-" the rest of what he had to say was cut off by the car jerking to the left.

I didn't know what had come first: the sickening crunch of metal on metal or the jerk of the car. Whichever wasn't important. I dropped the phone as I tried to regain control of the vehicle.

"Son of a bitch!" I shouted.

Tyler's tinny voice came from the floorboards mixed with the grind and crunch of car on car. Then the car that had hit me regained control. I regained control of the wheel and took a shaky breath, starting to pull over so we could assess damages. The next crash made me more mad than surprised. Something was seriously wrong here. As I fought for control of the vehicle, I looked over to the next car that I realized was fighting to keep on the narrow roadway. It was a woman with a crooked nose and short brown hair. Something about the hair sent off warning bells in my head. The car jerked away, and I righted the car again. Darting a look at the other car again, I realized what was off. The person looked very familiar.

A car honked and was coming right towards us. He laid on his horn as the lights shone into the car. With bright lights, I realized it was John Jeffries in disguise. He was wearing the wig and nose prosthetic that he'd bought from Jazzy. Shock recoiled through my system. It couldn't be. I don't know if he knew he'd taken me by surprise or not, but the next thing I knew, the car sped up and swerved over, knocking the front of my car, pointing it to the ditch. I didn't have any time to react as my car sailed into the ditch. The seatbelt dug into my ribs as I braced myself. Crunching and crashing filled my world as I flipped, once, twice, three times, and the world went black.

CHAPTER 15

"Wakey, wakey." Came a voice that was all too familiar.

I was too tired to give it much credence.

"Get your ass up, girlfriend," it said again.

This time I recognized it clearly as Bab.

"You're damn right it is. Now, get out of this car before I get you out of here myself," said Bab in a stern voice.

Grumbling, I opened my eyes. Where in the hell was I? It took me a second, but I realized I was hanging upside down. Putting one arm up to prop myself up, I unclicked the seat belt with the other arm, catching myself before my face implanted itself into the ceiling. I lowered myself with tired arms and turned my legs to crouch on the roof. I peered through the window into the night. I couldn't see any dangers, but just in case, I pulled energy into my body and pushed just enough to light a thin glow into the darkness.

Nothing. Not even a stopped car.

Jeffries must have taken me for dead and kept going. It was probably in his best interest since I'm sure the car that had almost run him off the road had witnessed the whole thing. As if on cue, I could hear sirens getting closer and closer. Confident that would scare off Jeffries in any event, I pulled the latch on the door and pushed it open with my forearms. Just as my head popped out of the door opening like a prairie dog, blue and red lights lit up the side of the road right before coming to a stop.

It was getting easier to move already. I could tell I was already starting to heal from the few injuries that I had. I looked down and saw some new rips in my jeans that had more to do with the blood staining my jeans and less to do with a fashion statement. Hopefully, nobody insisted I go to the hospital, or this was going to turn into "fun to explain" real quick.

CHAPTER 16

I walked into Iris's shop feeling like it had been a lifetime since I had been here last. Had it really only been less than a month ago? The smell of lavender was overpowering as I ducked past some herbs that hung drying from the ceiling.

It was an unlikely place for me to be after the car wreck, that was for sure. All I could attribute it to was shock. After having talked to the police, one of them, which had been a very panicked Tyler who had been sweet enough to track my phone when he'd heard the car wreck, I'd gone home and told Sven that I had to come to Knockaine and could I borrow his car? He'd looked at me like I was insane. I couldn't help it, though. It felt like there were just one too many people out for my head, and that was getting as old as dancing with your Uncle Walt at your Sweet 16. If I could put just one of those mysteries to rest, I would be the better for it. I could feel a little more at ease.

And currently, the mystery that was eating at my head that I actually might be able to find out the answer to was the goblin's increasing presence and threat on my life. Right now, they were manageable, but if they kept scaling in number and in an attack like they were, it wouldn't be soon before I would be too outnumbered and too unaware to do anything about it. So I was here to find out from Iris if any of the bone was left (I was hopeful but doubtful), and if there wasn't, how did I go about getting them to stop. Given all of her knowledge of the fae, she was sure to know something. Well, more than I did anyway. I had been a piss poor student in school. Something I was really regretting right now.

Not seeing her in the shop, I ducked my head into the kitchen off the front of her shop that doubled as her spell cooking area. A giant, cast-iron cauldron bubbled noisily on the flat cooktop. What was she cooking up in there? A duplication potion? An enhancer potion? A *love* potion? Gods was I curious to know. I'd never known any witches before, and I'd always been insanely curious as to how one went about making magic.

"Well, then what are you standing there for? Go find out!" Egged Bab on.

I could tell from his tone of voice he was just as curious as I was.

"Oh, alright," I said in an exasperated voice. "Let's do what *you* want to do."

Then I giggled at the absurdity of it all as I all but tiptoed over to the steaming cauldron. The steam heated me up quickly. I took my thick winter jacket off and set it next to the cauldron, making sure to keep it far away from the cooktop. I quickly realized the cauldron was too tall to see inside on top of the cooktop. My hopes sank until I saw a plastic step-stool to the left of the gingerbread-style counter. Taking care, I plucked it up and set it soundlessly onto the ceramic butter-yellow, glitter, and grime-covered tile. I climbed up onto it and peered in. A dark magenta colored liquid bubbled and smoked swirling iridescent shimmer in its depths. Every so often, the smoke would come together to form a heart that would float to the ceiling to hit the glass and then dissipate into nothing.

"A love spell," I whispered in awe. "I wonder who she's making it for?"

"That's none of your damn business." Came an irritated voice from the doorway.

Looking up quickly, I saw Iris's disapproving face right before my sudden movement threw me off balance. I reached a desperate hand up as I started to tumble off the foot-stool. I caught myself just in time, my hand closing around something squishy. I almost didn't dare look up, but I had to. I was holding onto a bushel of eyes that were roped together and dangling from ligaments. Horror reverberated throughout me as I realized I'd squished one of them in my palm.

"Eye of newt," Iris explained calmly.

I, however, was not as calm as I started to wildly wave my hand around, sending the squished eye into the cauldron with a healthy plop. The hot liquid splattered on my forearm (whose glass scratches from the accident were healing way better than it should have), and I looked in horror at the pot as it changed from magenta to pitch black.

"Gods, I'm sorry, Iris," I said, turning to her.

As I turned to her, I could feel the world pitch a bit, and I felt like my arm...hummed for lack of a better word. I reached out to steady myself. My arm hit the cauldron. The cooktop hissed as the dark liquid splashed out from the sides. The cauldron wobbled violently. I threw my hands out to stabilize it by the handles. Boiling hot liquid sloshed down my chest. I screamed in agony but didn't let it go. There was no telling what was in this pot and what reactions it might have with everything else. When the heavy cauldron was stable again, I ignored the searing pain on my chest and grimly surveyed the contents. Barely any liquid simmered in the bottom. Shit. Looking around didn't change that assessment. The coat I'd just bought last year with the fluffy hood was ruined, the new potion simmering in pools on the black fabric. That wasn't the least of the destruction either. Liquid coated every available inch of space on the island. Guilt rode me as I turned to Iris to apologize.

"Close your eyes. This second!" Iris said, panicked.

I squeezed them closed at her command. The panic in her voice made *me* panic.

"What was that?" I asked the darkness behind my lids, not wanting to know.

"Did you see me afterward?" She asked, the dread in her voice palpable.

"No, I closed my eyes when you told me to." I was relieved to admit.

She seemed just as happy to hear that as I was to say it. "Thank the gods. That's a binding love potion I was toying with, and as much as I'm unfortunately starting to like you, the last thing I want is for you to become my slave."

"Slave?" I about squeaked in response.

"Yeah, you heard me." She said, and I felt her hand take mine. "Come with me."

I kept my eyes closed as she helped me off of the stool. Glad I hadn't killed myself getting down.

As she led me into another room, I tried to ignore the burning of myrrh, "What in the hell are you doing making a potion like that?"

I had difficulty forming the words because the vibrating and humming was getting so ferocious it was hard to operate over.

"I have the unfortunate task of finding a cure for a woman who got too close to one, and now she is a slave to her half-brother for all her life unless I can break the spell.

The best way to break the spell is to replicate it to find the exact signature. That way, you can deconstruct it and create a cure with the opposite ingredients." She said as I heard what sounded like water turn on. Then before I knew what was happening, I was being thrust under a steady stream.

I would say it was water, but it was too sticky and foul-smelling to be liquid. It smelled like rotten eggs. I gagged.

"Take off your clothes," She instructed.

I hesitated only a split second before complying. Being bound to Iris was far worse than her seeing me naked. Any hesitancy I felt was dispelled by the immediate reduction in vibration. The liquid on my burn hurt like a bitch, though.

"Iris, my chest burns," I said through gritted teeth.

"I can see why," she said grimly. "Stay there with your eyes closed. I'll be right back.

I heard her footsteps leave and return after a moment.

"Hold out your hand," she instructed.

I did as directed, and an icy cold goop plopped into my hand.

"Rub that where it burns," she said.

I took the thick substance and smeared it around my chest. The relief was almost immediate.

The buzzing and vibrating were but an echo, and the burning had stopped entirely. My arms dropped to my sides in relief. Thank the gods.

After a few more moments, Iris turned off the liquid and thrust a towel at me. I could feel the plush terry against my arm and reached out to grab it.

As I rubbed myself down, the buzzing feeling faded away completely. It wasn't the most straightforward task to do without sight. I heard her going out and coming back into the room in silence, busying herself while completing my task. When I was reasonably confident all of the moisture was gone from my body, I stood there.

"Just set the towel down." She instructed.

After I complied, she waited for a few heartbeats before asking, "How are you feeling?" She asked.

"I feel fine now," I said.

It was the truth too. Besides a dull ache from the burning, I felt surprisingly good. No burning, vibrating, nothing.

"Open your eyes," she said.

I opened my eyes to find her two inches away from my face. She put the pad of her thumb on my eyelid and shone a small penlight in it. First one and then the other. Satisfied, she tossed it back in the pocket of her apron and patted it.

"Put this on," She said, thrusting a dress into my hands.

I didn't bother looking at the dress. I was grateful to have something to wear. It hit the ground in a curtain of skirts, a panel of turquoise running down the front only interrupted by a network of ties around the middle. I pulled them as tight as they would go. It was surprisingly comfortable. She let me work, going in and out of the room, using a pair of giant tongs and a sunflower adorned garbage can to dispose of my clothes.

"Try not to do anything stupid like that in the future." She said as she made her way back into the kitchen.

"I won't," I said, eyeing the cauldron warily as we passed it. "By the way, sorry I messed up your potion."

She waved her hand and kept moving. "I'm more concerned about your coat. You can't go out in the winter without some warmth."

She wove through the seemingly randomly placed racks in her store; she said over her shoulder, "You know, if you have an interest in potions, I'm more than happy to have you come cook with me some time."

I stopped, shocked. "Really?"

"Of course," she said, not bothering to wait for me.

The kind gesture held me speechless for a couple of

heartbeats. It had been so long since someone had invited me into their world. And this was clearly an invitation. I blinked back the sudden tears that pricked my eyes.

We'd reached the front window. It took only a few seconds for her to pluck one of the glowing potions from the front display.

She held it out and said, "Drink that right before you go outside. It will keep you warm for 24 hours."

Swirling reds mixed and shimmered with oranges as I took it. It fit neatly into my palm the word WARM scrolled into a yellow label.

"How much do I drink?" I asked, not deceived by the small size of the bottle.

She looked at the bottle and said, "For that bottle? Just a sip."

Just a sip? There had to be over 10 doses in there. "Fair enough. How much can I tell the Treasurer you will be sending the bill for?"

Rolling her eyes, she moved past me back into the shop again. "Don't be silly. You can have it."

I blinked at her parting form. Potions were expensive.

"But why would you give this to me?" I asked after her, increasing the length of my strides to catch up with her. "I ruined my coat, not you."

She made a disgusted sound in her voice and said, "Friends don't make friends pay for things."

Her words made me stop and blink. Such a sweet sentiment. I couldn't believe that she would be so kind as to overlook our previous issues so wholly. She rounded the corner, oblivious to my shock. Then her next words made me think maybe she wasn't so oblivious to it.

"Besides, I have a feeling you're going to be needing more than that before all of this is said and done. I heard about the vampires," she said with a long, meaningful look as she took a seat on the same swivel stool she'd sat at four fateful weeks ago when we found out we'd accidentally opened the door to the Never.

"Speaking of which," her turquoise eyes pierced me, "what brings you here? I know it wasn't my otherworldly talents."

"I wish it was," I said with a sigh.

How did you admit to someone the level at which you fucked up? Especially when you were so fresh off a previous fuck up that was the magnitude of opening up a magical door to another realm.

I decided to start from the beginning. "Do you know that goblin bone I collected for the potion?"

"Yes…" she said, stretching the syllable out like she could see the car-crash of a fuckup coming.

I just hoped it was a fender bender of a fuckup and not a full-on wreck.

"Well, I didn't exactly tell you where I got the bone from," I said.

I knew I was dragging it out, but I felt so dumb at this point. Talk about a complete lack of forethought. I blamed my ability to make snap judgments in high-stress situations. Those usually resulted in a reliable 70/30 result. 70 to the good and the 30? Well, that could range from 'holy shit, you've got to be kidding me" to...not so good. Planning and forethought was my specialty, though. That had more of a 95/5 result. I could logic the fuck out of a situation.

Iris apparently got impatient with me rattling around inside my own head and said, "Ok...where did you 'exactly' get the bone from?"

"From an altar," I said, wincing as I admitted my error.

Iris looked towards the heavens, a long-suffering look on her face. Finally, she shook her head and returned wary eyes to me. "That probably belonged to someone important."

"That's putting it lightly," said Bab, and he started laughing.

"Like Goblin God, important, apparently," I agreed.

Confusion ran across her face, so I explained, "Goblins have been chasing me all over the city. They told me as much."

"Of course, it was." She said, shaking her head. "Girl, you can't win for losing."

"Well, that's why I'm here, actually. I'm hoping you still have some of the bone. I could give it back to the goblins, and they could return their god to his final resting place. Happy goblins equal goblins who are not trying to kill me. That way, I can go back to dealing with only one crazy lunatic at a time."

"That *is* a good plan…" Iris said, her lips twisted wryly to the side.

"But…" I prompted.

"But I don't have any of the bone left. It all went into the potion. Because it was an old spell, it didn't list any amounts. Think of it like your grandma's cookbook. It's an art. I put it all in to increase the effectiveness."

Her words settled like a tree stump in my gut.

"I'm so sorry." She said at my crestfallen face.

"It's not you," I said, waving away her concern. "You were just doing what you thought was best by me."

"Well…" she said, waffling her hand back and forth.

It took me a second to remember she'd hated me before the start of our journey a couple months ago. Funny how trauma can bring people closer together. If I had to be honest, I liked her spirited personality. And I'd grown to rely on her for help and advice.

I found myself pouring out my grievances to her. "It's just…I can't seem to do anything right. When I stop thinking about what other people want, crazy things happen, like me outing our entire species to the vampires or opening a door to a completely new *realm*. Between being inevitably found by the vampires and the persecution of our kind to who *knows* what kind of travesty could come through if I opened the door again, that's clearly not the way to go."

I threw my hands up. Just getting started, I said, "Then I try to do what I *should* do. And that goes just as awful. I'm *supposed* to be with a faerie. Well, I tried that. And what did that get me...huh?" I didn't wait for her and instead started pacing. "I'll tell you what. Nothing. A big, fat nothing. In fact, it *lost* me a friend. One of the few people I'd ever been close to. Now, he's just gone. Just because I don't want to be with him as part of a couple. I don't *want* to be with him, though. I want to be with a *vampire*. A gorgeous, sweet vampire."

I raked my hands through my hair. "How am I supposed to be with a vampire and still be Queen one day? I can't. It's just not possible. He would have to leave his people. And our people would never accept him. How could they? No one would agree to live in constant fear that he would go rogue one day and kill everyone. And I can't stay on the outside forever. Mother is degrading. She isn't aging, but she is...changing. I've heard stories of how she had changed from before. I'd never really believed it, but now....now, I can see it. One day, she will have to be stopped. I just pray to the gods it's a long way out. Because the thought of being Queen scares the shit out of me. I don't agree with almost any of what we are doing. Hell, that's why I left in the first place. We aren't *supposed* to be caged up like animals. We are meant to run and fly wild and free. Dance in forests. Have our midsummer night's feasts wherever the gods may take us. We aren't *supposed* to protect ourselves with human inventions. We aren't *human*. We're supposed to protect ourselves in the great wide world with the tools that the gods gave us. Not some damn martial arts. And you're supposed to be happy about all of this repression. The powers that be ensure you are through brainwashing. Brainwashing to accept less than what we are meant to. Brainwashed into thinking you are less than who you are. But I can't accept the brainwashing. I can't stay caged in this place. So how am I supposed to leave everything, everything that makes me who I am, just to do what I am "supposed" to do? Especially when every time I attempt to do what I am "supposed" to do it bites me in the ass?"

Iris looked at me, looked like she was looking through me, straight to my soul, and said. "Maybe the answer is somewhere in between."

My emotional tirade had spent me; all I was able to manage was a tired shrug as I said, "I don't know how to do that."

"All will become clear in time," she said, coming around to pat me on the shoulder.

I shrugged her hand off my shoulder, not feeling completely worthy of her comfort right now. "I don't know. I just feel like I've done a great job of fucking things up. Of pushing things away. Lately, I feel like I've just gotten one thing wrong after another. It's...too much, you know?"

"What makes you think it's too much?" She asked gently. "We can handle much more than we think we can."

Her unwavering patience in the face of my negative onslaught made me smile. Maybe I'd been wrong to think I didn't have any friends left. I had to laugh at her naivety, though.

"What's so funny?" she asked, her brows furrowing together and pulling her hand away.

"I'm sorry. I'm not laughing at you. It's just that I know it's too much. I've... I've been hearing voices." I admitted, feeling like I was at a confessional. "I'm not a doctor, but I'd have to say if your brain starts finding other ways to cope with things, then you are in over your skis."

That made Iris grow still. Couldn't say that I blamed her. Everyone always joked about going crazy, but it was an entirely different game to be talking with someone who *was* crazy.

"You're going to have to explain what you mean by hearing voices," she said, stepping back behind her counter, her eyes never leaving me.

That wasn't easy. How did you explain something like this to someone else?

"Tell her it's like having a really fabulous house guest who goes with you everywhere," Babs added.

"You're not helping," I said under my breath with a sigh.

Iris blinked, taken aback. "You'll remember *you* came to *me* for help."

Great. Now, she thought I was mad at her.

"No, not you. I'm not talking to you." I said, starting to tap my foot in agitation.

Frustration curled my fingers. Why couldn't things be easy?

"The...voices?" Iris guessed.

I pointed at her, a tight smile on my face. "Bingo. Except its really just one voice."

"Since you were just talking to this...voice, I can assume it's safe to say you are conscious and aware when the voice is around?" Iris asked.

It was understandable that she would be curious. It's not every day you met someone with a multiple personality disorder.

"Absolutely, everything is functioning like normal. Well, if you don't count these two times, it took over my body. Then it was like I was fighting for control of myself. I felt...possessed." I said, unable to find an appropriate word for what happened to me.

"Maybe, that's not too far from the truth of it." She said, turning and making her way into the room to her left.

Oh, no. She couldn't leave on that note. I followed her in. The room was covered in floor to ceiling bookcases. Books of all sizes adorned the shelves, loose scraps of paper punctuating the wall of leather bindings. As soon as I crossed the threshold, I felt a pull. It felt like a giant hand wrapped around my midsection, pulling me into another direction. Considering the magical disaster I'd caused just a few minutes ago, I had a second to wonder if I'd tripped another of Irises' spells. Then as it continued to pull and actually dragged me a couple of steps back, I realized it was Purdy. Call of the People. It was a bitch power. Too bad, I was immune to it. It pulled at me hard, and I had to wonder if she didn't have an enhancement charm because this pull was stronger than usual.

Bracing my hand on the door jam, I brought myself back to the present reality and asked, "What are you talking about, possessed?"

She grabbed a leather tome and set it down on a cluttered desk and looked at me and asked, "Does the voice say or do things that seem off?"

I couldn't help the almost-hysterical laugh that tore past my lips and said, "You mean besides taking over my body and mind?"

She shrugged and cocked her head back and forth. "Bad choice of words. How about this: does he say anything that seems out of touch with the modern-day?"

Then what she was getting at hit me like a ton of bricks. "Possessed. You think the Goblin God bone could have had the spirit inside of it."

She looked up from what she was reading. "Frankly, yes.

Ah- here's the list. Does he have a different personality than yours?"

I tried to push the jumble of crazy out of my head and focus on her question. "Uh...yeah, I guess he does."

"Do you have any new knowledge or skills that you didn't have before?"

I thought back. Immediately, his quirky phrases and knowledge of the goblins came to mind. I sighed.

"Yes," I admitted.

"Does he ever refer to you to as 'we.'" She asked.

"He does it, and I do it." I had to admit again.

"Well, I think that gives us our answer." She said, closing the book with a resounding thud.

I jumped, processing this new information. "So, you think there is a Goblin God inside me?"

She motioned to the book with a sweeping hand. "I don't know. These books aren't always right. Why don't you ask him?"

She led me back out to the store's floor. As thoughts swirled in my head.

Ask him. An unnamed emotion turned in my stomach. A goblin god. Could it be? On the one hand, it would prove I wasn't insane, but on the other hand, it presented a whole other slew of problems. A jingle turned our gazes to the door. Horey stood there, outfitted in his station's suit of armor. Between his presence and Purdy's call, it was apparent my possible possession wasn't a problem I had time to think about.

$\mathcal{I}$ had a steady stream of the Fuck Its running through my core as I stood in the throne room. The white marble underfoot and sheathing the long chamber had black veins running through it. All of the veins ended at the edges of the room. Even they were looking for a way out.

My mother was sitting on her throne. When I walked in, I was taken aback at the sight of her. Her hair was black instead of the deep amber it had been before. And her hair looked nothing like a sheet of glass. It separated into sections and seemed to be...oily. A word I'd never have attributed to my mother before now. She was the Queen. Appearances were everything to her. Even her skin looked paler than usual. And slightly sallow. It wasn't the mother I was used to seeing.

Despite her, dare I say, ragged looks. Everything else was status quo. She had enough of her power on either side of her, so you knew who you were dealing with: The Queen. Her right-hand guards were there, Guinevere and Bromwell; they were not at her side. Three of the departments were there: Justice from the Department of Truth was there. A twisted lipped Purdy from the Department of Fae Services was there. (She was clearly still peeved I'd not heeded her call.) Magus from the Department of Magic was there. The first two were as corrupt as the day was short. Magus was solidly on the fence; he pretty much did whatever he pleased unless it struck a chord in him. What constituted a cord strike for him I'd still yet to figure out.

And last but not least, Anthony was there. As Messenger of the Crown, his inclusion in these types of gatherings wasn't standard. However, I knew my mom had brought him because she'd heard of our falling out, and as a result, she had him here to unnerve me. To rub it in my face.

Between the fae of authority flanking her throne and the lords and ladies gathered along the edges of the rooms in speculative huddles, the Queen had just enough people to be a formal display of power. However, it lacked the numbers and buzz of a formal reprimand. It was the kind of production she used to remind you that she was in power. That she was Queen. I'd seen it enough times. I wasn't impressed.

Mother talked to Bromwell as other faeries drifted down from the crossbeams above, settling in for the spectacle to come. Since I was given The Call a good half an hour ago, it just proved the now-delay was all cleverly orchestrated to make me feel as uncomfortable as possible. As a lesser rank than the Queen, I knew I was supposed to accept it. And to a degree, I had to, as part of my station. However, that didn't mean I had to make it easy for them.

"So Purdy...the call still doesn't work, huh? That means either," I looked up like I was thinking, "your powers have decreased with your ever-increasing age or that I am, in fact, still more powerful than you."

My voice cut through the din and effectively silenced the congregation as I spoke. Everyone was clearly hanging onto the words of the rarely seen AWOL Princess. Everyone, that is, except my mother. From the rigidity of her spine, I knew she'd heard me, but she refused to give me the satisfaction of her attention. The assembly started when *she* said, not by anyone else.

Purdy was perpetually worried about age and the presence of it in her face, so I wasn't surprised when she responded on cue. The smooth skin of her pale face reddened.

"Kundalini Energy still runs just as fierce through my veins." She said, her eyes squinted at me like she wanted to strike me dead on the spot.

Kundalini Energy was how we referred to the process of pulling energy from ley lines. The more powerful your Kundalini was, the more powerful your magic. Think of it as more juice. It's why I was so easily able to pull ley line energy; my Kundalini was strong. It had been since I was born. I'd accidentally electrified more than just toasters when I was a toddler.

I nodded, "Oh, so that just means I'm stronger than you still. Nothing new there, I suppose."

Her robes swayed as she started towards me, clearly wanting to tear me from limb to limb. Justice stopped her with a hand on her bicep. Her head looked from his hand to his face in a silent threat that clearly said she would be happy to take her anger out on him rather than me. He just gave her a steady look and a quick shake of his head. It was enough to settle her, and she jerked her hand out of his grip. She was calm enough now, though that she stayed where she was. I watched the exchange with mild curiosity. Purdy had always been as corrupt as the sky was blue. Still, if this exchange was anything to go by, Justice was either on the same path to going down that road, or had been swayed and was solidly in her camp already. It made me wonder if she was on a campaign to corrupt the entire Knockaine Court. My eyes flicked to Anthony, and my course of thought was derailed. His eyes were on me. The force of their gaze made me take a step back. The regret there made my eyes do a lot of blinking. I couldn't cry now. Not here.

Either mother saw the exchange or thought she'd waited long enough because she dismissed Bromwell with a wave of her hand. He fell back in line behind her, ever a good soldier.

With her full attention on me, I returned her gaze. I could almost feel her triumphant anger radiating from the dais.

"We have brought you here before the Court to answer for oddities that have presented themselves since you have left the mound." Mother said, ever the picture of royal superiority.

Oddities? That was vague as hell. And since when did I become responsible for what happened when I wasn't around? Last I checked, I didn't have control over anything but myself.

"How can I answer for things that had happened when I wasn't here?" I asked.

Not bothering to answer my question, she nodded to Magus.

Magus stepped forward. "Disturbances in ley lines around the globe have been recorded...unusual activity twice in the past month. Both instances were at the tail end of your...visit at Knockaine."

Visit. I laughed out loud.

"Oh, I don't know if I would do that, sugar," Bab said, clearly uncomfortable with the accusations being hurled at me.

I couldn't help it. It was either laugh or walk up there and punch him. It was too ridiculous to comprehend. I'd hardly call being kidnapped a visit, but call it what you like.

"Pick your battles, electric lady," Bab advised.

There was a lot of truth to that. Before I could decide what I wanted to do, though, Purdy jumped into the conversation so fast, I looked for verbal skid marks. "And there have been reports of a Bargot roaming around the forests of Pilot, NC."

It didn't take me long to remember from my Ley Line studies that the Arcadian Ley Line and the Serpent Ley Line connected at the Pilot Mountains in North Carolina.

I scoffed. "Did you bring me here for bedtime stories? Everyone knows Bargots aren't real. Maybe you should screen your informants for delusions."

Denial climbed up my throat. I didn't want to be the cause of real shit going down in our world. If there really *were* Bargots and they were loose in our world, who knew what else could be out there.

"There have also been a record number of people reported as dying in their sleep," Justice added smugly.

Shit. That certainly *sounded* like a Bargot. Legend had it that Bargots were malevolent geniuses that put clammy hands over your face while you were sleeping. Even though I couldn't count on him being on the straight and narrow, I could trust the information. As the Department of Truth, he would be up to date.

"It is our belief that magic was used to remove your wings, and as a result, you have set into motion a chain reaction that will doom us all." Mother said.

I expected her to relay the news with relish, enjoy her proof that I was a fuck up. There was no joy in her delivery, though. If anything, regret marred her brow. I didn't know how to feel about that. My stomach flipped as I tried to process it. Then it hardened. Despite her soft heart right now, she was as unstable as a cup of coffee on a water bed. I couldn't let it wiggle its way into my heart. It was only setting me up for hurt. I'd seen that show enough before. I wasn't buying tickets to it again.

Instead, I tried to focus on the situation at hand. There was a chance, however small, that by opening the doors, fae had passed through. But I couldn't admit that to my mother. If I did, she would surely lock me up. Again. I'm sure she'd make some sort of excuse about how they needed to tame the magic, but that was bullshit. All she wanted was to see me under her thumb. That was all she ever wanted. And I couldn't go back to a life of captivity. Between being kidnapped by the vampires and my own mother (twice), I'd had enough of that to last a lifetime. Besides, I wasn't going to use the magic again. I'd been warned by Iris already, and I knew the consequences would be super dire if I did.

"Anthony," Mother called. "Search her for magical markings."

Murmurs ran through the crowd.

Shock took my breath away. The only place I would be marked was on my body. She wouldn't strip me down in front of all of these people. There was no way she would humiliate me like that. AWOL or not, I was still Princess of Knockaine. Still her daughter.

"My Queen?" He asked, hesitancy stopping him.

"Do you question me, Anthony?" she asked; an edge in her voice said that would be a very unwise move.

"No, my Queen," he said.

I could sense his hesitancy as he fought with himself. He knew just as well as I did that he would find no magical markings. He also knew that I had indeed used magic to get rid of my wings. He'd known my mother as long as I had, though. He knew telling her the truth was as sure of a death sentence as anything. I prayed to the gods he wouldn't say anything. Would just let me accept the humiliation that was coming. It only took the space of a few seconds to make his decision.

He stepped off the dais.

As he made his way down the half-moon shaped stairs, thoughts of another time and another place flooded my face with embarrassment. His eyes collided with mine. I took little comfort that he didn't want to do this as much as I didn't want him to.

"If it was due to me losing my wings, why would there have been two disturbances in ley lines?" I asked, grasping at straws.

Anthony's feet faltered, but when no response was forthcoming from my mother, his steps resumed.

No, this couldn't be happening. I could hear the murmurs around me turn to outrage as Anthony reached me. Our people clearly were outraged by what was happening. Any warm and fuzzy feelings brought on by their support were wiped away as he moved behind me.

It wasn't as much the thought of being naked before all of these people that upset me. It wasn't even that I was worried they would find something. I knew they wouldn't. I'd taken a potion, not had a spell cast on me. What really bothered me, though, was the thought of Anthony's hands on me. I don't know who it would scar more: him because I'd rejected him, and now, he had to put his hands on my naked body even though he could never have me again. Or me because I knew that I didn't want him, and I knew that I would personally be responsible for this tortured image for who knew how long. Whatever it was, I threw caution to the wind when I felt his hands come up to remove my coat.

I blurted out recklessly to my mother, "What if it was your doing?"

Anthony's hands stilled.

"Excuse me?" she said, pulling herself up to all her queenly glory.

Desperate to prolong the torture, I pressed on.

"Do you think it could have been your own actions around that same time? We'd all witnessed the display at the Midsummer Night's Celebration. Who's to say there wasn't another incident when we weren't around."

When my mother didn't say anything, I turned to the Court and asked, "Did you ever think about that?"

When they all shifted uncomfortably on their feet and averted their gazes, it hit me. "You have. Haven't you? You're just too afraid to speak your truth. Too afraid if you said something that you would be held responsible for pointing it out, almost like you'd committed the act yourself."

I knew it was right from the looks on their faces. My mother was a disease to this Court. There were no two ways about it. Anthony seemed to sense the change in tenor and moved to the side. I breathed a sigh of relief, but it wasn't for long.

Any of her earlier regret was gone, replaced by harsh words that cut through the murmurs that had started at my declaration, "Having your wings removed was a disgraceful act. You should be ashamed of yourself."

Her words sent a knife into my gut. Not because of her hatred for me. No, because on some level, she was right. Granted, it wasn't for the reason she was saying. It was because you shouldn't change who you are. I should have left them on. I regretted taking them away. My thoughts flickered to Avalynn and then to Anthony. On top of it all, their removal had caused far too much pain and heartache for so many people who had been close to me. I should have looked for a way instead to live with them. I should have them still. My eyes sought out Anthony. His eyes bore into me, pity and something else I didn't want to acknowledge shining in them.

"Ashamed is not a punishable offense," I said, my eyes never leaving Anthony's face.

His eyebrows pulled together as if in pain. I know he didn't want me to feel bad, but I did. I didn't make it a habit of ruining people.

"I'm not surprised you aren't willing to take responsibility for your actions. You never have been. A Princess shouldn't be off galavanting around the world doing gods' know what. You should be here. Where you belong." When she finished her speech, the corners of her mouth pulled down.

It was as if the thought had just occurred to her that I belonged here, and the idea didn't sit well with her. So she wanted me here. The gods only knew why. Maybe, she just wanted me under her thumb. How could she be all-powerful if her own daughter wasn't under her command? Or maybe, just maybe, she missed me. From the way she looked at me, it was highly doubtful. Did it really matter anyway? Of course not. Still, the question squirmed inside me as I focused on the decision I'd made a month ago.

"I do plan on being here more," I said.

That was the truth too. I decided even if I couldn't be in their lives every day. I wanted to be here for the faeries. They needed someone who would fight for them. Be for them when they needed it most.

"Oh, sure. That's why you've been so present the last month and a half," she said, sarcasm dripping from her words.

She had me there. However, I wasn't about to go into why I hadn't been around as often as I'd vowed to. The last thing I wanted public knowledge was that I heard voices. Talk about a one-way trip to the Tearmann.

"Ok, I'll admit I haven't been here much, but I do plan on it," I said, knowing my voice sounded defensive.

"You haven't been here for years. Now that your wings are gone, you don't plan on being around any more than you were. Admit it." She said, getting louder.

I started to explain again, "I do-"

"Admit it!" She shouted, standing up, pointing a shaking finger at me.

She was visibly upset. I wanted to give her something, give everyone some assurances. But I didn't know how to explain what was happening to me. Anything I said now would only hurt my cause, not help it.

Mother seemed to realize she was standing and started to pace the length of the dais. "You think you can come and go whenever it pleases you. Come and wreak havoc on people's lives, then just pick up and leave again. Leave as if everything's the same. As if you haven't just ruined people's lives."

Her words hit me like a punching bag, ringing my ears. I could see Anthony all but squirm in my peripheral vision. It had to be the height of embarrassment for him to have his broken heart trumped out in front of everyone. It was this realization that made me realize one of the most shocking things I'd ever thought.

My mother was right.

For all of the things she got wrong, for all of the bad choices and decisions she'd made- in this- she was right. On the heels of that thought, after seeing the anguish and injustice on her face, I realized she was talking about herself. That hit me like a freight train. How selfish could I be? Here were two people who were affected by me, and I was just going to walk away? Again?

"I'll eat the bitch," said Bab, bringing me out of the sadness beating at my heart.

His presence was a sharp reminder that I had to take care of myself first no matter how much I wanted to be there for others. I wouldn't be any good to anyone if I wasn't mentally healthy. But how did I explain that?

"Look, I didn't mean to cause anyone any pain. I'm just trying to figure things out. I want to stay. I really do. But I can't right now." I said, by way of explanation.

My mother stopped. The force making her robes swish with the abruptness.

She brought a hand up to gesture to the ladies and men in the audience. "These people rely on you. You said you would protect them. But you haven't, have you? You've given them nothing. After you gave your word, you would. Your promises clearly mean nothing."

I knew I was breaking my oath to them, knew I wasn't giving them what they needed. Knew I needed to be here. But I couldn't come home right now, who knows what would happen if I did? John Jeffries had already murdered once, and he'd tried to kill me too. There was no doubt in my mind he would kill again. I had to stop him.

"I want to. I really do, but I can't right now. There are too many things going on. Someone just tried to kill me last night." I said, trying to get her to understand.

Gasps scattered through the crowd. My mother was having none of it, though.

"Isn't that a pretty excuse? Someone trying to kill you again, are they? What is this? Twice in as many months? Poor you. Your life is so hard, isn't it?"

She sat back on her marble throne. "Try running a whole kingdom. Try figuring out magical disturbances. Try figuring out what to do now that vampires know we exist. All sources say they are on the hunt for us now. We are in the middle of a very real faerie hunt, the likes we haven't seen for over 250 years. And who is that thanks to? Oh, yeah.

That's right." She leveled a stare at me. "That would be your fault."

The reality of her words weighed my shoulders. All of it was my fault. I needed to get things fixed ASAP and get back here to help out. But still, I hesitated.

"But by all means, go find your would-be killer." She said with a pertinent wave of her hand. "Go put your head on some other chopping block. It's not surprising. You have forever been nothing but a selfish brat, only thinking of your own welfare. You've never done anything for anyone here. Ever since you killed your father-"

Outrage filled my breast. "I didn't kill father-"

But I might as well have been an ant on the floor for all the mind she paid me as she kept on talking, "-and your sister. You've been nothing but a burden, nothing but a problem. Day after day. So yeah, go. Don't trouble yourself with us here in faerie."

I could barely breathe for the fury that pumped in my chest. The world had pin-holed down to her face in the world of rage that had taken over me at the wild accusations. I knew she'd held bitterness towards me for my living instead of my father. She'd prized her husband above all. When you added that I had lived instead of her "better" daughter, it was just icing on the cake. But I couldn't believe she was pinning his death on me. I had nothing to do with it. The king had saved me that fateful day. I'd be damned if I let my mother not only distill my entire existence down to an event that happened when I was young but also take away my father's bravery.

"I've been a burden? How do you think I feel? I watched my very own sister and father be murdered by those..." my thoughts flickered to Kitty, and I changed the hateful words "pixies. I only stand here today because of the king's bravery. He saved me, knowing full well it was his life or mine. A life that I've repaid the best I can by risking my own life to save over a dozen faeries' lives-"

Mother's words were like a blunt knife cutting me to the quick as she interjected, "A life you would never have risked if you wouldn't have been a vampire whore. But that's easy for you, isn't it? Just spread your legs and having any man run to you."

Fury ate at my gut. It was a blatant dig at Anthony. I could feel his answering heat of embarrassment even though he stood feet away. I tried to remind myself that this was very typical of her: to lash out when she wasn't getting what she wanted. That I shouldn't be upset. But this time, she wasn't just hurting me. Hurting me, I could take. Hurting someone I cared about wasn't ok. I swore to myself she wasn't going to get away with this for much longer. People deserved respect. And they would get it: one way or another.

I straightened my shoulders and looked down my nose at her as I said, "Typical, Mother. Not getting your way, so you hurt people. Doesn't that get old?"

"People's poor decisions have no bearing on me." She said. The indifference of her words would have been believable to anyone who hadn't noticed her subtle shift in her seat.

"And that's what it boils down to, isn't it? You. It's all about you. It has been for as long as I can remember." I said.

She shrugged a delicate shoulder, her oily hair swaying with the movement. I knew she wouldn't deny the words. They were as true as the sky was blue. That was fine, though. I didn't say the words for her. I said them for the other faeries. I needed them to see that she didn't care about anyone else. She only cared about herself, and that truth would affect everything she did. Every decision she made. Mother seemed to understand there was censure in my voice because she sneered.

"Do you expect me to apologize for this? You? The faerie

who single-handedly has put our whole race in jeopardy? Reports of vampires traveling outside their normal haunts have been coming in. Reports are flooding in. It's our belief that there may be more...farms out there like the one you were foolish enough to burn down. We can only pray to the gods that there are enough to where they don't feel the need to find us." she said.

Her words and cries of affirmation from the congregation lashed at my heart, pulling sorrow.

Flabbergasted, I said, "First of all, how can you say that you pray more of our people are locked up? How can you say you hope their freedoms have been stolen from them? How can you say you pray for them to be treated like cattle? How can you pray for the mental and even possibly sexual abuse or your people?"

At my words, others in the congregation cheered. Tension coiled in the room like a snake.

"I'll tell you how because at this point. It's the only way to prevent the destruction of our very existence. Don't stand there in your self-righteous indignation when you are solely responsible for this predicament." She said.

Her words were hot on my cheeks, but I ignored them. It was my turn to continue on.

"Secondly, I recognize that my...relationship with the vampire was...selfish. For this, I deeply apologize. I can't say that I would do it differently if given the same choices. He is a good person. Vampires are not all bad. I recognize I put us in the situation we are currently in." Guilt attempted to crawl up my chest. I took a deep breath and let it out slowly to push it back down before continuing, "This is a situation I have every intention of rectifying when I am...in a better place."

Mother did something I don't think I'd heard her do in the last 75 years. She laughed. It wasn't a joyous laugh, though. It was derisive and filled with contempt. "How rich. I have to know: just how do you plan on 'rectifying' the manhunt of our species?"

I didn't have an answer before she asked, and the ease at which the answer sprang to my lips shocked even me. "I shall lead a movement to make peace with them."

Shocked murmurs rumbled through the congregation at my declaration. Some people laughed like I was insane; some just shook their heads. But I didn't back down from it. I braced my feet and let the words stand. Because even though I hadn't had any previous plans to make peace with the vampires, I knew as I said the words that I meant them with all of my heart. I would help facilitate peace with the vampires. I would help faeries live again.

CHAPTER 18

The transition from marble floors to earth was abrupt and jarred me a little, so single-mindedly focused was I on the thoughts racing around in my head. How dare she? I know my mother was not one to be gentle-hearted, but this was going too far.

I was so entranced in my thoughts that I didn't hear someone until they were right behind me. Spinning around, I sucked ley line energy into me, ready to unleash it. Instead of a threat, Oren stood there, his hands raised and his eyebrows raised equally high in a sign of truce.

I immediately let the energy flow out of me. "My apologies, Oren. I did not know it was you."

"Nor did I expect you to, my Princess," he said with a bow.

Not used to the display, it made me slightly uncomfortable. Conscientious of how Mother had just tried to make me look, I tried to keep my face carefully blank as I waited for his steel-colored hair to rise again. For a split second, I wished it was Anthony. I really should talk to him. Maybe, it was for the best that I didn't speak to him. I'd already said everything I could.

When Oren came back up, I nodded my head towards the exit, indicating he should walk with me. Dutifully, he fell into step beside me. It felt good knowing I wasn't alone.

"I tell you. I'm as frazzled as a knot around here." I said, trying not to rub my arms against the cold that I suddenly felt creep up my arms.

"Because of Avalynn?" he asked casually as if we weren't talking about someone who'd tried to murder me a mere month ago and was now dead as a direct result.

I shook my head as we crossed the clearing to get the thoughts out of my head, and we began heading down the dirt path towards the exit.

I nodded in concession. "Well, yeah. That and the people who must now hate me as a result of what happened with...Sven."

Even though Oren had been saved by Sven and myself, it still felt awkward to mention Sven in the space of these walls. He was, after all, a vampire. Even if I had made peace with him.

"But those are nonsense things to worry about in comparison," he said with a shake of his head.

Feeling like I'd been slapped, I stopped so hard my boots kicked up dirt from the packed path.

"In comparison to what?" I asked, half indignant that I was clearly being judged.

Again.

"In comparison to the wrath of your mother. You must take care not to get on her bad side, my Princess," he warned softly.

"I don't think I have much of a choice there. Everything I do seems to irritate my mother," I scoffed as I started to head down the path again.

Even as the words came out of my mouth, I knew there

was more to it than that. I provoked her, intentionally at times. I couldn't help it. It was the only emotional defense I had. Maybe, someday I would be strong enough to let her insults wash over me. To not be affected by her insults and twisted words. Today wasn't that day.

This time Oren stopped me with a hand on my arm. "I don't think you understand, my Princess. It's been rumored...well, you see, people have been saying that she is... she is turning.." he looked to the left and the right and stepped close to me.

Hairs of foreboding rose on my arms as he stepped even closer still and whispered with volume barely above the wind. Still, it was unmistakable, "Banshee."

The word and all of its horrific implications had me recoiling in horror.

"But...but that is simply not...possible," I said, haltingly unable to stop the thoughts that were rushing me at the revelation.

Everything from the almost golden-haired goddess I'd remembered from my childhood to the black-haired beauty I'd come back to my after my 5-year hiatus, paraded in front of my memories. It was a stark contrast to the faerie I'd just left in that throne room: the one who looked like a shadow had settled over her. Shock seeped into my veins, leaving me ice cold. It certainly looked like it was true.

My mother? A banshee? It's not possible. I didn't even know I'd whispered the horrifying thought out loud until Oren was answering me.

"It's not as impossible as it may seem, actually." His voice softened as he explained. "As you know, we are all sidhe. Faeries can experience things that cause them to...evolve through the course of their lives to become more. When your mom lost her goddess powers after the death of your father and sister, I would have thought she would take the path of Leanan sidhe. She was the fertility goddess, after all. It would make sense that the tragedy would twist her goddess powers into use for killing. But that was not to be her fate. Alas, it looks like she is taking the path of the bean sidhe, the banshee."

He had a point, but it got me thinking about other pieces of the puzzle.

"But she has the power of Darkness and Illusion. How did she have those powers and the powers of fertility? They seem...counterintuitive." I couldn't help but ask.

Oren sighed a big sigh and said, "We were all just as shocked by the transformation. It's widely thought that your mother had that gene lying dormant inside her because Bile, the god of Darkness and Death, was the consort of Danu."

Just when I thought this couldn't get any more shocking. "You're saying you think Bile is my...great grandfather?"

"Who's to say? But that would explain a lot of things." Oren said with a shrug.

"Like how my mother is turning into a banshee," I said, with utter disbelief.

Oren just nodded bleakly.

I processed the information, dully noting the network of tree roots above us that the path had been burrowed through. A black beetle scurried along the reaching limb, its shiny back catching the only light in the tunnel. After a minute of watching it, I looked down at my own skin. That same potential for death and darkness flowed through my own veins. A feeling flipped in my stomach, and it took me a second to realize what it was. Fear. I was scared of...myself. For the potential of death and destruction that sang in my veins like it did my mothers and her grandfather before her.

No. I couldn't think that way. I wasn't my mother. I had more control over myself than that. Boxing up the fear and putting it away, I met Oren's gaze. He was gauging me to see how I was taking the news.

"So what do we know? That my mother is a crazy loon. Nothing new there. Now, we just know what kind of loon." I gave him a shrug of my shoulders to mask my own pain and to say what could we do?

"The question isn't 'what do we know,' it's 'what do we do?'" Oren said, his hands held wide. The tips of his dark fingers brushed the tendrils of roots that trailed down the side of the narrowing path. "More specifically, what 'what do you?"

I laughed and started walking again. "Me? Why does it have to be me?"

"Because whether you believe it or not, your mother cares for you. Your one of the only people she has any feelings for anymore. Your presence here could be what keeps her from completing her evolution into a banshee." he said, careful to keep his eyes forward.

He knew the tensions between us, and from everything that had transpired, I'm sure he could figure out my feelings regarding them. I bit my tongue to keep from launching into a tirade of what I thought about the notion that my mother cared for me. I'd known for as long as I could remember that whatever care she had once possessed for me had died along with my father and sister years ago. But Oren was a smart faerie. That much was obvious. I found his words wormed their way into my heart. My mind touched back on a few times where I had to admit it seemed like he just might be right. Maybe my mother was lashing out at me because she felt abandoned? Perhaps she felt...alone. It was a mind-fuck of epic proportions.

I shook the thoughts away as we reached the stairs inside the hollow of the tree.

"Look, I'd love to help," I said as we started to ascend up

the rough-hewn steps. "There's no way that I can do anything right now, though. There's just too much going on. Let me figure this situation I have going on right now. When I come back... I'll see what I can do."

"With all due respect, my Princess. Once your mother is a banshee, there's no bringing her back. She needs you now. By the gods, your people need you now. Do you remember what it felt like to be captured and held against your will?"

Sickening memories slid down my throat at his words as I swallowed the memory of helplessness and terror I'd felt.

"I will come back, Oren. I will. I will not leave our people to such a fate. As soon as my...business outside the mound is concluded, I will start to clean up this issue. You have my word." I finished, unable to figure out how to word that.

I didn't want the goblin threat to be common knowledge and instill more fear in our people.

We'd reached the door to the outside world. A stoic faerie stood, unmoving. Guarding the fabric of our peace. Oren and I turned to each other.

Not able to say much now in the company of others, with a somber set of his lips, Oren said, "I fear that may be too late for your mother."

The horrifying possibility of the goblins tearing apart New York City looking for me lapped at the edges of my mind, and I said, "Let us pray it will not be."

"Let us," said Oren with a bow.

With a nod to the guard, I was on the winter wonderland that was the outside world. As the wood door became one with the tree behind me, a chill enveloped me, despite my coat. Reaching into my pocket, I pulled out the jar of warmth. My fingers were shaking as I unstoppered the top and drew the glass to my lips. How much again? A sip? That was such a vague amount. I tipped the liquid back quickly and brought it back down. The drink was surprisingly cool as it coated my lips. I waited for the potion to take effect as the wind bit my skin.

Nothing.

It probably wasn't enough. Indecision warred in me. But what if I took too much? It was a warmth potion. How bad could it be?

Conversely, I could freeze to death on the way home without it. That made my decision, and I took another gulp. This time I was warm before the bottle came away from my lips.

Much better. Toasty even. Perfect. I started down the stairs, my head a yarn ball of thoughts. Threats on my life, goblins, vampires closing in on us, faerie farms, my banshee mother. Things were starting to roll downhill quickly. I tried to prioritize and make sense of the thoughts in my head. Two pressing matters needed to be handled before I could come back to faerie and figure out the rest: First things first was the threat on my life. I couldn't do anything if I was dead. That meant neutralizing Jeffries. Now that I had more information to go on as far as what triggered him, I felt better about that vein. That made me stop. What kind of messed up world did I live in where I considered an attempt on my life a positive sign?

Next, I had to put this disaster with the goblins to bed. The goblins. The conversation with Iris had been enlightening, to say the least. The barely shimmering stairs leading to my descent back into the ordinary world flared with energy as my foot came in contact with each step. Thoughts flitted at the edges of my mind. I concentrated on the phenomenon step after step as I descended. When my foot finally touched the dead October grass, I knew it couldn't be avoided any longer.

"You're a goblin god, aren't you?" I sullenly asked the voice in my head that had been suspiciously quiet.

He chuckled quietly in my head and said, "No."

I could feel the tension leave my body until he spoke again.

"I'm *the* goblin god." He finished.

CHAPTER 19

The car idled on the street in front of my apartment building as I waited for Sven to come down. My impatient foot tap was muffled by the rental car's mat. I wasn't in love with the car, I didn't typically like big cars, but the interior was comfortable. That was pretty much the only thing that was necessary for a stakeout. I went through the mental checklist. Snacks? Check. Beverages? Check. Cards? Check. Portable phone charger and cables? Check. Blankets and pillows? Check. All ready. I'd been on so many of these, I pretty much had it down to a science. I ran my hand across the stitching on the steering wheel. I wasn't excited about the prospect of having to go into car buying again. But since my car had flipped when Jeffries forced me off the road the other day. That limited my options. I popped my lips and then sighed. I knew I was avoiding the elephant in the room, or should I say the G. O. D. sharing my mind, but the whole thing freaked me out still. How did someone start to even be ok with sharing your head with another being?

"I can spell, you know. I'm not an idiot." Bab said, with a tone halfway between amusement and irritation.

"I didn't say you were an idiot," I said.

I flicked down the car's heat as I felt heat creep up my face. I'd done precisely that by trying to spell it out, but hell, how was I supposed to keep any of my thoughts to myself if I was sharing a mind? Just because I wasn't already crazy didn't mean that wouldn't make me crazy. Eventually, or not, crazy was crazy.

My mental hamster wheel was interrupted by a large growl. I fidgeted in my seat. When was the last time I'd eaten? I couldn't remember. I directed my thoughts at the god in my head. I really shouldn't put this off any longer.

I decided to start with the basics and asked, "So...who are you...exactly?"

It felt bizarre to be asking about someone who I had been living with for over a month now, but here we were.

"I'm Baboloki, God, and Protector of the Goblins." He answered in a voice that confirmed that he wasn't probably lying about all of this goblin god business.

I nodded my head as I processed that, absently watching a group of carolers stroll by. That seemed like a pretty...optimistic hobby for New Yorkers, but whatever turned their crank.

"Yeah, you're probably better off going with Bab. Loki is already taken by Marvel. You don't want to be sued by someone with that much lawyer power." I said, only half-teasing.

"What is this suing you speak of?" Asked Bab, confused.

I shrugged it off. "You're better not knowing. So does that make you like...a demi-god then?"

I knew there was god, and there was the Devil, and I knew how they worked. But I just wasn't sure how all of the in-between stuff worked.

"No, a demi-god is when a god has an off-spring with an earth-dwelling creature." He said.

"You're using 'a god' in a different context than 'God,'" I noted.

"That's right. God creates lesser gods to look after different pieces of his world," he explained with surprising patience.

That made a lot of sense when I thought about it. It was like ranking officials.

"So you were always a god then?" I asked to make sure I had the details hammered out.

"Yes, but I did not know it. God had placed me with those I was to rule. It wasn't until I reached about 16 and understood all of my powers and talked with god that I came to understand what I was and what he wanted me to do."

"How long ago was that?" I asked, thoroughly entranced now.

"About 500 years ago," he said, a note of wistfulness in his voice.

"So young!" I couldn't help but think.

"No, that was quite a bit into adulthood back then. Remember, races of the time didn't live as long as they do now." He corrected.

"So what happened?" I had to ask. "When they found out you were given to them from God to look after them?"

"Well, they weren't exactly...overjoyed at first..." he said, his voice taking on a far-off quality with a tinge of sadness.

I was trying to think about a way to bring it back to a happy place when Sven walked down the stairs. There should have been no reason I saw him walk in. I wasn't looking for him. I was too entranced by Bab's story. But I'd felt him. It was a blink of awareness, like a door, had been opened, and I'd felt the draft. And once I was aware of him, I couldn't take my eyes off him. I felt the pull to go to him. I stared at him as he came towards me, backdropped by someone's sad attempt at Christmas lights hanging down a brick wall. It was almost like his pelvis was moving towards me before the rest of him. I couldn't stop staring at him, half noticing the way he walked and half trying to figure out what in the hell was going on.

"It's the mark," said Bab.

"Mark?" I asked, mesmerized by his dress shirt pulling taut over his chest when he moved out of the way of an excited kid in a Santa hat who bustled through. Then it hit me. The vampire mark. "Oh, that." I breathed. "Is that why I'm so…" I watched the way the front of his jeans pulled across the width of his thighs. "Attracted to him?"

Bab laughed and said. "Oh, no, sweetie. A vampire mark doesn't make you more attracted. That's all those hormones you got firing. A mark just makes you more…aware of him. The more marks you share, the greater the distance in which you can tell where he is."

I tried to be scared by that, but instead, I was fascinated. Either that or I was fascinated by the way his forearms corded as he put a hand out to grab the door handle. Whatever it was, by the time he sank into the seat next to me, I was fairly panting.

"Hi," I said, in what was far too breathy of a tone for a grown woman who wasn't in a black and white movie.

The blast of cold was cut off as the door shut behind him. A grin spread over his face, and his eyes roamed over my face. I became very aware that my head was tipped up like I was waiting for a kiss. Just a kiss of those perfect lips. I could almost feel them on my lips.

"Hi, to you," said those perfect lips.

"You've got it bad, girl," Bab said with a laugh.

That was enough to button me up. I couldn't have it bad for Sven. We'd tried that. It wasn't going to work. Despite my pep talk, I still felt too many butterflies in my stomach as I pulled out into traffic.

Sven's head craned to see the street signs. "Can we take Southbound Fredericks Ave?"

"No sweat," I said, turning onto the street he'd indicated.

I wasn't sure if it was the car's heater pouring into the cabin or if it was the heat I felt from the sexy specimen sitting next to me. Whatever it was, I had a hard time focusing on the conversation as Sven started to chat. When we'd talked on the phone, he'd sounded positively excited to come on a stakeout. I hid a smile by turning my head as I made a show of turning down another street Sven indicated. He was about to be disappointed. The biggest threat on a stakeout was usually of dying from boredom. However, with Jeffries having already made one attempt on my life, I wasn't taking any chances. And on any other day of the week, I wouldn't have given it another thought. I'd taken out vampires. I could certainly take out one human. But things were different now. I didn't trust being alone with Bab, let alone protect myself while worrying about him.

"No offense," I said to Bab.

"You do what you feel like you have to do, honey," he said. "If it means this delicious morsel gets to come with us, I'm all for it."

"I'm sorry, what?" asked Sven, interrupting my dialogue with Bab. He didn't realize I'd been talking to Bab.

Heat flushed my face. I'm sure I looked insane to him. It was a damn miracle he was even around at this point. I turned the temperature dial on my side of the car. I was going to combust if I didn't.

"It's just..." I tapped my brain, not wanting to say the words.

Recognition lit up his gaze, and his lips pressed together in pity, "Oh, I see... how's that going anyway? Is it still status quo?"

I rolled my eyes. "Oh, boy. That's something to talk about

for sure. We'll have plenty of time on the stakeout, though. We'll get into it then."

I wasn't comfortable with saying more. It was a hard thing to admit to someone. Not to mention, how much was someone supposed to be able to take before they decided you were too much of an emotional drain and went as cold as hour-old fries.

"Speaking of which, stop here," he said.

Since we weren't anywhere near Jeffries's shop, I was pretty confused, but the urgency in his voice had me cutting off two cars so I could pull over. I pulled the boat in front of a disapproving hot dog vendor. I smiled an apology to him.

"I'll be right back," Sven said as he ducked out of the car.

Before I could open and close my mouth, he was out of the door. The cold December air blowing into the door made me throw the vents open. Where was he off to? I tried to peer around the vendor, but all I saw was a wall of aluminum. Damn cart. It wasn't long before Sven was throwing the door of the car back open, though.

"What was that-" I started to ask but was cut off by a box preceding Sven into the car.

I squealed in delight as I snatched it from his hands.

"Gods, Sven, you shouldn't have." I gushed as I threw open the box top.

The unmistakable smell of pepperoni caressed me as I ogled the pizza that sat inside. Cheese and pepperoni beckoned to me. I closed the top before I did something stupid, like grab a piece and eat it while driving. Sven grinned from ear to ear. He knew how amazing he was. I handed it back.

"You're not supposed to be irreplaceable, you know." I accused him with slitted eyes.

He settled the box back on his lap and angled the vents to

the mouth-watering gift. "Oh, that's exactly my goal," he said with a devilish grin.

"Can't we keep him?" asked Bab with a hopeful lilt to his voice.

I ignored him and pulled back into traffic, shaking my head. Dream men. Who needed them? The intoxicating aroma of pizza said maybe I did. Before I knew it, we were on Jeffries' street. Switching into bounty hunter mode, I slowed down. The house looked deserted. No lights were on. In fact, it looked much the same as it had since the last time I'd paid a visit.

Sven must have noticed how hard I was scoping the place out because he asked with an incline of his head, "Is this the place?" he asked

I nodded and kept driving. When we'd clearly passed the house and were turning down another street, he was clearly confused.

"Isn't that where we are doing the stakeout?" he asked in halting sentences.

"It sure is. We just have to pass by the first time as to not arouse any suspicion." I said as I circled the car back around the block.

"That's pretty smart," Sven said with a smile.

"Gee, thanks." I said, then because I realized that had made me sound like a jerk, added on, "There's a little thinking that goes into the whole bounty hunting thing."

I'd never been good at taking a compliment.

He merely shook his head and said, "I had little doubt."

I wanted to kick myself for the faux pax, but since we were back at Jeffries', I took the diversion and pulled to the side of the street. There were half a dozen cars parked on the road with us. I breathed a sigh of relief; we didn't look too conspicuous. Throwing the car into park, I killed the engine. It took two seconds to scan the sidewalks and the home fronts. There was no sign of life. Not even a rustle of a leaf. All was quiet. I gave another quick look to Jeffries' house. It sat as silent as the dead. Typically, I wanted to see the opposite, but this time I was more than ready for a break.

"Ok, how about that pizza?" I said, so needing a piece, I could almost taste it already.

Sven flipped open the top, fished out a slice, caught some cheese tentacles on a napkin, and handed the whole delicious mess to me.

I knew I was smiling as big as a newly crowned queen as I gathered the mess up and said, "Thanks."

"My pleasure," he said with a smile that almost made me believe him. Then he added with a depreciating smile. "I thought it might go over better than the food I tried to cook the other day."

"It was pretty bad." I laughed, remembering the debacle. "It was awesome of you, though. It just proves that you aren't always perfect."

"No, I think we've proven that fact well enough," he said, a dark look coming over his face.

I noticed it immediately as regret. He felt terrible about marking me. It didn't make things right, but it sure as hell went a long way towards making things better. I folded the slice of pizza in half and stuffed it into my face as he replaced the lid. He handed me a napkin and laughed as grease dribbled my chin. I just got the napkin under my chin right before it dropped onto Iris' dress. Princess or not, there was no civilized way to eat a New York-style pizza. It took me a second to realize he wouldn't be sharing in the pizza. As a vampire, he didn't eat. He'd bought the pizza just for me. My heart swelled. Maybe it wouldn't be so bad if I made him feel a little better about his own fuckups if he heard mine.

Finishing the last bite of pizza, I wiped my face and said, "Well, you're not the only one who makes mistakes."

"What do you mean?" He asked.

His words appeared innocent enough, but from the way his back became even straighter (which I hadn't thought was possible,) I could tell he was uncomfortable, like possibly I was going to say that us getting together had been a mistake. On the one hand, I was glad he didn't dismiss what he had done to me. However, it was up to me to beat him up. He shouldn't beat himself up so much about it, mostly since I'd already forgiven him.

"Do you remember me telling you about the potion I had to take to get rid of my wings?" I asked.

He nodded, "yeah, the one you had to go on the world's craziest scavenger hunt to find."

"Right. Well, one of the ingredients I had to get was a goblin bone."

"A what? Did you say a goblin bone?" At my nod of confirmation, he shook his head. "That's crazy."

"Oh, that wasn't even the worst ingredient to find." I assured him, then with a shrug, I said, "I suppose everything makes us stronger."

"That it does." He said with a laugh. "So what was it about the goblin bone that makes you say it was a mistake."

"I...I lifted it from an Altar." I said, rushing through the sentence as I said it.

It sounded worse and worse every time I told the story.

He shook his head. "Lifting a bone from an alter...yeah, I think that can safely be considered a mistake."

He had no idea.

I took a deep breath and said, "Oh, that's not the worst part..."

I trailed off as a car appeared in my peripheral. It was driving way too slowly. Making a decision, I released my glamour and let my hair bleed back to purple. I made a show of reaching in the center console, letting my hair fall in front of my face to conceal it. When their red tail lights lit up my peripheral, I craned my head to get a look at the vehicle. They were turning.

"What is it?" asked Sven, instantly on high alert.

I tapped my lip. "That car looked very familiar."

"I noticed it too. Did you recognize the car?" he asked.

"I'm still trying to figure that out. Was it familiar to you?" I said.

He shook his head. "No such-"

Adrenaline jumped into my throat. I threw out a hand to stop him. "Here they come again."

The silhouette of the car's hood was unmistakable this time as it rounded the corner to come back around. It was the Jeffries' family car. Whoever was driving the car obviously hadn't realized it was me in this car, and I couldn't chance that they would notice me this time around. Not when if this was Jeffries, this crazy could be over in a matter of minutes. Thinking quick, I reached across Sven's lap.

He threw his hands up in a gesture of innocence. "Cy...what are you-"

His words were cut off when my fingers found the seat lever, and he flew back into a reclined position.

Scrambling out of the driver's seat, I took a deep breath and moved to his side of the vehicle. Straddling him, I looked down into his wide eyes. From the way his nostrils flared, I could see he wanted me and was fighting it. That's not what I needed right now.

My heart in my throat, I said, "They can't see my face. Kiss me."

I didn't know why my voice came out in a whisper. There was no one there to hear me. The truth was that I wanted him to kiss me. I ached for it so badly I could feel it in my toes.

"In that case, you should be under me," he said with a growl but complied anyway.

He cupped my jaw and threaded his hands through my hair, freeing it to fall down over my face on both sides. Between the hair curtains and the purple hair, it was the perfect coverup. His thumbs stroked the sides of my face in slow, knee-weakening circles. It took all of the focus I had to keep an eye on the car to make sure it hadn't seen us. It pulled into the Jeffries' drive. The ploy worked. What I saw next was no surprise, though. Tillie hopped out of the family car and made her way to the front door. What came after that, though, *did* surprise me. Becca popped out of the car after her. Looking both ways, she inserted a key into the lock and made her way inside. After I'd been sure she shut the door, I turned back to Sven.

"I didn't see that coming..." I trailed off when I saw the look in his eyes.

"Tell me in a minute." Desire was raw on his face as he said, "I haven't kissed you yet."

With gentle pressure on the back of my head, he brought my lips down to his. The rush in my head was the only sound as his lips moved across mine in a slow claim. My mouth fell open in desire, and he took advantage of my weakness. He slid his tongue over my lips in a move that pulled a groan from my throat. My hips pressed into his as I urged him closer. He moved a hand down to cup my ass in a slow grind against the evidence of his arousal. We stayed like that, our mouths, tongues, and hips greeting the other like it had been a decade.

Finally, I tore my lips from his. My breath was ragged in the silence of the car. That was amazing. That was a mistake. I dropped my head to his chest, unable to look him in the eyes again when my emotions were so caught up and confused.

"Gods alive," I exclaimed quietly.

"You said it," he said, bringing up a hand to gently touch my hair.

Oh, yeah. That's right. My hair. It gathered too much attention when it was purple. Not a quality you want when you're undercover. With a thought, I turned it back to blonde. He didn't make any move as I moved off of him, but his disappointment was palpable. I couldn't just go back to how we'd been and pretend everything was the same. No matter how badly I wanted it.

Shifting my focus, I turned back to the Jeffries' house. There were two lights on, one upstairs and one downstairs. A quick calculation said it was the living room and same room with all of the disguises. Bingo. She was helping Jeffries.

"You see that light on upstairs?" I indicated to Sven with a nod of my head.

"Yes," Sven answered, clearly trying to collect himself.

"One of Jeffries' sisters is in that room. That's where all of his disguises are at. That means she has to be helping him." I said with a nod to the house.

"In what way is she helping him?" Sven asked.

I tapped my lips. Searching the house, as if that would give me the answers, I said, "That I don't know. What I do know is that they are trying to maintain a level of normalcy. When they leave, we're going to go in and see what's missing and see if we can piece together Jeffries' next disguise. Then since it's clear Jeffries isn't going to come back here, we'll need to start staking out the Jeffries family home since they are obviously in contact with him."

"Hey, Cy?" Sven asked.

"Yeah?" I asked, my mind still transfixed on the house and our next plan of attack.

"You mentioned earlier that stealing the bone wasn't the worst part." He hedged.

"That's right," I confirmed, sitting up a little straighter when I saw movement in the living room and a flare of a screen.

Was that a computer screen?

"Is the worst part that you now have goblins following you trying to get it back?" he asked.

Stunned. I turned my eyes away from my surveillance.

Turning to him, I asked. "How in the hell did you know that?"

"Oh, let's just say I put two and two together," he said between laughs as he pointed out the window to the side of the street we were on.

Down the sidewalk was the unmistakable silhouette of two goblins. I didn't have to see them close up to know it was Kut and Maybe. They were heading straight towards us. The only thing that was slowing them down was Kut kept pointing to the houses and sending Maybe scurrying over the grass to the homes that had seen better days.

"What kind of homing beacon do these relentless little gangsters have that they could find me out here?" I mumbled under my breath.

"They need to know where I am," pointed out Bab. "I can't abandon them."

"Fucking, of course, it's you. The hell you can't. We're in the middle of catching a murderer here, Bab. We can deal with your little G's after that." I about spat, watching Maybe make his way back to Kut, throw his hands up, and shake his floppy ears.

"One doesn't pick and choose when they're a god." huffed Bab.

"Did you name the voice in your head?" asked Sven,

giving me a look that said, 'ok, yeah, you're insane, but I like you anyway.'

"Not exactly," I said, darting a look back to the goblin's nearing us. Maybe was currently hanging on one hand and a toe hanging from latticework, "Turns out there's not actually a voice in my head. As luck would have it, there was the spirit of a god in the bones on the altar, and now since I...ingested the bone, he's...inside me now."

I turned back to Sven as I finished the last, not wanting to see Sven's reaction but having to see it like a train wreck. Sven did a slow blink. You could see his brain whirring. I bit my lip to keep a nervous laugh from bubbling out.

"So you're...possessed," Sven said, testing the word out on his lips.

"Possessed has such a negative connotation," said Bab.

I resisted the urge to roll my eyes at Bab and answered Sven instead, "In not so many words, yes."

After a few seconds of mulling this new information over, he pointed at the fast-approaching Kut and Maybe, "Do *they* know that?"

Kut had her hands on her hips and was shaking her head in quick, jerky motions to a Maybe who was pointing at a house two houses in front of us that had no lights on.

"They don't, no," I admitted.

"Well, I think it's about time we tell them, don't you?" Sven said gently.

I couldn't help the laugh that burst out of me. "Tell them that their god is inside me? That's a terrible idea. They'll just take me down to their wretched home again, but this time they won't let me leave." At Sven's admonishing look, I added petulantly. "Look at me like that all you want. I'm not about to set myself up for another round of kidnapping. That's quite a blow to the ego, you know."

I snuck a peek out the window. There was only one house

in front of us now, Maybe running on unsteady stubby legs up to the dilapidated Victorian.

"I won't let them do that to you," he said quietly.

"With all due respect, you weren't able to prevent it last time." I didn't want to say it, but it had to be said.

He bristled at the mention, and then it led to an expression of almost pain, "For that, I ask a thousand pardons. It was inexcusable."

I put a hand on his shoulder. "Hey, it's not your fault. Faeries aren't given enough credit, but they're the real deal. You don't want to fuck with them."

"So I can see," he said with an admiring glance.

"I think that you're right, though. I need to tell them something." I contemplated what as Maybe came defeatedly back, his shoulders slumped. "Listen, I'm going to grab the one. You grab the other. We'll bring them back in here and scare the bejesus out of them. Can you do that?"

He grinned at me, his canines growing as he did. "Madame, that is my specialty."

I ignored the shiver that ran down my spine at the sight. Meanwhile, Kut and Maybe started to pad past the front quarter-panel.

I reminded myself he was on my side as I swallowed and said, "Ok, on my word."

When they were just past the front door, I said, "Word."

Hearing the click of his door open, I thrust mine open too. Two sets of surprised eyes met mine. As I reached out to grab Maybe, the one closest to me, the other ones disappeared in a blur. Blinking to make sure nothing was wrong with my vision, I laid hands on the other goblin and hauled him into the car. Little arms swung at me. I wrestled them and pinned them behind him, grabbing the door and shutting it with my other hand. I threw the seat down and turned him around, putting a knee into his back.

To my shock, Sven was already back in his seat, pinning Kut under him, with bared fangs. She cowered beneath him. It was a good thing that my knee was in Maybe's back because I had a moment of panic enter my heart too. I was back in Jerrick's place, Thomas leaning over me, prepared to bite.

I jostled my head, bringing myself back to the present. Their grunts and snaps filled the car.

"Enough!" I shouted.

The noises were muted to heavy, labored breathing and quiet grunts.

"You can die, pretty princess." Kut spat at me.

She was surprisingly not perturbed by the snapping vampire in front of her. I had to admire her fervor.

"You listen close, Kut," I said to her. "We are going to let you go, but only if you never come back again."

"We'll never go. We'll never give up getting our god back." Maybe said, his voice muffled by the car seat.

"You want the bone, right?" I asked for clarification.

"You know we do, faerie." Maybe said from.

"That's my point," I said, trying to get them to see reason. "You don't seem to understand. You aren't getting the bone back because I ate it."

Silence met my proclamation, followed by guffaws. Maybe was laughing so hard, his body twisted beneath my knee. I had to put pressure into it to keep him in one place.

"Yeah, right, pretty princess gnawing on a bone like a dog. We believe that, all right. As soon as we believe that Maybe is the champion of our land." Said Kut with a healthy laugh.

Maybe however didn't find so much humor in this comparison. How did I get them to believe me? I looked out the window. That's when I saw Tillie and Becca were heading down the walk.

"Sven, down!" I said, flattening onto the seat.

The goblin squirmed under me. Sven had followed suit, and I saw Kut get very still under him. I didn't have much time to think about that, though because Maybe was starting to rock the car with the violence of his movements. That had to stop. Pronto. Before the sisters noticed it and conversely, us.

I pulled some ley line energy into me. Bringing a hand in front of his face, I released some of it in front of his face. Lighting danced in a small arc in front of his face. "You will be still until I tell you otherwise," I whispered, the threat unmistakable. Then I directed my harsh whisper to Kut. "That makes both of you."

There was something along with the anger in her eyes, but I didn't take time to flesh the feeling out. We sat like that for a minute as we waited for the Jeffries' family car to pull out of the driveway. It wasn't until they had rounded the corner that I continued.

"How I ate the bone is not important. However, let me be extremely clear: There is no more bone of your god. So go back and ask for forgiveness at his altar. I am sure he will grant you leniency for your efforts to retrieve it."

"You know nothing." Whispered Kut, obviously taking my threat seriously because she didn't move from her position.

"Everything? No, but I do know some things. Let me tell you what I do know, for a fact: 1. That bone is not coming back. 2. If I see you or any of your other little friends around, I will kill you on contact. My life is mine, and gods alive, I will get control of it back."

Kut stared daggers at me. I looked down to see an identical expression on Maybe's face. Here I was again, just making friends. I released the kundalini energy, and the lighting vanished like it had been stamped out by an invisible foot. I opened the door and got out. Sven followed suit. The goblins crouched inside the plush interior, out of place, like eternally angered statues from some pampered rich boy's dreams.

"Now, go. And just be glad this isn't the day you died." I said with a stare at them that told them next time they wouldn't be so lucky.

Maybe, his eyes wide, looked like he believed me. Kut was up almost as soon as Sven had let her up. At my words, she didn't release my gaze but helped Maybe up. They jumped out of the car and stalked away. Throwing glares and measured glances over their shoulders to watch us the whole time. Sven came over to stand next to me and watch their departure.

"Why is it that I feel like this isn't the last of those two?" I asked with a resigned sigh as I saw them start to bicker between themselves with large hand movements and head bobbing.

"Because you're smart," Sven said with a wry smile.

"Smart enough to eat a god bone," I said with a wry smile of my own. "Come on, let's get on with this investigation, so we can figure out what to do about this whole God thing."

"Oh, don't worry about me," said Bab with a laugh. "This is the most fun I've had in centuries."

Fun at my expense wasn't my favorite kind of fun, but at least someone was having a good time.

CHAPTER 20

*I*nside the Jeffries' house, the first place I went was to the living room. I'd noticed a light was on in the room, even though I'd seen both women leave the house. Oddly, the living room light was off, but the computer was on. On the computer was a Facebook post. It was a picture of a young Becca, dressed up as a green witch. The caption said, "Reminds me of better days." I clicked on the comments. I scrolled past the 'Looking great, girl." and "Slaying it, sister." comments but stopped when I saw, "Reminds me of fishing at Goddard State Park with dad while you, mom, and Tillie went shopping." Becca had replied to the comment saying, "Lol. There was nothing that made us feel more grown-up than brunch and boutique bra shopping." He responded again by saying, "Ah, it was A Fitting Experience, was it?" she replied back with "Oh, haha." More scrolling said that was the end of the communication. That the other comments were just more rah-rahing.

I sat back. "Why do you think she wants us to see that?" Sven asked from over my shoulder.

"I don't know," I said, breaking out my phone. "But she had capitalized Fitting Experience."

After a quick Google search, I held out my phone. "Bingo. A Fitting Experience. It's a bra shop in East Greenwich, RI."

"That's only about...3 hours from here," Sven said after a thought.

"3 hours and a lifetime away if the pictures of this town have anything to say for it. It's definitely a place someone could go to build a new life and avoid detection." I said. "Here, let's go see what's missing from the upstairs costume room, so we can see what we should be looking for."

"We?" He said with a smile in his voice.

"Well, yeah," I said, unable to keep the smile out of mine either. "Until I can figure out how to get rid of Babo here, I'm going to have to keep you around in case he tries to take over my body again or something. That is...unless you don't want to."

I added the last because it foolishly hadn't dawned on me that he might now want to be around. However, after everything we had been through and how I'd shunned him in the car, that was a genuine possibility. I hadn't realized my steps had faltered too until Sven responded.

"Of course. It would be my pleasure to accompany you anywhere and everywhere, Cy," he said, and I could hear the sincerity in his voice.

It warmed my insides, and I could feel my steps grow lighter again as we finished our ascent.

"How are we going to know what's missing?" Asked Sven as we entered the room.

I waved my phone in the air. "I have the pictures from before here, so it should be pretty obvious that whatever is missing is what we are looking for."

A quick perusal of his costumes and scouring of my

pictures showed that a set of buck teeth, a blonde surfer wig, and horned rim glasses were missing.

"So we're looking for a glasses-wearing surfer?" Sven guessed.

"It would appear so," I said with a laugh. "Probably, not his ideal disguise, but I guess you don't get many choices when someone else is picking out your costume for you."

Sven smiled at the irony of it, but it wasn't long before his smile disappeared. "Do you smell that?"

"Smell what?" I asked, sniffing the air. No sooner had the words left my mouth than I smelled it too. "Smoke."

Sven nodded in silent confirmation. He grabbed my hand in his, his long fingers enveloped mine. We rushed to the stairs, but we both stopped short at the sight that greeted us. Flames licked up the stairs. The heat grew unbearable. I immediately covered my mouth to protect myself from the smoke. Smoke was the number one killer in a fire. And I didn't plan on dying today.

"This way," I said, pulling his hand this time, deeper into the house.

I kicked open the bedroom door since I didn't have a free hand. Bingo. I pushed past the deceptively normal-looking bed and made my way to the window. Dropping his hand and my shirt, I pushed open the window, letting blissfully clean air into my lungs. Thank the gods. I gulped it like a starving man.

I stuck my head out the window and saw we were above the garage. Perfect. A quick glance showed the coast was clear.

"Come on," I said, over my shoulder as I lifted myself up onto the window sill and lowered myself out the window.

It took a few seconds to find purchase on the old shingles, but when I was confident in my ability to stay on the roof, I lowered myself down. Adrenaline pumped into my veins. Lowering my full weight onto the roof, I immediately looked up. Sven crouched onto the window sill and then dropped onto the roof without a sound.

"I could do with a little less of the vampire theatrics, but good enough. Let's go." I said with a twitch of my lips to keep from smiling.

The twinkle in his eyes said he knew it too. We made our way to the back of the shed. I eyed the stretch warily. It was the kind of distance where you weren't sure if you were going to break something, but there wasn't much choice. I swung my arms and lept. Only to be caught by a pair of arms and pulled to a muscular chest. I looked back to glare at Sven.

"What do you think you are doing?" I asked. "We have to get down from here before this part of the house catches on fire too. I don't feel like being a Cy, Sven shish kebab.

"Me either," he said with a smile. "I can think of much better ways that I would rather find myself pressed up against you. But I think I can be of assistance here."

Scooping my legs up, he cradled me in his arms and pulled me close. It felt good to be cuddled against him. Then, with a velocity that made me catch my breath, he propelled us off the garage room. I had the feeling of the wind blowing through my hair as we freefell then we hit the ground with little more than a thud. I blinked, scarcely able to comprehend that we were on the ground and in one piece. I could hear the sirens in the distance. Rescue was on its way. I laughed in relief. We did it. We'd made it out alive. He pulled me close with a squeeze. I could feel the hesitancy in his arms as he released me. I put my feet on the ground, not wanting to be free of him but knowing we weren't through with the drama yet. I looked wildly around the plain but normal-looking back yard. There wasn't really anywhere he could hide.

"Look, you have to poof like a bat or something," I said to him.

"What are you talking about?" he said, a furrow developing between his brows.

"As a bounty hunter, I have legal jurisdiction to be here. "You, on the other hand, are not. Being that you were so closely affiliated with your Uncle, I don't want them getting the wrong idea and throwing you in jail and asking questions later."

His Uncle had been a known drug runner. Faerie blood was a drug to vampires. Just because it was a human law didn't mean he wasn't mixed up in all other kinds of...activities. It was my experience that when you were involved in one, you tended to be involved in more.

As I heard the sirens pull up, I pointed to the trees and said, "Go." He stubbornly stayed, a set to his jaw. I gave him a bit of a push, panic rising inside me. I hissed furiously. "Now!"

Giving in, he jogged to the line of trees that separated the adjacent property. It was just in the nick of time, too, because Tyler came around the bend, a scuffed gas can in hand. Thank the gods. I waved at him but immediately dropped my hand when I saw a stocky man with a cigar in his mouth stalking after him. He stopped when he was close enough to where I could smell the tacos he'd had for dinner.

Burdock.

"Ms. Vanguard. I should have known," he said as he chewed on his cigar. "You're supposed to catch them, you know. Not kill them."

"I wasn't trying to kill anyone," I said through gritted teeth.

"Is that your Buick out front?" he said with a nod towards the front of the house.

"It is," I said, not liking where this conversation was going.

The gleam in his eye said he knew it too. He threw his head back to Tyler. The small kid whose birth certificate must have said he was at least 20 (otherwise, how else was he a cop?) held up the gas can in a helpless gesture.

"That's what I thought. We're going to have to take you in for questioning. That was found by your car." he said with a sly grin.

"Of course, it was," I said, not believing a word of it.

"Mooney, cuff her and bring her downtown for questioning," he said, with a satisfied smile on his face.

I heard a growl come from the treeline. Sven. Shit, he must be losing his mind. Another siren joined the last. From the clinging and clanging, I could tell this one was the fire truck. I tried to push the confusion from my mind and held out my hands to Tyler to show Sven I was going willingly. All of the ruckus made people nervous. I prayed the gesture would tell him and Sven both not to do anything stupid.

Tyler looked like a scared kitten as he came over to me. I was surprised I couldn't hear his knees knocking together. He took my wrists in his soft grip and pulled them behind my back.

"Sorry," he whispered for only me to hear as men started to shout and bustle.

"It's fine," I said to Tyler as rain from the hose sprayed from over the house and started to drench us.

"Do you want me to take him out?" asked Bab.

I could hear the readiness in his voice.

"It's *fine.*" I reiterated for him this time.

Gods alive, I'd just started to feel like I'd gotten my shit together again since finding out the voice in my head wasn't of my own making. However, if anyone did anything stupid, I was going to lose my carefully held together shit.

Misunderstanding I was talking to him, Tyler said, "I heard you. I heard you. We're just going to take you down for questioning, is all. Nothing to worry about."

His words, meant to soothe, had the opposite effect.

CHAPTER 21

"*N*umber 4, please come forward." I heard through the loudspeaker.

I looked down the line of girls who were all holding numbers like me. With their squat frames and blonde hair, they could have all passed for my double.

"Number 4?" the loudspeaker said again, this time with less patience.

Blinking, I looked down at the number that I was holding. Number 4. Of course. I stepped forward. My combat boots lifted precisely off the floor and set back down with finality as I faced the two-sided mirror. Heat sufficed my cheeks. I didn't know if it was still remnants of Iris' potion of embarrassment, but it didn't go away. I wanted to bore hate into the glass, straight into the soul of the person on the other side of the glass, but I didn't give them the satisfaction of a response. I maintained the calm of a queen.

"Thank you, that will be all." came the loudspeaker.

At the command of the loudspeaker, an officer appeared at the door. The line shuffled out behind him. I made sure to take careful, precise steps. When we were back in the holding cell, I practiced Muay Thai level patience as I waited. Finally, Tyler ambled into the room. He looked like he would rather be having a root canal, but I was glad he was here. At first

He read names off a list. My name wasn't on the list. All of the women from the line-up filed to stand in front of the door. It didn't take a genius to see what was happening. I got in line and went with them, but he stopped me with a hand when I got to the door.

"Not you."

My stomach growled over him as he spoke, but I'd heard enough to decipher the gist of it.

"You can't honestly mean to say you're keeping me here?" I asked.

I tried to remain calm, but I could hear my voice rising in octaves as I asked the question as he closed the bars of the NYPD holding cell. I could feel ley energy rising into me, unbidden. I must have been pulling it without being consciously aware of it because my hair started to float.

Before a petrified looking Tyler had a chance to answer, a red-face Tillie walked out of one of the closest interrogation room. There was no hiding my shock at seeing her here. It didn't take a genius to know that she'd come out of the room that had to have the two-way mirror to the room I'd just been in. Ripples of shock resonated through me.

Burdock followed after her and said, "No, thank *you*. Miss Jeffries. Your eye-witness account will be critical for keeping her behind bars."

He gave me a meaningful look. No way was he going to take my word over hers.

"She's a liar," I said to Tyler, desperation entering my voice.

"Look, I know you're upset, but I have to say the evidence isn't mounting in your favor," Tyler said, trying to reason.

I had to add evidence to my case.

"Look, they want me out of the picture. John Jeffries tried to kill me the other day." I said. "Don't take my word for it. Go look for his car. You'll see the marks that match mine from the wreck the other day. Ask Wesley for the file for the make of his car and go look in some junkyards. I guarantee you'll find it."

"Wesley, the bail bondsman?" Tyler asked, taking out his notepad and scribbling in it.

I nodded, and he made a couple more scratches.

When he looked up again, I pled to his sense of justice and said, "You can't believe for one second that I started that fire."

Tyler, ever the rookie, said, "It doesn't matter what I believe. It matters what the courts decide."

"That's bullshit, and you know it!" I screamed, smashing the flat of my hand into the bars as hard as I could.

They bent a little under the force. Tyler's eyes got the size of milk saucers, and he ducked his head and left the room too. I was alone. Completely and utterly alone.

"Fuck," I said.

I started pacing the now empty holding cell. It didn't take more than a couple rounds before I stalked to the back of the cell and rested my head against the wall. The brick ate into my scalp. I'd just scared off the one person in this place who could have helped me. What was I going to do now? There was nothing left. No hope. They were going to lock me away for the rest of my life. And even if I *did* find a way out, I would be a fugitive on the outside. A criminal on the outside and a pariah inside Knockaine. My life was distilling before my very eyes, and I didn't like what I was left with. If I wasn't snagging bad guys, what was the purpose in my life? Hell, even if I did catch the bad guys, was that really the most impactful difference I could make? Oren's beseeching image popped into my head.

As I was on the edge of an existential crisis, it was then that the answer was brought to me. The answer came in the form of a crack and a flash of blue from behind me. It lit up the entire wall in front of me.

I almost couldn't dare to hope. Anthony? It couldn't be. It had to be my imagination. As ridiculous as the thought was, I still couldn't help turning around. My body was pulled like a doll on a string.

Hope materialized, first in the tips of enormous, blue wings, then bare shoulders that dripped with muscle, and then the full-on spectacle that was Anthony. Shoulders that dipped and jutted in sinewy glory. Blue sift dotted his chest. He was all man, that was for sure. My fingers flexed with the memory of those collar bones underneath my fingertips. Warm and fuzzy feelings didn't come with the thought. No, it was shadowed by how I'd left him.

I didn't want to raise my eyes to see the accusation in his, but I made myself. Being strong meant doing things that weren't always comfortable. His eyes were guarded but not angry. That was a good sign.

As we stared at each other, it felt like neither of us wanted to break the fragile silence.

The seconds ticked by, though, and someone could come in at any moment, and they would freak.

I broke the silence with an awkward, "I guess you're the rescue squad?"

He gave an overly long shrug and twisted his lip up into a sardonic smile that said, "that's me."

"That's cool." When he didn't make a move, I said, "We should get out of here then, shouldn't we? Before anyone comes in?"

I paired actions with words as I stepped towards him in an odd dance that clearly said, How Do I Touch You Without Touching You. Popping through the Space in

Between with Anthony required you to be close. Too close for exes. But between the choices of staying in jail and not touching my ex or touching my ex and getting out of jail, I'd take the latter.

"We've got to talk." He said, his chiseled frame remained that of a statue, as he didn't move a muscle.

Impatience screamed in my muscles. "Can we talk later?" I implored as I heard steps in the hall and pulled some ley line energy.

"No, it has to be now." He pressed.

"Oh, for the love of the gods," I said under my breath.

Why could things never be easy? Out of time, I released the kundalini energy I'd stored in a flood of glamour. To the outside world, it looked like an empty cell, save for me napping on one of the benches. I don't know who would buy that because those benches had the cozy property of a mountain of rocks, but it was the best I could do in a pinch. To fae eyes, the glamour made the world pulse and glimmer, the air saturated with a steady flow of magic from the never. Not an ideal environment, but none was going to be for this talk.

"So talk," I said, crossing arms across my chest.

"Since you left, Queen Aine' has started a campaign to squash faerie training of using their powers as weapons."

His words shocked me. Partially because this wasn't the conversation I'd expected and partly because of the news.

"Why would she do that?" I asked.

It didn't make sense that a Queen would take away her people's ability to protect themselves.

"I think it's because of you. She doesn't like how people are rallying around you. What you've said makes a lot of sense and is clearly best for our people...it gives them a purpose again. And some fairies aren't shy about backing you in this. And that's the thing people kill for."

I swallowed hard. "Has anyone...died?" I was almost unable to speak the words; they stuck in my throat.

I didn't want to be the cause for more killing.

"No, not yet. The Queen recognizes the rise and sees it as dissent. She wants to kill it before it grows out of control." He said. "And she will use any means necessary to do that."

His words were calm, but I could see his fear for me in his eyes. I glossed over the concern. It wasn't me I was concerned for.

"It's hard to imagine words have such an impact on people," I said, rubbing my arms.

"It's not just your words that move people, Cy. Look at the faeries you saved, look how you used your own powers to open our eyes to how we needed to use ours, look at how you stood up to the Queen for what you believe in. People aren't dumb. They see these things. And they are with you."

This all made my head spin. "This isn't how I wanted things to be. I need to get back to Knockaine and set things right."

I went to move towards him, but he stopped me with a look.

"We aren't going to Knockaine, are we?" I asked.

He shook his head. "No, I'm to bring you to Sven."

Sven's name on his tongue immediately made me uncomfortable, especially thinking about the kiss we'd shared. Sure, Sven and I weren't a thing, but that didn't mean every fiber in my body wasn't screaming to make that happen. I wanted to ask how that had happened, but I thought it was best to let it rest. I didn't know if it was the struggle or the constant flow of kundalini energy flowing through me, but I felt suddenly drained.

Anthony read my discomfort because he said, "Look, Cy, I want to start over. I had a lot of time to think, and I think I was always just so in love with the idea of you growing up that I didn't stop to look to see the woman you had become. While I adore that person as a friend, I've come to realize that this...excitement isn't what I am looking for in a significant other. I want to spend countless hours with them sitting in the fields watching kittyhawks catch their meal. And...that just isn't you."

Ouch. That stung a bit. Nobody liked to hear they were a strain, but it wasn't something that everyone was cut out for. It was hard, but I nodded my understanding. This was best for both of us.

"I'd like to start over," I said with a small smile.

He smiled an answering smile. "Then it's done. Now, let's get you out of here."

That was something I could get on board with. Breaking out into a big smile this time, I stepped into his outstretched arms. He closed his wings around me, I dropped the glamour, and we were gone.

Wind flew past me in the nothingness that was the Spaces In Between. Since we hadn't left in a hurry, there was no pain this time. There was a weightlessness to it that made me take a breath to get the reference point. There was almost nothing to it, though, because we were there in the space of seconds. The second we surfaced again, I knew two things immediately. One, we were outside. Even though we were still in the cocoon of Anthony's wings, I could tell by the smell of the air. It was pungent and cloying. I was thankful for Iris' warm spell that protected me from the no doubt freezing air. And two, Sven was here. I could feel his presence like a buzz in my veins. I was so grateful he hadn't had to bend the Spaces In Between quickly, and as a result, we were both clothed. That would have been an awkward scene I'd have wanted no part in.

Anthony dropped his wings, revealing Sven's tense form. From the set of his lips and the way his hands were balled at his sides, I could tell he didn't like Anthony's arms around me. I could tell from Anthony's chuckle that he saw it too. But he didn't drop his hands right away. Men. I could beat the lot of them. I knew from our conversation that he didn't want me anymore, didn't mean as a friend he approved of Sven. Why did things have to be so complicated? I wriggled in his arms, a subtle tell to let me go. He did then.

I stepped out of his arms, and Sven instinctively moved towards me. I smiled at him tentatively. I wasn't sure how all of this transpired, but I was eternally grateful. When he reached my side, he searched my gaze assessingly.

"I'm fine."

I could see the relief in his eyes.

"I'm being framed for arson," I said.

"I gathered as much." He said, with a wry smile.

I turned back to Anthony. "Thanks for your help."

"Anytime," he said. Then with a meaningful look to Sven, he added. "I've always got your back."

I could feel Sven stiffen next to me. I tried not to roll my eyes because I really did appreciate the sentiment, even if it did have a double meaning. Being at Court made me a bit of an expert at them.

Instead of addressing it, I added, "I appreciate that. If you could go back and try to…" do what? Make things all better? Tell people to not kill each other? "…just make sure things go as smoothly as possible. I'll come back as soon as I have Jeffries dealt with and have cleared my name. We will get those who are ours and bring them home. I will unite our people again."

"I'll let the people know, my Princess," he said.

Then he did something that surprised the hell out of me. He bent at the waist. All kinds of uncomfortable feelings bubbled up inside me. I couldn't tell if it was because my childhood friend and former lover was bowing to me, because I was being acknowledged for the title I'd tried years to avoid, or both. Whatever it was, tears prickled my eyes.

"Oh, get the hell up," I said, trying to get the sensation to go away.

I could see the corners of his eyes crinkle as he bowed deeper. Then he came back up, the smile gone.

This time his words for Sven. "Keep her safe this time."

A growl reverberated from Sven's throat. Before I had time to wonder if things were going to get out of control, Anthony had wrapped his wings around himself and was gone, in an explosion of blue sift.

Alone with Sven, I turned to him. Before I had time to process anything, he had me enveloped in a hug.

"I'm so sorry I failed you." He breathed against my hair.

"You didn't fail me," I said, my words muffled against the softness of his button-down.

"I did, but it won't happen again. This, I promise." He said.

His words were so filled with vehemence that I didn't say anything to dissuade him. Now was not the time.

"We need to find Jeffries. He's on the run, and we have to get him before his trail goes cold..." My voice trailed off as the earth started to shake under our feet.

"Earthquake?" Sven questioned.

"I've never seen one in New York," I said.

I had to raise my voice because the rumbling started to become loud enough that I couldn't be heard over it.

An explosion came from 40 feet away in the form of a manhole cover thrown into the air. A dark and eerie mist poured like tar out of the hole. Eyes peppered the thick fog. I didn't know if it was the gas or their otherworldly aurora, but the eyes glowed a sickly green. They layered one on top of the other, unblinking and unholy.

The mist parted. A gasp was wrenched from my gut. Goblins. Dozens of them. One tiny male rolled out of the pile. He somersaulted leather bottom over wrinkly, bald head, ending on his butt. Blinking with wide eyes, he looked around. The noise of the growing horde behind him finally grabbed his attention. The bones on his armband swung wildly as he pushed himself up. Without so much as a backward glance, he ran back to the mass, mud, and asphalt sticking to his leather. The wayward goblin might have eased my tight nerves if it weren't for the growing dump truck-sized mound in front of us. Grunting and teeth chattering like a skunk with too many teeth, they climbed over themselves in a desperate attempt to be the first ones out. No, not out. I realized as they turned like the tide and rushed towards us in a stream of guttural screams. To me.

Looking desperately from side to side, I searched for an escape. Nothing. We were in an alley. There *was* no way out. We were going to be trampled to death.

Before I knew what was happening, Sven had scooped me up into his arms.

"Hold tight," he gritted out right before his legs started pumping, and the world became a blur. He was rushing us into the approaching hoard.

CHAPTER 22

My heart pumped against Sven's chest as adrenaline coursed through me. Even though I hadn't been the one running, I felt like I'd sprinted a country mile. I reached into my pocket and grabbed the coin there that Gaige had given me. I transferred it from one hand to the other over and over again in an effort to calm my mind.

Sven was as cool as a spring daisy as he strode into the lobby of his apartment. The only way you could tell anything that had happened was his hair was windblown. He still walked with a steady clip like he was on the way to a business meeting with a briefcase in his hand instead of a very-capable looking woman in his arms. At least that's what I told myself, but I could feel my eyes were a little too wide and my forehead a little too-pinched.

However, that didn't make me any less conscious of the stares as he strode me over to the elevator. When we passed, an older lady with a puffy poodle who looked as affronted as its owner had her hand to her throat like she was being choked out. I wanted to tell her to move her own hand. She'd be just fine.

It did make me drop my arms from around Sven's neck, though.

We passed another resident whose eyes were about to roll out of his head. What was this? Tea time? Why the hell were all of these people just standing around here? Sven had reached the elevator and punched the Up button. It lit up like it was just another day. Elevator lights lit up, goblins chased you by the hundreds down the street, and you were accused of a crime you didn't do.

See? Normal.

We had to start somewhere, though.

"Ok, you can put me down now." I hissed through smiling teeth.

The elevator doors whooshed open, and I felt the air open up behind me more than heard the doors open. He took 3 strides to get me inside and pushed the Penthouse button. Very efficient, but he still hadn't responded to my prompting. I wriggled in his vise grip.

"Sven," I said; I knew my voice had an edge to it that screamed I-was-two-seconds-away-from-losing-it.

Whether he heard the edge or finally felt like we were safe, I didn't know. All I knew was that he brought my legs gently to the ground like he was handling a fragile doll. I hated that feeling, and I wanted to move away from him. However, all thoughts of pushing him away fled when he cradled my head and brought his other arm around to pull me close. I rested my head on his chest in silence. We stood like that, reveling in the closeness as the metal box we were in shot us high to the safety of his apartment. When I could feel it slowing, I pulled away, regret in my bones. I didn't want to leave the safety of his arms. There was a peace there I just couldn't find anywhere else. My eyes sought him. His hand allowed the movement, finding its home on the base of my neck. He must have felt the pull, too, because his eyes were clouded with unspoken emotion. An emotion that buzzed my spine as his thumb reached up to swipe across my lips. It was an unmistakably possessive action. Every molecule hummed with the thought, but doubt made me step away, using the opening of the elevator doors as the convenient excuse they were.

He seemed to need to touch me, though, and dropped his hand to the base of my spine, the exact spot that had been buzzing with the electricity of his touch just a few breaths ago. I couldn't deny the same need inside myself, so I let it be. It seemed safe. Safer than pulling him to the floor. If I did that, I'd for sure lose myself to the thoughts and emotions that made up the storm inside of me.

He ushered me forward with the sweep of his hand. An overly gallant motion considering the events of the night. I giggled. With a shrug, I moved on. Some games were fun. A smile played at the corners of his own mouth as I passed.

A silence opened between us as we came to the door. I remembered the last time I'd been here. The city lights had twinkled behind him, as his lips had devoured mine. It had all happened as he'd dropped my pants to the floor. Right on top of the first image was the sensation of him pressing into me for the first time.

Sven unlocked the door and stepped to the side, interrupting the memory. The images had been visceral. The weight of them pressed down on me like a physical thing. I had to blink it back just to operate in the presence. I walked into the small hallway into the two-story entry with sure steps like I wasn't on the verge of a nervous breakdown. Funny thing about nervous breakdowns, though. You don't get to say when they are done, and my brain wasn't done with me yet. An image of him on the bed below me covered in shimmering mounds of sift as I flew above him came right behind the first.

My steps faltered. He was at my side in a second.

"What is it?" His hands danced around me like they weren't sure what to do.

That made two of us. I blinked back the visions that threatened to overtake me. Honestly, his house wasn't helping, though, and I struggled to find my voice.

"Here. Come sit down." He ushered me to the living room, and that damn glittering city backdrop from my visions rose up to choke me from the floor to ceiling windows.

With careful hands, he guided me to rest on a couch that defied all odds of its boxy architecture and was actually comfortable. He moved a footstool closer, and I obliged by putting my feet up, even though I really didn't want to. Getting too cozy only led to things I didn't want. Dangerous things. On second thought, I put my feet back onto the floor.

At a loss, he sank down next to me. "It's been a rough night. I wish there was something I could do to make it better."

His hands clenched and unclenched in my peripheral. I was doing everything I could do not to look at him, not to touch him. I didn't want to trigger my visions again. He didn't even know the truth about what had happened at Knockaine. If he knew, he probably wouldn't even want me. Not that I would blame him. It was a moot point anyway. You can't be with someone you don't trust.

He popped up from the couch like a piece of bread in the toaster and said, coming to a decision, "Water, you need water."

I allowed myself the luxury of watching him walk away. In a world where so much seemed unreal, at least that much seemed real.

I felt so alone. But I wasn't. If I was honest with myself, I had friends. Anthony, Kittie, hell, I could probably even count Iris as my friend, if I stretched. But everything in me wanted to be friends with the vampire who was banging around in the kitchen. He was opening and closing cupboards like he'd never been in there for the entirety of his undead life.

If we were truly going to be friends, he deserved to know the truth. All of it. I'd fought demons, outran a dragon, outwitted werewolves. I could do this. Couldn't I?

I breathed deep, the scent of cinnamon and earth filling my nostrils. A smell so very Sven it made my heartache. I could do this. I perched on the edge of the sofa, waiting for Sven to return When the slamming of cupboards stopped, Sven was back.

As soon as he stepped back into the room, I blurted out, "I slept with Anthony."

The second the words left my lips, I wished I could put them back in like chewing gum. Just great, Cy. Wasn't there a kinder way to tell him?

"No, that was way more fun," Bab said, his apparent break from torturing me over.

Ignoring him, I turned my focus to Sven. It was so much easier to do when I knew it wasn't my subconscious talking to me.

My words stopped him short, and his expression shut down as firmly as a garage closed for the night.

I started to rise. "I'm sorry-"

He cut me off with a wave of his hand. Obediently, I closed my mouth. For good measure, I sat back down. He resumed his path to me, walking more sedate this time. When he reached me, he held the glass out to me. Condensation was already starting to slip down the waved edges. I took the cup from him, its frigid temperature matching the cold fear snaking its way through my veins.

This could be it. The end of any chance I could have to salvage any sort of a relationship with Sven. What had I done?

"I know," he said simply.

I couldn't help but blink. "You know? But how-"

He sat down. I almost wished for one of those cheap couches that sagged when another person sat down next to you. Anything to stop this gap I felt growing between us. He sighed and ran a hand through his hair.

"Kittie," he said simply. I could see the hurt in his eyes, though, and it pulled at the strings in my heart. "When she saw you two together, she thought she should 'let me down easy.' Was that ever wishful thinking."

I could hear the self-condemnation in his voice. The actions of the past month flew through my head. I knew I hadn't done anything wrong because Sven and I had broken it off, but it stung like I'd cheated on him. I hadn't, but my heart still loved him. Even now, when I couldn't have him.

He was lost in a moment of his own reflection. I watched him, head bowed, but then he straightened.

"I get it, though. I messed up. I betrayed your trust. What hurt the most, though, was that I felt like I was just starting to get to know you...like really know you. You know, beyond all of that..." he paused, and I could feel the air almost shimmer between us, "infatuation bullshit. And what killed me the most is that I really, really loved the person you are. And I'd just fucked that up."

I breathed a ragged breath. If we were honest, I guess it was my turn to be totally honest. "I think the thing that hurt most was that you weren't the man I thought you were. I thought you had my back through thick and thin. I thought if there was one person in this world I could count on...it was you. That you loved....cared for *me*, not just the person you thought I could be. The potential I had. For who I could be."

He turned to me this time and took my hands in his. There was a fire that lit his eyes as he said to me, "But I *do* care for you. I don't give two shits about who can be or will be. I care for the person you are today and the person you will be tomorrow."

"Then why did you try to do the same thing to me that so many others have? Why did you put me in your own little box?" I couldn't help but ask. I knew the torture was in my voice.

This time it was his turn for his voice to turn tortured. "Because I was scared. I was scared of losing you."

He didn't understand. Clearly. Frustrated, I started to take my hands out of his in frustration, and he gripped them firmly.

"I see now that was wrong, though. By trying to hold on to you too tightly, I now see that I was pushing you away. And I am sorry. Sorry for putting you in such an impossible place. Sorry for destroying the beautiful thing we had. I know we can't get back what we had, but I vowed that if you ever, ever reached out to me again. I would be different this time. I would be someone who would be worthy to be next to you."

"Sven..." I faltered, my thoughts warring with my emotions, "I... can't. I can't do it again."

He leaned forward, his eyes bored into me. "Listen, I don't give a shit about Anthony-"

"Anthony and I aren't together." I cut him off. With all of the painful emotions swirling around, I didn't want any misunderstandings between us anymore. I had to tell him the whole, raw truth. "I think I was more in love with the idea of a picture-perfect future than I was with him. He was convenient, easy. He was everything that my life *should* be. The white picket fence. But I didn't want it. I didn't want *him*."

I saw the light of possibility enter his eyes. I so badly wanted to flame that light and feel it burn bright inside me, but even though I realized I didn't need the picture-perfect life anymore, that didn't mean that the future was with him. No matter how much that thought shredded my heart.

I looked him square in the eye and was proud my voice only wavered slightly as I said, "But that doesn't change things between us. I can't trust you. Being everything that you are- everything that *I* am. I can't take that chance again. There have been many ramifications of my...lapse, and I have to face the hard reality that I have to take control of my life. I can't make rash decisions anymore. I see what comes of those actions, and I'm not going to be that person anymore."

His expression was guarded as he looked at me. "Do you still feel...the same about me, though?"

Even though his expression was guarded, possibly because it was so, I knew how hard the question had been for him to ask.

Pity and an unnamed, raw emotion pooled inside me like a cracked gas tank. My heart squeezed my insides, trying to rid myself of the feeling. It was no use, and my voice contracted around the words as I said, "Of course I do."

Emotions broke like a flood gate, running across his face at a pace that was hard to follow, but finally, he looked up and said, "I can't change the past, but I can change the future. I will show you that you can trust me. It's up to *you* how to proceed from there."

Love flooded through me in a warm wave at his determination to keep me in his life. It made me feel special. Like I mattered to him. I didn't need that to be the whole package. It felt so good to actually matter. Me, for who I was. Not who I used to be or who I could be. Just flawed, messy me. I would give anything to keep that feeling.

"I'm telling you right now, though: I'm not going to

pretend that I don't want you back. I do. With every fiber in my being, I do. I'll be in your life in whatever capacity you want me to be, but you'll always know that I want you. All of you. And I always will."

This time his desire was unmistakable, naked in his eyes. He let me see all of it, feel it deep inside. The rawness made my heart skip a beat. The need for him built up inside me. I couldn't move for fear of going to him. This was going to be the hard part. The stuff to get over. Taking an unsteady breath, I let it out in a shaky release. After I was more sure of myself, I nodded my understanding.

"Good, now that we have that out of the way. Let's get you to sleep." He gave my hands a light squeeze.

The touch was reassuring and planted a seed of comfort into my belly. Though, it rooted something else too. It nestled deep inside me the knowledge that he respected me. His speech hadn't been just words. He would take me on my terms, nothing more. It had been more than anyone had given me before, and it made my throat tight with unshed tears. He stood up and started towards the stairs that led to his room. "I'll prepare the guest room for you. You're probably tired after all of that...drama." He finished with a wave of his hand.

I stood up, too, feeling his absence on the couch. "That would be nice."

I stared at him as he started to walk away, blinking back the tears that threatened to spill. Women thought they wanted a bad boy who would take what they were too scared to give. But they didn't. What they really wanted was a man who would make them beg for him from their pedestal of dignity and respect. Not because they had to, but because they needed what only he could give. Then he would give them exactly what they craved and treat them like the fierce, clever beings that they were, not like some caged doves to be protected. Sven was exactly that man. This was the man women dreamed of.

"Awww, come on," Bab complained. "You aren't even going to kiss him?"

Just hearing the words made my pulse run. Remembering the way he'd scorched my senses in the car, I swayed towards him. My mouth went dry. I wanted the wetness of his lips on mine.

I licked my lips a couple of times before I could get out the words. "It's not like that."

I knew he sensed the change because his body stopped with a corded tension. He turned, ever so slightly, like he was afraid to move.

"What's not like that?" He asked, the quiet sound falling in the hush like a boulder.

His reaction only served to ramp me up. It was taking everything in me not to cross the distance and be close to him again. At that point, I didn't know if the words were for Bab or myself. I could feel him against my body like a physical thing. I remembered our kiss in the car, and my palms sweated.

I shook my head to clear the fog of desire. "It's... it's just Bab."

"Yeah? What does he have to say" he asked, turning more fully to me, clearly wanting to come to me.

"He wants me to..." I tried to think of the best way to word this.

"Fuck him." Bab supplied unhelpfully.

"...kiss you," I said instead.

I thought it was better to go with the PG version he'd supplied earlier. It put fewer images in my head.

Sven smiled, clearly not against the thought. Outlandishly, he tapped his lips, clearly pretending like he was giving the matter real thought, and he walked towards me like a panther on the hunt. "You know what I think?"

I bit my lips to keep the smile that threatened to pop to myself and simultaneously wanted to reach out to him. "Hmmm?"

"I don't think it's Bab telling you that." He stopped when he reached me. Even though he was a foot away still, he made the space seem impossibly tiny by leaning in. "I think you want to kiss me again."

"Oh, you do. Do you?" I said so quietly I wasn't sure I'd said it out loud until he leaned in.

"I do. I think you're thinking about my lips sliding over yours right now. I think you'd give anything for it..."

"Is that right?" I asked, afraid he was right.

This time he did step in. I swayed towards the heat of him.

He reached up a hand to thread his hands into my hair. "Oh, yeah. In fact, I think you'd let me take you, right here...right now."

His words whispered across my lips as he lowered his head. I didn't have any way to argue against that. I would. Gods, but I would. I groaned in response. We sat there, sharing breath, breathing in the scent of each other. My pulse pounded in my ears. Then he pulled back with a wistful look.

"But I'm not going to. I don't want you to come to me in a moment of weakness. I want you to come to me with every...voice in your head screaming the same message: that I'm the one for you and you're the one for me. Then and only then will I give you what you need."

At his words, he kissed the top of my head. My heart tripped all over itself at his declaration. I wanted him. Needed him. But I couldn't convince myself I wanted him in every way. I realized just how hard this was for him, too, when he took a few deep breaths of his own before coming away. His eyes collided with mine, both of ours searching for something the other couldn't give. Then with a small compression of his lips and a stiff nod, he turned on his heel and left me again. This time it felt much colder than it had before.

THE SHRILL of the telephone pierced my eardrums. Who thought it was a fun throwback again to get an old-time telephone ringtone? It couldn't have been me. My legs slid over too-soft bed sheets as I stretched my arm over to grab it from the side table. My arm sailed through the air as it didn't meet the intended target. What the hell? I cracked my eyes open to get my bearings. The sight did nothing to aid me. Spartan yet masculine surroundings met my tired eyes. Where in the hell was I?

"For the love of God, you are at Sven's," Bab said, and I could practically hear his eye roll.

Oh, yeah. That's right.

"Thanks for leaving him alone last night," I said to Bab, recalling how Bab had taken over my body during our last sleep-over excursion with Sven.

"No problem. I figured you'd need some sleep after yesterday." was his nonplussed reply.

The events of the night before came flooding back. I couldn't decide what disturbed me more: being a fugitive for a crime I didn't commit, the goblin horde we'd narrowly escaped, or the vampire sleeping down the hall that was mine for the taking if I just said the word.

Each was insane in its own right; together, they made me feel like I was auditioning for Wonder Woman. First things first, though. I got out of bed as quickly as I could make myself and moved the box from last night's Chinese delivery to find my buzzing phone. It was a Restricted number. That cleared my mind a bit. Typically, I didn't answer calls from Restricted numbers, but this one gave me a funny feeling, so I swiped to answer it.

Holding it up to my ear, a gruffer than intended "hello?" came out.

A terrified voice on the other end had me awake in a heartbeat.

"Cy?" She asked. Then as if seeming to pull herself together, she continued on with only a slight tremor in her voice. "This is Becca."

Becca Jeffries. My pulse quickened.

"Becca, yes. Are there any new developments?" I asked as I looked around for something to take notes on.

I spotted my purse and some of my other belongings on a stuffed chair in the corner. Bingo. Sven had apparently gotten them from the middle of the night from my car. Gods, I adored that man. Moving as quickly as my less awake legs would allow as I made my way to my purse and pulled out my notepad. I flipped it open and grabbed my pen.

"Yes, we're supposed to meet John at our childhood vacation home in Charleston, SC." She said, clearing her throat.

I remembered a vacation home, but Charleston? That didn't sound right. Scanning through my notes, I saw the comments from the Facebook post I'd seen. It said East Greenwich, RI. Something wasn't right here.

I had to ask her about it. "Charleston? Becca, are you sure? I have-"

"Yes, that's right. Why wouldn't I be sure? It was where I spent my childhood." She said, cutting me off in a hurry, her voice rising in octaves.

I blinked. Something wasn't right here. Her voice sounded...strained. A light knock came on the door, followed by Sven's head a moment later. At his appearance, I gave him the shush finger and ushered him in with a brisk wave of my hand.

"Becca. Is everything ok?" I asked quietly. "Is someone there threatening you?"

"It's a fitting experience." She said, ignoring my question.

Ice flooded my veins. She was in danger.

"I said it was a Fitting Experience. Do you understand, Cy?" she asked, her voice too even.

A Fitting Experience. That rang a bell. I went back to my notes. Bingo. There it was, a Fitting Experience was the place they'd gone to, and it was for sure in East Greenwich, RI.

"I understand," I said, trying to keep calm for her.

"Mom is leaving at noon, Cy, so you have to hurry. She's leaving at noon." She said, her voice the same dead tone, but this time there was a slight waver to her voice.

The waver said she was more scared than she was letting on.

"At noon. Got it." I said, scribbling in the book furiously.

"Please make it on time. Don't let her leave..." She whispered.

Then the line went dead.

I stared at the wall, trying to figure out the puzzle that had been laid at my feet: 1) John, Tillie, or both knew I was out of jail and was trying to throw me off their trail 2) Her mother was in danger. Something was going to happen at noon.

We had to get there. Immediately.

Calculating, I turned to Sven. "It's about 3 and a half hours to East Greenwich, RI from here, isn't it?"

"Give or take traffic, why?" he asked.

"I don't suppose you could run me there?" I asked, already knowing the answer.

"I'm afraid not," he said, with a twist of his lips. "I can only pull that party trick for short distances, maybe 10 miles, max."

That left us less time than we needed, but it would have to be enough.

"That's where Becca is, and we have to get there," I said, grim lines rimming my mouth.

At his confused look, I shook my head. "I'll tell you about it on the way. Let's go."

Determination fused with my spine, and I strode to the door, Sven in my wake. I would save that girl. I would.

CHAPTER 23

I threw down my phone in disgust. I couldn't get a hold of anyone. Not The SAW. Not Kittie to go to Anthony. No one. This not having a way to communicate to people in my network sucked ass. I supposed it didn't matter anyway at this point. We were minutes away from being there. It just frustrated the hell out of me that I couldn't get a hold of ANYONE in the last three hours. It may have been nervous energy, but I'd have thought I could get a hold of SOMEONE before then. Who I really needed was Anthony. He could have had us there by now. I hated that I needed Anthony. Hated that I couldn't get a hold of him. Hated this helpless feeling roiling inside me. I looked outside, and it dawned on me that we were pulling off the highway. In my desperate attempt to reach someone, I hadn't been paying much attention to where we were.

My eyes flicked to the digital display on the dashboard, 11:43 shone back with an accusing brightness. We were almost out of time. Dread ate at my spine. My hand reached for Gaige's coin in my pocket.

"How much longer?" I asked as we pulled into a quiet strip that made up the town.

"We're here," he said with a nod to the left.

"Thank the gods," I said under my breath.

As we pulled into the very suburban-America looking strip mall, I craned my head around, looking for a sign of the Jeffries. Any sign. The only sign of life was across the street. A woman who got out of her Cadillac and walked big hips into a shop. However, the whole strip mall was very dead. Dead. The thought sent a shiver through my spine.

Maybe they were outback. Time threatened to close in around me, and I started to jog to the back of the building. Sven, glorious Sven, picked up his pace alongside me. A minute later we saw there was only one car in the back of every shop. Two minutes later confirmed those cars had to belong to the workers in each shop. I jogged back to the car, nervous energy-demanding the pace.

"This makes no sense. I *know* she wanted me to come here. Where are they?" I asked no one in particular.

Sven answered me anyway. "It looks like they aren't here."

Since it was a rhetorical question, I ignored his response and pulled my notepad out of my pocket.

I was missing something. But what? Smoothing the wrinkled edges of the notepad, I scanned through the unprincess like scribbles there. Witch costume. East Greenwich, RI. Fishing. Wait. Goddard State Park. I slipped my phone out of my pocket and punched the map app.

"Uh, Cy?" Sven said.

I held out a finger. "Hold on a sec. I think I know where we have to go next."

Routing to Goddard State Park showed we had 9 minutes. Desperation dropped my stomach.

"We have to-" I swallowed my words as Sven grabbed my arm and shoved me towards the car.

"Go. Now." he finished for me.

Shocked at the urgency and his handling, I opened the door. "Yeah," I agreed as I looked up.

The sight that greeted me had me in the car and the door slamming behind me, shouting, "Go, go. GO!"

The goblins had followed us. And there had to be hundreds of them. Dozens flowed out from behind trees, and even more poured out in a wave of death from the sewers, their feet shaking the earth. The goblin shouts and war cries started as we pulled away.

Turning to the left, Sven moved the car away from the mass. Panic tore at me.

"No, we have to go left," I shouted over the roar.

"Are you crazy? Do you see how many goblins are over there?" Sven said.

As if to emphasize his point, a goblin thudded into the side of the car.

"We can't let anything happen to Becca!" I shouted, grabbing the wheel and yanking it.

Sven stared at me. I saw him out of my peripheral as I steered the car around a swarm of approaching goblins. When we were past them, I snuck a glance at him and saw something completely unexpected in his eyes. Love.

"You are an incredible woman, Cy Vanguard." He said.

The unmistakable thump of bodies hitting the front of the car gave a drumroll to the thought. I giggled.

He grinned back, from ear to ear, as he gunned it. "You're for sure going to be the death of me."

"Hey, can we have a *little* sympathy for my goblins you're treating like bales of hay?" Bab said irritably.

"Take the next left." The navigation answered back for me.

Arms and bodies beat at the car as we reached the end of the parking lot and where the goblins were the thickest. I locked the door. The exit was impossible to spot, and the car screamed as it bottomed out when Sven didn't guess correctly. Goblins took the slow down to press their advantage, and two jumped on top of the car. Three more tried to climb onto the roof but were too short. Helplessness balled my fists. I wish I could just use my lightning to electrocute the car. Talk about a way to clear a path. I couldn't, though. The electricity would come up through the steering column and electrocute Sven if I did that. And I wasn't willing to see if vampires could die of electrocution.

Rolling down the window about two inches, I pulled ley energy and got out two shots before a goblin hand tried to worm its way into the crack. I rolled the window up, effectively pinning it. Its yellowed eyes went wide, and its mouth turned down in horror as the car picked up speed again. Sven had gotten us through. I wanted to shout with joy. Instead, I rolled down the window and let the panicked goblin go. As soon as I slid it down a crack, his arm slipped free, and he disappeared from sight. I looked in the side mirror and saw his body hit the road and bounce two then three times before it came to a stop. Right before we rounded onto Old Forge Road, I saw the goblin lift its head, reeling from the unexpected ride it had taken.

I couldn't pay him any mind, though. We had to focus on other things. Like how to find and save Nadine. I looked at my phone. Clear, impassive letters showed an 11:56 arrival. And we had 4 minutes to do it in. I wanted to shake the damn thing. Slipping my hand into my pocket, I smoothed my fingers over the coin nestled there.

Trees sped past as we picked up speed. Sven didn't brake for the corners, and I swear we went up on two wheels at least twice. I gritted my teeth as we screeched around the corners and dug my other fingers into the armrest. I wouldn't say anything about the crazy driving. It would all be worth it if we could get to Becca's mom in time. Another glance at the clock burned back 11:57. It had just been a minute, but my heart climbed higher into my throat. Every minute that passed was one less minute closer to Nadine Jeffries' leaving this world for good.

Then dirt patches were visible through patches in the trees.

"There," I said, trying to infuse calm into my voice.

When we neared the clearing, though, the parking lot was empty. Dread dropped my stomach.

Instinct had me saying, "Keep going."

"What?" Sven asked with his foot still on the brake.

I banged the dashboard of the car. "Don't stop. This isn't it."

He gunned the gas, even as he asked, "How do you know?"

"I don't know for sure," I said.

I bit my lip as I looked back down at the directions. I pinched to zoom in on the map. To my stark relief, another parking lot appeared.

"A quarter-mile down the road, there's another lot. That has to be it."

It had to be. I assured my twisting gut. Shortly after, I let out an audible breath as we careened into the next parking lot. There was Jeffries' car. And right on time, 11:58. As we passed signs showing the way to the point, I pulled a gun out of the holster in the small of my back. There was little humans understood better than a gun. As Sven pulled up behind the car, blocking them in. Even though I could tell from the absence of the silhouettes in the car that it was empty, I still stayed low as I dropped out of the vehicle. I hustled near the undercarriage. Sven wasn't one for precautions. He was out of the car before I'd even hit the pavement. As he came around the corner, I saw a piece of paper on the ground. Picking it up, I saw the blood staining the crumpled sheet. My pulse quickened. With shaking hands, I turned the note over. A single word was scrawled there. POINT.

"Are you interested in displaying more of those lightning speed vampire running skills?" I said, waving the paper.

He pulled the paper from my grasp. With a solemn nod, he scooped me into his arms with the ease of a world-class bodybuilder, and within seconds we were off down the dirt path. I threw the safety on my gun, so I didn't accidentally shoot one of us. As the wind pulled my hair away from my face, I struggled to keep hope. It was no doubt noon. If something happened to Nadine, I would never forgive myself. Nobody had to assure me I'd done everything possible to save her. I didn't have to hear those words. I already knew I had. What I was feeling wasn't logical. It was pure emotion. And emotion wasn't clean like logic. It was messy, painful.

When we reached the signpost, multiple signs pointed to different areas. Sven slowed down to read them. Anxiety crawled in my gut.

"We don't have time for this," I said, fear lancing through me.

"You are quite right, Miss Vanguard." said a voice from a thicket of trees.

John Jeffries stepped out from the trees, dragging Becca behind him; his gun trained on her. He was disguised, but there was no denying it was him. Shit.

"Put her down," John said to Sven, meaning me.

Sven looked at me, his eyes narrowed. I nodded. He swung my legs to the ground, his lips compressed. He obviously didn't like this, but I didn't want to put Becca in danger, not after she'd gone through all of this to help us. Tillie stepped out from the trees, along with their mother, who wouldn't meet our eyes.

"She was never in trouble, was she?" I couldn't help but ask bitterly with a nod to Nadine.

Tillie tossed down a thick rope she'd been clutching in her long fingers.

John didn't answer me; instead, he nodded the gun at the rope. "Tie them up," he said to Becca.

Tears streamed down Becca's face as she gathered the rope from the dead leaves and mud. Her gasps traveled across the space of the path to us, pulling at my heartstrings.

"Stop!" John said his gun shaking. To busy himself, he pulled off his fake nose and tossed it to the ground. Seeming to take comfort in the action, he moved his wig and did the same. "You don't get to cry. It's you who betrayed me. *Me.* I gave everything up to support you girls, sacrificed my *life* for you, and then you betray me? Twist your knife into me with your self-righteous indignation. You had the luxury of such a thing. I *gave* that to you. No one gave that to me. I gave you everything. So no, little sister. You don't get to cry. If anyone gets to cry, it's me."

When he was done, there was a graveyard of prosthetics at his feet. That wasn't what had my attention, though. He was on the verge of breaking. The edge to his eyes made that as evident as the frozen ground beneath us. I had to do something.

Even though it was very much not the case, I said, "It's all right, Becca."

I infused reassurance into my voice, even though I had none for her. I didn't see a way out of this that didn't involve the death of them or us. Or both.

At that chilling thought, Bab piped up. "You need to electrocute his ass."

"I can't do that while the gun is trained on Becca," I responded in my head to Bab.

"You just said it yourself: it's them or us. And I don't know about you, but I like this walking around thing. It's infinitely more entertaining than sitting on some altar waiting for someone to need something."

"If I hit him, he's going to shoot her. I can't live with that." I said.

I must have said this out loud this time because Sven said, "Well, you need to figure something out because I'll be damned if you die today."

Nadine did something surprising. She shuffled forward. "John, what are you doing with these people?"

John double-blinked at her unexpected words. "It's none of your concern, mama."

She wasn't to be dissuaded, though. "I think it is, John. Your papa would not approve of this."

"But he's not here, is he, mama? I have to be the man now. And these people mean us harm. We don't have a choice here."

Her pale features fought with this information. A resolute look hardened her delicate frame. "I think-"

"There's no time for this!" Shouted Tillie shoving forward.

Indecision had frozen Becca. She stood unsure halfway between her family and where Sven and I stood, waiting for the opportunity to pounce. I hoped the distraction would have given us the much-needed space to make our move, but throughout the tirade, John didn't waver from his train on Becca.

A familiar rumbling soon let us know that was the least of our worries, though. A sound that changed everything. A sound that made all of our lives forfeit.

Throwing my hands to the side and shoving energy into them, I pulled on Sven's arm. "Get us out of here!"

It was too late. Goblins burst through the trees, swarming us and overrunning the Jeffries' family. Even though the goblins only came up to the human families' waists, there were so many of them, they'd yanked the unfortunate group off the ground like rag dolls.

"Stop!" I screamed, throwing lightning into the horde.

All it succeeded in doing was taking down one goblin, only to be replaced by another, in the space of a blink.

"Bab, do something!" I screamed.

No sooner had the words left my lips than I felt what could only be described as a gerbil crawling up my throat. I clutched at my throat and fell to the ground. Cold mud-soaked my knees, but that was the least of my worries. Something was coming.

A voice, deep and scratchy from thousands of years of disuse, erupted from my throat. "Goblins. My people, stop!"

Elation threw my eyes open. It was Bab. My euphoria was short-lived when the goblins kept coming.

"Bab, you *have* to stop them." I pleaded in my head, no longer having control over my voice.

It was Bab's turn to answer out loud this time. "I... can't kill my people."

He was torn; I could feel it in his being, hear it in his voice.

"It's either them or us," I said in my head, panic edging my thoughts.

I had my answer when I felt the feeling leave my throat again, and I could speak. I had to save us. There was no running away now. We were out of time.

Thinking quickly, I said to Sven. "Hold on to me."

As he pressed himself to me in the sweetest caress possible, I sent a prayer to the gods.

Prayed this would work one more time. Spreading my fingers wide, I arched lightning between them. Moving my arms wide, I connected the strings in a cage that circled us just as the goblins reached us. The scream that hit my ears let me know my plan was working. Thank the gods.

They formed a barrier around our cage. I could see their eyes reflecting back the lightning that kept them out. I couldn't tell what was brighter. That or the rage that burned in their eyes. At least we were safe. For now. Dawn wasn't going to save me like before, though. How were we going to get out of this one? Maybe we could move the cage to safety.

Any thoughts of movement were quelled when the most unbelievable thing happened. A goblin put a hand on the lightning. I waited for him to move it away. From the way he winced, I could tell it bothered him, but he didn't move though. Instead, he put his other hand on the cage. Then afoot. Then his other foot. My mouth hung open. What was happening? Fear ate at me as he started to climb the cage.

"How?" I asked in desperation.

It was Bab who answered me. "They are used to the lava down in the caves. They have highly resistant skin."

I didn't have much time to reflect on this because something else soon became apparent. His weight on the cage was making it harder to hold together. I gritted my teeth and threaded another chain into the cell.

No sooner had I finished than another goblin out of my peripheral put his own spindled fingers on the glowing rope. I prayed he couldn't climb it. That he was special. That Bab would be wrong. But my prayers were in vain. He was soon following the path of the one before him. With the utmost care, he climbed to the top of the cage. His weight bore down on me and made my back bow. Sven saw my consternation.

"What is it?" He asked concern etched into his face.

"Their weight. It's too much." I ground out as the weight of another goblin joined the two above them.

Then to my horror, the unthinkable happened. The cage started to shrink. The weight of their bodies pressed on the cell. In on me. The pressure of it was too much. Too much to bear. In fact, if it wasn't for the inhuman strength Sven had given me when he'd bitten me, I would have collapsed by now. We'd already be dead. If only Bab would do what I'd told him to do in the first place, we wouldn't even be in this position.

Then a terrible idea hit me. It slammed into me with the force of a boulder. And my eyes grew wide. It was a long shot, but what if...

More goblins added to the cage, making me scream out and bow my back. It was either that or die. That made the decision easy.

Nothing brought clarity quite like death.

"Sven." I managed to squeeze out. "Closer."

Confusion knitted his brow, but he did as I'd asked and closed the last foot between us. It was none too soon either because another goblin joined the others. I groaned under the unexpectedness of it, and the cage collapsed that foot.

"Holy gremlin testicles," Bab exclaimed.

I ignored him. Sweat dripped down my brow and dipped into my mouth. Salt tinged my tongue as I managed to nod him closer. Uncertainty wrapped itself around him. He fought it for a few seconds, but after the space of a breath, he overcame it, and emotion rolled him as he folded me into his embrace. He folded me in like a broken man. I wanted to relish the flood of love I felt in his arms. The rightness of it. It felt like coming home.

I couldn't, though. There was no time for it.

As if to prove my point, the cage shrunk again, and the smell of chlorine assaulted my nose. It had to happen now.

I bared my neck to Sven and said, "Mark me."

The rejection on his face was instant as he said, "Cy, no. You don't want that."

Considering his bite was why I'd cut him out of my life before, I didn't blame him for the rejection. It was our only chance at survival. We didn't have the luxury of choice here.

"Now's the time to spit it out if you've got other options," I said through gritted teeth.

Indecision warred on his face. The cage shrunk. He screamed, squeezing his eyes tight as the lightning bit into him. I knew in my bones it couldn't happen again. Next time, our fragile protection would break.

"Just do it!" I screamed, pushing my neck at him.

A tortured look washed over his face before he closed his eyes. The muscles in his neck jumped as he bent to my bared offering. Seconds passed. Shudders wracked his body. Yet, he didn't move. He wasn't going to do it. We were going to die.

Pain flared in my neck. I almost wept with relief. Never in my life did I imagine I'd be so grateful to be bitten by a vampire. That was my last thought before I was flooded by a mind-melting pleasure.

Nothing happened. I didn't feel any different. Though the cage wavered at how weak the loss of blood was making me.

When he pulled away, I asked dazedly, "Is...is that it?"

I smelled my hair as it was signed by the fast-shrinking cage, and I knew that this was indeed it. For us.

"Not quite," Sven said, his voice dark with the drug of my blood.

Then he slit his wrist and pressed it against my lips. I could feel the change roll over me and out in waves. It roiled over Bab too. He cried out in agony as the two fought for a place in my body. In my brain. It was like trying to fit two things into a space that would only accept one. For all his torture, pain pierced through me as I expanded to hold it all. Yet still, I held onto Sven's arm and drank for all I was worth. Filling myself up. Beyond capacity. Beyond what was possible. The flood of pain made holding the cage impossible. The cell broke with a thunderclap, and goblin bodies fell, burying us in a blanket of death.

Bony parts that could have been knees, elbows, skulls, or

even fists writhed and pressed into me. They were nothing compared to the pain inside though. Dimly, I became aware that Bab's cries had gotten louder and louder, building to a crescendo that clawed at my insides.

Finally, I couldn't take it anymore. My mouth tore from Sven's wrist, and I joined him in a blood-curdling scream that ripped itself from my mouth.

As soon as my lips opened, energy flowed out of my mouth in a deadly wave. A wave that lifted and blew back the goblins in a hailstorm of bodies.

The absence of noise was deafening. It had to be for Sven too. I could feel him squirm in discomfort next to me. I flinched, turning my head to the side to stop the imaginary onslaught. Blood dripped from my lips onto my arms as I brought them up to press my hands to my ears. The muffled sound of skin on cartilage, providing the relief I so desperately needed. I had to keep going, though. As crazy as that blast had been, there was no way it had taken out everyone.

I managed to get a knee under myself. I unfolded myself like a marionette, which I was convinced I had become because there was no way anything other than strings was holding me up at this point. I made it to my feet. It wasn't until nothing else was touching me that I realized power flowed through me. My whole body pulsed numb, like a super-charged glow rod. Simultaneously charged and drained by it. I could go for a nice coma.

Shrugging off my discomfort, I surveyed the clearing. Or non-clearing as it would appear, I corrected as I took in the inordinate number of goblin bodies around. However, there was still a horde of very-much-alive-thank-you-very-much goblins on the perimeter of the woods. My stomach sunk. There were still plenty alive. Enough to ruin your day, without a doubt. I hated being right.

"What now?" asked Sven; his eyelids were heavy, clearly, affected by the drug of my blood. His words were slurred as he attempted to continue, "Do you want me to use your lightning to pick them off, one by one?"

The sound of his voice gave me a start. Two thoughts crept into my consciousness at one time.: 1) I didn't have the foggiest clue when he'd stood up. 2) There was Oh, yeah. I was so not cut out for more fighting. I'd done all of the tricks I could at this pony show.

Outloud, I said, "No, even with two of us shooting, we'd still be outnumbered."

We were still surrounded too. Gods knew where the Jeffries were, but I couldn't be concerned with them right now. I'd figure out how I was going to explain that piece of crazy to the authorities later. There was really only one option.

"Bab, this is where you come in," I said out loud.

Sven shrugged and then nodded his agreement. It really was the most logical choice. He was their God, after all. After a few moments with no response, unease started to creep in.

"Bab?" I asked again.

What if something had....happened during the mark. What if he was gone? What if I'd killed-

"It'd serve you right if it did," Bab said, his voice rich with indignation.

Relief poured over me. "Oh, I knew it wouldn't kill you." I chided.

"You did not." He said, calling me out on my bullshit.

"Ok, so I didn't." I acknowledged, trying to not feel guilty. "But if you would have just helped to begin with, I wouldn't have had to turn myself into a faerie-bomb."

After a few begrudging seconds, he conceded. "Fair enough. What would you have of me?"

I pushed down the sigh of frustration. Why was I the one

always having to come up with the answers? Just once, I'd like not to have to be the one to figure things out. Just once.

"Why don't you..." I waved my hand in the air like the movement might trigger me to think of what to say. Finally, I settled on, "talk to them?"

He gave a belabored sigh and said, "Ug- fine."

I went to respond but realized I couldn't get anything out of my throat. Clearing it didn't produce any results either. Because of that, I wasn't surprised when my body sashayed forward without any help from me. Boy, that was quick.

"Children of mine, cease your attack on these creatures." He said in his booming voice.

"Pan be damned, you've some gumption, Princess." Maybe said, from a cluster of trees to the left.

There was no mistaking the admiration in his eyes. Next to him, Kut rolled her eyes.

"If there was any confusion, this is your God, Baboloki," Bab said, high-stepping through the goblin bodies and throwing his hips in a way that I wasn't sure my body had ever moved before.

Goblins dropped to their knees in a wave of confusion and respect.

Bab took this as his due, barely paying them any heed as he continued on, "This senseless onslaught needs to stop."

"But your holiness, the faerie, has your bone. You cannot rest while it doesn't reside on the altar."

Internally, I did a lot of swallowing hard at that. How were they going to take that I'd eaten their God, for lack of a better term? Thankfully, Bab avoided that possible disaster with a wave of his hand.

"Preposterous. I am clearly standing here in front of you, stronger than ever. No longer am I weighed down by a set of bones. I have freedom again. I have been reborn inside this body. This vessel is me, and I am this vessel. We are one." He said, raising his hands to the sky.

His words gave me pause. I didn't like the way this conversation was starting to turn whatsoever. What was said next did nothing to quell my building anxiety.

"She is to come with us then?" This from Kut, who folded her hands across her chest, but I could see the twinkle in her eye.

I held my breath, very aware that I didn't have a leg to stand on should this go south.

"Of course not. We can't be having earth dwellers living underground." He said with a dismissive shake of his head.

A goblin, with a red cap that dripped with what suspiciously looked like blood, stepped forward.

The air seemed to grow stale as his eyes narrowed. "So are you saying you renounce your duties to goblin kind, God of mine?"

"A carefully worded question. One would think twice how you word things, my dear Mast. You wouldn't want me to misunderstand your question for insolence." He deliberately turned his back on the angry goblin and spoke to the general assembly in harsher tones. "Let me say here and now that I do what *I* want. I will not be questioned. Anyone who dares to do so will feel the full extent of my wrath."

An angry goblin, who was larger than any goblin I'd seen before, even larger than Kut, stepped forward. His body vibrated with repressed rage.

His voice was impossibly high-pitched yet grated like sandpaper as he said, "That isn't our holiness. It's more fairie tricks, and I won't stand for it, I tell you!"

Shit. I'd no sooner thought the word than Bab had shot my arm out. The goblin clutched and clawed at his throat as he rose off the ground.

"What kind of Darth Vader shit is that?" I said, unable to believe what I was seeing.

"I have control of them," he said simply as the goblin thrashed.

Revulsion roiled in my gut. "Ok, you've proved your point. Put him down."

But Bab wasn't listening. The goblin's thrashes grew less and less until they finally ceased altogether. Until he hung there limply. Bab dropped my arm, and the body fell to the ground, motionless.

"Now, I have proven my point," he said to me coldly.

He let his actions hang like a pendulum over the stunned crowd. Ignoring the outburst, he said, "As your benevolent God, I understand you, my People, will need to know how to move forward."

Swinging his gaze over the crowd, he leveled it at one after another. As each of them cowered under his eye, I had to agree: that had most certainly gotten his point across.

Continuing on in a louder voice, he said, "Since a bone is required to be on the altar, it is my choice to stay with the faerie. When and if I grow bored, I will return. Until that time, I am appointing Kutulun and Mabye Royal Messengers. If you have a need of me, send them to call on the Princess. As my vessel, you will treat her as your God, for I am her, and she is me. She will answer your call. She will take care of you."

My stomach dropped at his words. This was not happening.

I thought hard at Bab. "Oh, no. I will not be a glorified, goblin babysitter."

"You fucked up, Princess. Now, you must pay the price. We all have to answer for our sins." He said simply. Then, as if his metaphysical guilt trip hadn't been enough, he added, "Besides, there is no way they are going to let you walk out of here if they don't hear these words. They are scared. They need to be taken care of. Since it was you that made such an egregious error, it only makes sense that the person to do that is you."

I tried to think of a way to argue that, but he was right. I had messed up. It was up to me to make it right. I was the only one who could.

It was nice to know I didn't have to fight him anymore. That, as crazy as things would sometimes undoubtedly get, that we would always be on the same page. I let out a sigh of relief at the knowledge, and the weight of control of my body came back over me.

With the weight came a calm. Today, I'd made peace with the demons inside me, vampire and goblin alike. The freedom of that realization made me positively giddy. It most certainly wasn't an appropriate time for it considering there were two areas where it was clear pieces of the Jeffries clan law. A quick deduction helped me to see it was Nadine and Tillie. This was further clarified when I heard grunts and screams behind me. I spun on my heel the same time Sven did, albeit slower. I was simultaneously horrified and relieved to see Becca and John strung between a cluster of goblins. Their intention to mimic what they'd done to the other members of the Jeffries clan was clear.

"Wait!" I cried out.

At my voice, the goblins hesitated, clearly uncomfortable with following orders from a faerie. I continued on anyway, adding steel to my tone, and said, "That isn't how things work up here."

"Well, they should," Bab said, grumbling in my head.

A thought hit me. I focused hard to make sure the next question I asked would only be in my head.

I couldn't keep the smile off my face as I asked Bab, "Does

this mean I have subjects who will obey my every command?"

I could feel his mirroring smile as he said, "But of course."

I unsuccessfully tried to swallow my smile as I said to the goblins, "Tie them up and bring them back to my car."

For a second, they stood, motionless. I held my breath. Would they actually do it? It only took a second to pass before I got my answer. Shouts were called out, and they scrambled around the clearing as they scurried around to obey my order and find something to secure them with. A satisfied smile fell over my face.

Sven shook his head next to me, crossing his arms over his chest. "You're liking this too much."

I merely shrugged, not bothering to deny it.

He cocked his head to the side and asked, "How did you know my marking you would do that?"

I held my breath, waiting to feel that familiar uncomfortable feeling at the mention of being marked. When nothing came, my smile grew even wider. I'd done it. I'd gotten over my fear of being marked. I'd made peace with the new me. Demons and all.

Feeling pretty damn good, I turned back towards the car and started walking. He fell in step beside me.

"Well?" he prompted.

I looked at him, heat welling in my chest. Gods, I wanted to kiss him. Revel in his taste. Thank the world for him.

Instead, I answered his question, "I didn't. But from everything I've seen in my life, I knew it had to do *something*."

Sven looked at me for a couple more blinks then shook his head, a smile flirting at the edges of his lips. "You're something else, Cy Vanguard."

A pack of goblins rushed by us, saving me from admitting how I felt the same way about him. I laughed as I kicked and squirmed in their raised hands. By the time they'd rounded the bend, they'd almost dropped him at least a half a dozen times. And to think usually, I would have to deal with all of that nonsense, but instead, I could just walk lazily back to my car and know that everything would be ready and waiting?

A girl could get used to this.

a fuzzed image appeared on the TV screen as Tyler and I made our way through the lobby.

The news anchor said with her plastic smile, "And in other news, the unidentified creatures spotted around New York City over the last two months have been identified. It's a half dozen brown-throated sloths. They'd gotten loose en route to the rain forests of South America, where they were being reintroduced to the wild. Their transport car had overturned, and they had escaped. The good news is they have all been rounded up and are now back on their way to live the rest of their days peacefully."

Sloths. Right. My eyes rolled so hard, I think they hit the back of my skull.

"I still can't believe you were framed." Tyler prattled on as we made our way through the lobby of the police station.

I stopped to give him the stink eye. His feet did a staccato shuffle to halt his perpetually peppy stride.

"You mean you actually thought I set fire to the Jeffries' house?" I asked, not bothering to keep the disgust out of my voice.

"Well, no." He sputtered. "What I meant was-"

Thinning my lips, I gave him a dead-panned stare and made my way to the door. Alone.

"Just tell Burdock he better have that press release stating my innocence like he said. And Tyler? Have it done like yesterday. I don't need to lose business over this."

The winter wind howled into the building as I opened the door. I hated winter in the city. There was no escaping the wind. The tightly packed buildings funneled it into an inescapable river. Buttoning the top button on my leather jacket, I braved the frigid blast. I ignored Tyler's mumbled "yes, ma'am" behind me. I didn't do, ma'am. I didn't need to feel older than I did.

Ok, at the moment, that was kind of a lie. My body felt better than it ever had. A perk of the second vampire mark, I guess. What other fun and exciting abilities had I gotten from the second mark? I'd have to ask Sven next time I saw him. For the first time, the thought didn't come with fear. I breathed a sigh of relief.

At the thought of Sven, I couldn't help the grin that came to my face. There was a man. Vampire or not. He was full-on man meat. I didn't know how much longer I could remind myself that we were just friends and believe it. He had, after all, literally put his life on the line to help me today. No questions asked. And he'd even tried to talk me out of the second mark. I shivered as I remembered the pleasure of his bite. Who knew being bitten by a vampire could feel so good? It made me 60 degrees warmer just thinking about it.

I turned down the darkening Park Row, lost in the memory of the chaos a mere eight hours ago. So much had changed. Yet, I was the same. Funny how life worked like that.

As I passed the Southern District Court, I saw a familiar glow in the fading light. A smile widened my face, and I changed my course to follow. The two sculptures Justice and Authority towered over me, their robes forever frozen in time like wings of an angel. Usually, their beauty brought me joy, but not today. Justice's shield seemed to scream "turn back," and Authority's scroll was at the ready, like a sword prepared to engage in battle. My feet slowed at the feeling starting to creep up my spine.

Then her light bobbed around the corner. I bit my lip to keep from smiling. I'd missed my surprising little friend. There was something to be said for a real friend. The kind that didn't have agendas or weird underlying currents. Just straightforward, honest friends. As soon as I rounded the corner, the glow appeared two inches in front of my face.

Kittie was wrapped up in a mink pelt scrap, complete with a tiny hat that sat in a spiral on top of her head. The brown looked out of place with her usual emo self. I'd sooner die than tell her that the color set off her hair like stars in the sky. A grin split her face.

Her permanently mischievous grin crooked as she said, "Hey, largie. Miss me?"

An overwhelming feeling of gratitude for her and her newfound friendship came over me.

I bit my lip and said, "Yeah, I think I did."

Blunt honesty with no witty banter was not the norm for us, so it made her pause. Her tiny face searched my eyes. After a second, she bobbed in understanding. Then a shiver wracked her body, sending pixie dust to the snow covered pavement. It was fresh snow here. People were creatures of habit and didn't venture off the path from the walkway to the door. Not to mention, the courthouse was closed now. Nobody was coming this way.

It was the perfect place to meet each other. I put out my hand so that she could land in it. No sense in her catching her death by coming out to see me. She landed on it, and I cupped my fingers around her, so they acted as a wind barrier.

The wind stopped whipping the fur on her hat around, so I knew I'd done my job.

"So is it true?" she asked in a rush, obviously dying to know. "Are you a goblin God now?"

I laughed and pushed down the uncomfortable feeling that came up. I reminded myself I was ok with this. There was nothing to be uneasy about. Instead, I focused on the positive parts, like having my own personal muscle. I was smiling sooner than I thought possible.

"I suppose it is," I said, with a wry grin.

I could almost feel Bab roll his eyes. "Of course, you get all of the credit, how typical."

His words just made me smile bigger.

She let out a low whistle. "Faerie princess and goblin God. That's quite the resume you've got there."

"Don't forget Bounty Hunter." I teased, wrinkling my nose at her.

She rolled her eyes at me. "Yes, gods forbid. Faerie princess and goblin God is nothing in comparison."

I laughed and tweaked her hat. "You'd be surprised."

The laughter disappeared from her face, and suddenly it was my turn to be confused. That hadn't made her mad, had it? She jammed her hat back onto her head, but it didn't take me long to realize her gaze was not on me. Instantly on the defense, I turned around. What I saw made my heart beat double time.

Standing there were two vampires. The blacks of their cloaks were stark against the white of the snow, but their pale faces stood out clear as the noonday sun in the rapidly darkening light. Shit.

"Don't worry your pretty little head," Bab said.

No sooner had he said the words than I could feel him

taking control of my body. I didn't fight it. My hand came out, independent of my doing. Could I actually not have to live in fear of vampires any more? Hope flared in my chest.

I waited for the vampire to lift off the ground, but nothing happened. Well, fuck.

"What in the hell?" Bab growled.

Kittie bobbed in shock. "Holy, deep voice."

We ignored her. Bab tried again.

I only let him try twice more before I said to him, "It looks like your only effect is on goblins. You're going to have to let me have this one."

Reluctantly, I could feel control return to my body. I ignored the rubbery feel of getting my limbs' usage back and started retreating to the back of the closed-off alcove, looking around for a way out. There was a trash can at the end. Maybe I could boost myself onto it?

The vampires advanced in on me as I backed away. I took the wallet out of my purse and flung it at them.

"Look, take my money, I don't want any trouble," I said in an attempt to divert their attention.

It fell without notice at their feet. They stepped over it and laughed.

"Oh, we're not here for your money. Are we, Pall?"

The one called Pall shook his head and licked his lips. Razor-sharp canines grew over his lips. "Not even a little. We're interested in a *faerie*. Going to get our own proper supply now that the supply in the city has been all but cut off."

"Faerie?" I asked, feigning confusion. I was almost to the cans. "I don't know what you're talking about."

"Bitch! Don't be coy." Pall said, slamming his fist into the cement wall. A fist-sized hole formed in the wall. "We know you're a faerie. And we're taking you. Finders keepers. Sven will just have to find himself a new whore."

"He won't mind." laughed the other one.

Hurt zinged through my chest at the mention of Sven's name. Gods, I wish he was here. My eyes flicked behind the advancing vampires. Some insane part of my brain thought if I wanted him there enough, I could will it. I put all of my energy into it. *Sven.* I felt a flutter in my chest, like a distant memory.

But he didn't come, and my knees hitting the trash can behind me told me time was up. I had to save myself. Fine. My heart slammed against my chest. I had two choices: fight or run. With my increased abilities, I could maybe have given one of them a run for their money, but not two. That left run. So be it. I jumped. My feet crashed onto the metal lid of the trash cans. I could hear the vampires scramble behind me. The top of the wall was easily still two feet over my head. Way too high to reach to pull myself up, but maybe...

Pushing with all of my newfound strength, I jumped again. To my shock, I soared above the wall. I laughed, relief cutting through me like a snipped kite string.

Shock dropped my stomach as I felt a hand close around my ankle. The force of it drug me down, and I fell back to the earth. Trash cans crashed and clattered seconds before I smashed into them. When I landed on a soft body instead of hard metal, it became apparent as to why.

Tucking and rolling, I pushed off the heap and leaped to my feet, right in front of the second vampire. His head tilted to the side, and he bared fangs that glinted off the street lights. That was the only warning I had. I'd just managed to get my hands up in time before he was on me. His jaws snapped and clicked inches from my neck. I screamed as he thrashed over me. Gritting my teeth, it took all of my effort to hold him at bay. Seconds passed. He was too powerful, and my muscles shook with the effort to keep those precious inches between us. Those inches meant my life or death. My arms began to buckle. The gleam in his eye was hard to miss. I shook my head in denial. This couldn't be happening.

"Cy, shut 'em!" Came Kittie's high-pitched cry from above.

Instinctively, I knew what she was going to do. I squeezed my eyes shut. In an instant, a storm of red light and shimmer flashed behind my eyelids. Pixie dust. The vampire screamed and let go. I could feel him thrash next to me. When the lights stopped flashing, I opened my eyes. The vampire clawed and scratched at his face. Now was my chance.

I went to dart around him to take a break for the street. With a gasp, I threw out a hand to stop myself. The other vampire blocked the alley, a cocky smile on his face. He wagged an eyebrow at me. There was no way I could take him out by myself. My eyes darted to the mouth of the alley again, half expecting to see Sven. Nothing. I don't know why I thought he was going to show up. It was almost a palpable buzz in my veins. It was a thought I was going to have to get out of my head. No one was coming to save me. I had to save myself.

My eyes fell on the garbage cans. They were crushed, useless. What was I going to do? The vampire at the end of the alley prowled towards me. I flicked a quick glance at the other vampire. He was pulling himself to his feet. Whatever it was, I had to do it now; I was out of time.

I only had this one chance. This second to getaway. There was only one thing I could do.

My hands shook as I braced my feet, said a quick prayer, and then shouted, "Never, never, never."

And just like that, I felt the weight of my wings, back again. I was ready for them and had them beating before a thought even had time to form. Weightlessness took over my body as I raised into the air. Right on time, too. The vampire had just opened his eyes. They were red and burnt.

"Come here, you little bitch." He shouted, jumping for me.

Fear bloomed in my gut as his fingertips hit my foot. I didn't know if it was the fear or what but the flutter I'd felt earlier intensified in my chest. Breathing deeply, I worked my muscles, giving all my focus to it. Then something hit my wings. Something large. Something solid. My wings brushed against them again and again, the effort to stay moving, to keep me in the air, increasing a hundredfold. It felt like they were hitting a wall. But there was no wall behind me that I would be striking.

To add to my confusion, Sven rounded the corner, lightning-fast. His black trench coat billowing behind him. It curled around him as he came to an abrupt stop. No matter how strange it was to see him, that wasn't what added to my confusion, though. It was the look of pure terror on his face when he saw me.

Things became as clear as a diamond when I turned around. Behind me was a face. I'm sure the mug must have been attached to a body, but I couldn't see it. The visage was massive and filled my entire field of vision. Panic fluttered my wings faster. I didn't have any time to think about the fact that giants existed. I had to get out of here.

"Oh, no, you don't!" shouted Kittie.

Not her too. I turned to her. To my surprise, she was making a bee-line to me, rose-colored pixie-dust trailing behind her like a flag in the encroaching night. Shit. That could only mean one thing. I curled my wings around myself to drop out of the sky, but it was too late. Hot, meaty hands closed in. It felt like a boa constrictor wrapping itself around me, and I bucked my body to free myself. It was no use. We weren't sticking around for pleasantries either. My stomach heaved as I was pulled back like a car on a roller coaster.

I'd only come to grips with the sudden backward movement when I realized I had something else to contend with. I wasn't being pulled through an inky night sky anymore. It was a dark magenta sky laced with swirling pulses of hot pink. No matter how fascinating the pulsing, blinding white pink was, I didn't have any time to focus on it. I could still see the inky night sky. I could see it through the fast-disappearing slit in front of me. It shrunk at a panic-inducing speed. And I couldn't tell if it was giddy relief or terror coursing through me as Kittie popped through the opening right before it closed with an audible pop. And then there was only deep magenta with the pulsing hot pink around us.

We'd clearly gone through a door. That meant I was in the Never. Correction: Kittie and I were in the Never. Dear gods, what had I done?

THE END

Thank you for reading *Goblin Cursed!*
If you can't get enough of the world of the Fae join our newsletter:
YOU'LL GET YOUR VERY OWN FREE BOOK *TODAY*!
Click here to join!

MESSAGE FROM THE QUEEN

Thank you so much for reading *Goblin Cursed*!
I hope you loved reading it as much as I did writing it!
Reviews are the life-blood of an Indie author.
If you could pop over and leave a review, it would mean the world to me!

Amble on Over to Leave a Review!

ABOUT THE QUEEN

Erica Reeder is a *USA Today* and International bestselling author of Urban Fantasy who uses glitter as a territorial marker. Kids, boyfriend, you name it. If it's got glitter on it, it's hers. Besides an infatuation with glitter and all things fantasy, she is a Queen with an unreasonable passion for writing. Whether throwing her characters a demon or hiding pixies in pants, there's always fun to be had. Come be a part of it in so many places either at www.ericareeder.com, where there's merchandise that will spellbind you, and of course, books that will steal your breath and enchant your heart. Or you could join our Facebook Group: Erica Reeders Fae Court to have daily fun. OR for less interaction but no fewer goodies, you could JOIN THE NEWSLETTER, WHERE YOU'LL GET YOUR VERY OWN FREE BOOK *TODAY*! Click here to join!

SOCIAL MEDA LINKS